Gun Guy

Alice Carlton

Book design by Diana Wade

ISBN: 979-8-9864054-1-4

Dedicated to victims and
families of gun violence

Advance Praise

There have been so many mass shootings in the United States, more than 300 in 2023 alone, that we become numb to the news of yet another one. In this work of fiction that weaves together the emotions of actual shootings, the reader is given the opportunity to feel the raw reality of awful death and shown the possibility of a change of heart when gun violence becomes real in a person's life.

—Max Carter, PhD, William R. Rogers Director of Friends Center and Quaker Studies (Emeritus) at Guilford College; author of *College Spirit: Essays in Campus Ministry.*

Gun Guy's engaging fictional story carefully portrays the recent, all-too-real history of mass shootings, the painful breakdown of family relationships, the ongoing crisis in mental health, and the broken political system that allows easy access to all kinds of guns. But this story also shows how older people can change, how young people can envision a better future, and how the United States could become a safer nation. And this thoughtful novel ultimately affirms that even the most tragic personal losses can lead toward social and historical transformations.

—Lloyd Kramer, PhD, Professor of History, University of North Carolina, Chapel Hill

Advance Praise

Alice Carlton has created a compelling novel that deals with the most painful crisis facing America—our classrooms have become war zones. Anyone interested in this issue will find Gun Guy a gripping read. The plot is well structured and the characters clearly delineated. This is a novel that tells an important story for our time. Guy Grant, the main character, has to deal with a life-changing event. As chief lobbyist for the National Rifle Association, he has fought any efforts for even minimal gun restrictions. However, two recent heart attacks have caused him to reassess his life and want to reconnect with his daughter and grandson. When a teenage loner does the unthinkable, Guy faces enormous grief, pain, and guilt. Readers will be quickly drawn into this story as Guy Grant begins to question his entire life.

—Sam Hardy Leaman, author of
DC Deals: A Novel of Greed, Love, and Espionage

Chapter 1

Guy Grant kicked the soccer ball back to his grandson. It was Saturday mid-afternoon in late September, and they were at his daughter's house in a modest Alexandria neighborhood. The houses were close together, but each had their quarter-acre of fenced yard. The six-year-old missed the ball and went scrambling after it as it rolled toward the edge of the grassy backyard. His blond curls bounced as he ran. He was slim and muscular and very quick on his feet. Guy smiled as he watched Little Guy's fierce determination to get behind the ball. As his grandfather had just taught him, he stopped it with his foot before facing Guy and kicking it back.

"Good job, son," cried Guy. The ball sputtered slowly toward him. He stepped his foot atop it gingerly and watched as little Guy barreled toward him, aiming his toe to take it away. Guy leaned down and snatched it up in his hands. "Let's take a break, Little Guy. Your old granddad needs to catch his breath." He tucked the ball under his arm and leaned his hands on his thighs, heaving. They had been playing soccer for nearly an hour, and he was done in. Nearing sixty, he had let himself get overweight and out of shape. His once-blond hair—straight, not curly like his grandson's—had more and more gray in it. He pushed it back from his face and resolved to get a haircut this week.

"Okay, Granddad," the little boy said with clear disappointment. He grabbed Guy's hand and led him toward the nearby bench. "You can sit here and breathe, Granddad. Want some lemonade? Mommy made some. I can get it."

"That sounds perfect. And did I smell fresh baked cookies as well?"

"You sure did," said Little Guy. "Before you got here, Mommy let me put the chocolate chips in and lick the spoon." In a flash, he was off.

Guy watched in awe as his grandson ran to the back door, where Guy's daughter came out with a tray holding glasses of lemonade and a plate of cookies. How he loved this little boy. He knew he hadn't been a good father to Laura. A "workaholic," she had called him once in anger when she was maybe sixteen, on one of the rare weekend visits he hadn't canceled due to work. Laura had been small, maybe eight years old, when his ex-wife, Maureen, had reached her limit and kicked him out. Maureen had also called him a workaholic, probably where Laura first heard it. He had to admit they were both right. He'd been driven and ambitious. He had risen to a pinnacle he had never dreamed he could achieve: chief lobbyist for the National Rifle Association. The climb to this position had cost him a marriage and two children. He was wealthy enough to provide for his children. Maureen's bulldog lawyer saw to that. But the flame burning under him had not dimmed, it had only grown stronger. He had worked hard to get here, but he had missed so much.

When he finally came to his senses and slowed down enough to realize his loss, Laura was in college and wanted nothing to do with him. His son, two years older, was hiking in Europe and even more out of touch. It was now years later. His son was living on the West Coast—he didn't even know where. Laura had married a less ambitious but hardworking man, Tom Ivey, and had a son. He knew she didn't approve of what he did for a living. She would never understand the importance of the Second Amendment the way he did. That subject was closed between them. But that she named her son after him and that she let him try to make up for it with time with her precious Little Guy felt like a miracle to him.

Laura set the tray on the small table next to the bench while Little Guy bounced and reached his hand toward the cookies. "Hold on, buster," she said. "Offer refreshment to your grandfather first. Remember your manners. He's our guest."

Little Guy quieted immediately. "Yes, Mommy." He turned his attention to his grandfather and touched his arm. "Would you like some, um, refreshment, Granddad?"

Guy tousled his hair. "Yes, I would, thank you. I would like one of those glasses of lemonade."

The boy took two hands to pick up a glass and turned carefully as he handed it to Guy. "Here, Granddad."

"Thank you, son, and I would also like a cookie on a napkin." Guy watched closely as the boy picked up a napkin and placed the biggest cookie in the center before handing it over. Laura was a wonderful mother, he had to admit. The child may be a ball of energy, but he was learning to be considerate and mannerly. It hadn't come from him, he knew, but he was glad to see what Maureen had surely passed down.

Laura sat in a lawn chair as Little Guy snuggled up beside his grandfather with his own cookie and glass of lemonade in a small lidded cup. "How are you feeling, Dad? Don't overdo it." She wore a simple shirtwaist dress in a red flowered pattern with a red apron. Her blond curls sparkled in the afternoon sun.

Her mother's curls, Guy noted. He took a long swallow of the sharp, sweet liquid before he answered. His heartbeat had finally slowed a bit. He was three months past his second heart attack and tired of taking it easy. He raised his eyes to his daughter. "I couldn't be finer getting to play with my grandson. This old ticker isn't giving up yet. I want to watch this boy grow up." He rubbed his side against the boy, who beamed up in response. "We have fun together, don't we, Little Guy?"

"We sure do, Granddad," said the boy with bright eyes.

"Don't you have a new book to read to your grandfather? Maybe it's time for a quiet activity."

Little Guy jumped up. "Yes! Granddad, Mommy got me a book especially for me to read to you. Can I now? Want me to go get it?" Guy barely had time to nod before the boy was gone.

"He can already read?" asked Guy, incredulous.

Laura smiled. "He sure can. And he loves to show off how well he can read."

"Thank you so much for letting me come today, Laura. It means the world to me." Guy reached for her hand. She let him take it, a limp fish. He released it. He studied her dark brown eyes. At least she had his eyes. She was blinking back tears.

"I know you love him," she whispered. "I want him to be surrounded by people who love him." She gathered herself up and met his eyes with a look that made him sit back. "Don't disappoint him. One time you don't show up when you say you will, and that's it. No second chances."

He cleared his throat and thought a moment. He put his hand to his heart. "I promise, Laura. Cross my heart. I'd love to have him sleep over at my house sometime if you'll let him."

"We'll see," she said. "We'll see."

The screen door banged as Little Guy shot through it, book in hand. "I found it, I found it, Granddad!" He settled in beside his grandfather.

"Let me see, what is this book?" asked Guy, bending toward it.

"I want to read it all to you, Granddad." He held the cover in front of them. "See? It says, *How to Babysit a Grandpa.*"

Guy chuckled and glanced at Laura. "*How to Babysit a Grandpa?* And you can read now? I can't wait to hear you read it to me."

Slowly, Little Guy began to read.

Ms. Kate Warwick was in the middle of a Monday morning arithmetic lesson with her first-grade class when she heard her principal's voice on the intercom. "Alert. Alert. Boys and girls, this is a drill. Please lock and secure your classrooms at this time. We are pretending there is an intruder coming into the office." All the children's heads popped up, and they glued their eyes to their teacher. Setting down her lesson plan and black marker, she went into action. She pulled down the black shade over the door to her classroom, locked the door, and directed several children to carry one of their tables to the door. Other children brought another table and their chairs and handed them to her as she piled them on top of the tables. She shepherded them to the side against their cubbies, where they all sat on the floor.

"Do you all have something to protect yourself with?" she asked as she counted heads. They held up pencils and books and scooted back against their cubbies and closer to each other. They remained unusually silent as they sat. "I will tell the principal we are all here in place." She texted on her phone and sat in a chair beside the barricade and waited. "You are safe—I'm here to protect you," she reassured the children as required. *But would we really be safe if this were not a drill?*

News images flashed through her mind of other schools, other children and teachers gunned down by automatic weapon fire from a gun held by a shooter gone mad from who knows what? Some childhood abuse and undiagnosed mental illness? A minute crept by . . . two . . . three minutes. She told herself not to be afraid. She knew some of her students did feel afraid. Some looked pale, others could barely contain their urge to fidget, and still others chewed their fingernails. Parkwood Elementary School had had these drills for years now. This year alone, only a month into the school year, and here they were, having their first active-shooter drill. Her students were well trained and cooperative. The clock on the wall showed her only four minutes had passed. It seemed like hours, days.

The intercom crackled, and the principal's voice broadcast that the drill was over. "Resume your lessons. All classrooms completed the drill in under five minutes. Well done."

The children moved quickly to replace the tables and the chairs and take their seats. They seemed subdued as they raised their eyes in unison to their teacher.

She cleared her throat and spoke. "You did a good job. Any questions before we return to our lesson?"

A small hand shot up in the air. She nodded to Gracia. She was a smart student who routinely asked such questions and expected answers. Her long black hair was held back in a ponytail she was forever pulling into her mouth as she pondered her work. Even now, she had it there as she lowered her hand to speak. As she opened her mouth, it fell down her cheek and dropped onto her shoulder where it stayed, held there by saliva. "Ms. Warwick, how will we know it really is a shooter and not just a drill?" she asked. Her bright black eyes locked on Kate's face.

Kate took a deep breath as she reflected on her answer. What to tell them that wouldn't scare them too much but would be honest? "It's very unlikely we will ever have an active shooter." She saw the class take a collective sigh and relax. No matter how many times she had said this over the years, her students responded to hearing it as if it were the first time. "Just like it's unlikely we will have a fire, yet we do have fire drills." She paused and studied Gracia's face as she decided how much to say. The girl clearly wanted more. Before she could ask for more, Kate said, "Just as the principal told us, this was only a drill; she would tell us if it was real."

"But, Ms. Warwick, she said an intruder came into the office. What if the shooter shot her first?" asked Gracia, unrelenting in her challenge. Another smart question.

Kate watched the class turn together to Gracia and then to her. "There is a plan, a very detailed plan of several people who would respond in order to alert us. The plan makes us as safe as possible, and it is very unlikely we will have a real shooter." Gracia sat back, seeming somewhat satisfied for the moment. The others began to squirm. "Any other questions?" She scanned the class. "All right then, who can tell me what two plus three is?"

Gracia's hand again shot up, as did several others.

Kate called on Guy, who usually did not raise his hand unless he was very sure he had the correct answer. And he did.

Chapter 2

Slamming the front door behind him, Sam Schuyler threw his books toward the coffee table, projectiles that missed their target and clattered onto the floor. Carla, his mother, watched from the kitchen door with a dish towel in her hand and saw him stomp up the stairs and disappear behind the door to his room. It closed with a crash. She stood still a moment, unsure what to do. She hated to admit it, but Sam had begun to have many of these outbursts once he had turned seventeen and started his senior year. The past month at home had been tumultuous, as had the past six months since his father had left.

Now it was only the second day of the school week and Sam was already blowing up. Last week he had made it until Friday. She knew he needed help but so far had not been able to convince him to agree to see a therapist. She had found a reputed good one, with the reputation for being effective with the most recalcitrant teenagers. She had talked to this Matthew Nichol on the phone. He had advised her to require Sam to come to one session. She just wasn't sure how to make that happen.

Sam's father had always been the strict parent, if only tuning in after she had reached her limit using a softer approach. How she longed to talk to her now ex-husband about Sam. But he had cut them both off completely after his seductive coworker had entranced him. She couldn't even be sure where he was now. He had taken that woman to Bali or Tahiti or some romantic place for most of the summer and she had no idea when or if they had returned. If her lawyer hadn't arranged for child support to be automatically deposited in her bank account, she didn't know what she would have done.

Her reverie was broken by a cold nose against her leg. It was Bailey, their little white dog. He was twelve pounds and stood a foot tall at the shoulder. She loved his velvety white coat and plush hair around the head. He sat, cocked his head to the right, and gave her his most appealing look, then whimpered before turning his head toward the stairs.

"Want to go see Sam?" she asked. "Did he shut you out too, Bailey?" She scratched behind his ears and could swear he began to purr. "Part cat, are you? Let's see what we can do."

He followed right on her heels as she climbed the stairs and knocked on Sam's door. In response, she heard the volume of the heavy-metal music increase. Bailey barked and began to scratch the door.

"Get lost!" Sam hollered.

"Bailey wants to come in, Sam, won't you let him in?" She rapped loudly on the door.

Sam opened it a crack, just wide enough to admit the dog, while remaining out of sight behind the door. Before Carla could get her hand on the doorknob, he slammed it shut. Heaving a big sigh, she returned to the kitchen where she had dinner preparations waiting. Checking her supplies, she decided to make spaghetti and meatballs with garlic bread, one of Sam's favorite dishes. Whatever had happened at school to set him off, she could usually get the scowl to leave his face at least briefly with a big pot of something he loved.

She chopped away her frustrations with onion, garlic, and celery on the cutting board. Fresh tomatoes peeled and cut up into tiny pieces enhanced the jar of sauce. Ground beef rolled into bite-sized balls. Fresh basil and oregano from her herb garden just outside the kitchen added the finishing touches. Some of the minced garlic she stirred into soft butter and applied to slices of Italian bread to toast in the oven. Soon the pot was bubbling and filling the kitchen with a savory aroma. This was usually enough to draw Sam downstairs. She tilted her head to listen. The awful music was gone, replaced by an eerie silence from the second floor.

With the noodles boiling and the timer set, she went to the bottom of the stairs and called up. His room was the first one at the top on the left. No answer. She pulled herself up with her hand on the banister. "Dinner is ready, Sam. We're having spaghetti and meat-balls."

The silence was broken by a faint whimpering. She turned the doorknob to find what she expected—the door was locked tight.

"Sam? Are you all right?"

Silence, then a dim voice. "I'm not hungry. Go away."

"I'd like some company." No reply.

Carla stood there, lost. What was going on? She paced up and down the hall a few minutes and then heard the timer. *Well, I'm hungry,* she mused as she hurried down to stop the buzzer.

She ate by herself that night without even Bailey begging at her side. It was delicious. She ate a second helping with a second slice of her toasted garlic bread, trying to drown the rising voices of worry growing louder inside her. After she finished and cleaned up, she dialed her ex-husband. He needed to know the mess he had left behind. No answer, then the recorded voice saying, "This customer's voice mailbox is full."

Sam scrolled to the playlist he had made called "Fuck it" and listened to songs of anger and rage with his earphones. The cord wound around his neck loosely. To the heavy bass beat, he pulled it tight, then let it go, pulled it tight, let it go, over and over.

Go ahead, you lousy prick, what are you waiting for? Strangle yourself, that'll show 'em. Count to nine nine nine nine or six six six six and be done done done done. Or six nine six nine six nine six nine and it'll be fine and then you'll shine and she'll be sorry she wouldn't tell you "be mine."

He pulled and felt the world turn black, then he let go and stretched out on the bed, arms wide, legs crossed, pretending he didn't have to be the one, they'd nail him. Let the devil take him. *Jesus wheesus you're dead too, just a pretty story, they nailed you too. Where are the Romans with the nails and vinegar? Don't leave me here all alone.*

Oh, shut up, you idiot, don't listen to him. What does he know? Nothing worth nothing shut up shut up go away go!

Bailey sat on the rug and watched. Sam felt his presence. He knew Bailey offered comfort, but he didn't want comfort. Bailey licked his fingers with his rough wet tongue. Pulling his arm back, Sam made a fist and pounded the mattress, then pounded his thigh. Bailey put his paws on the step stool beside the bed. Sam saw him, then shut his eyes tight. Tears rolled down his face and wet his shirt. Bailey stepped onto the stool and jumped nimbly onto the bed next to Sam, straddled him, and began to lick his face.

"No!" shouted Sam as he pushed Bailey's head away. "No!" he whispered.

Bailey didn't go away. He curled his small, furry body next to Sam and sniffed his armpit. After a time, Sam rolled toward Bailey, flung his arm across the dog's body, buried his face in the warm fur, and sobbed. Bailey snuggled his nose onto Sam's shoulder. The earphones slid off and settled around his neck, loosening the cord further. The angry rap sounds dimmed. Sam's muscles relaxed, and he fell asleep while Bailey remained still and on guard.

▷ ⊕ ◁

Her beautiful face filled the screen in his mind. He loved the way her ginger hair drifted in soft waves around her face and onto her shoulders. How he longed to run his finger through the strands, to cover her face in baby kisses. He stared into her eyes. She looked past him; she didn't see him. He moved to get in her direct line of sight. She scowled and pushed him away. He moved closer to embrace her. She slapped him hard across the face. He slapped her back, grabbed her hair, and pulled her head down to his crotch where he knew she wanted to be. She screamed and scratched him. He hit her hard.

He awoke with a start, flailing his arms and kicking his legs. It was Bailey's hair he held in bunches in his hands and Bailey yowling on the floor, his body bent in an impossible position. As he came from the grogginess of sleep into fuller awareness, he rolled on his side, shook his head, and focused on Bailey on the floor next to his bed. Bailey's eyes glazed over, and his body went limp. A wave of horror crashed over Sam as he watched his dog's body go still. Sam looked at the clock on the bedside table. Its bright blue numerals showed 3:17. Sam stretched on the floor next to Bailey and stroked his long fur. "Bailey, Bailey," he cried and began to sob. He laid his head next to the dog's head and sobbed until he fell asleep.

Buzzzzz! Carla rolled over in her king-sized bed and hit the snooze button on the bedside clock radio. She snuggled under the covers and spread her legs wide over the huge mattress. *I'm going to get a smaller bed.* She pictured herself in a queen or even a double bed. She opened her eyes and felt the bonds of sleep slip off. *Oh, Sam.* She began to remember the evening before. She never had seen Sam at all. She had worried and fretted and then binge-watched a few episodes of the latest rom-com until she had dozed off in her recliner and dragged herself to bed.

The radio came on. "Traffic is slow on the beltway due to an accident at exit 230," said the generic voice of the morning announcer. She turned it off and threw off the covers. Soon she made her bed, put her robe on, and padded to the bathroom. She tilted her head, listening for sounds of Sam's shower. He usually took one every morning, usually to the accompaniment of loud, whatever-they-call-music these days. Nothing.

Her usual routine was to roll out her mat, do her ten minutes of yoga, get dressed, and head to the kitchen to start coffee and breakfast. She had to be at the office by nine o'clock sharp, which was a blessing because it gave her time to get Sam out the door by 8:15 to catch the bus. Then she sometimes even had time to meditate before pushing through the city traffic to get to work. But the buzzing inside nagged at her. Yoga could wait.

Instead, she pulled her robe around her and went down the hall to Sam's door. Turning the doorknob, she found it was still locked. The silence from inside his room only made her inner buzzing louder. She stared at the door as if it held some answers she didn't have. Then she remembered. None of these inside doors stayed locked securely. She grabbed the knob and rattled the lock, wiggled the knob back and forth and back and forth. Finally, it turned. Slowly she pushed the door a few inches, then a few more, until she could step inside.

What she saw made her blood turn to ice.

Chapter 3

Guy Grant walked into the conference room in the Fairfax, Virginia, headquarters of the National Rifle Association. His lobbying team was assembled and waiting. It was their weekly Wednesday morning team meeting, and they had a lot of work to do. Laying his armful of color-coded folders on the table in front of him, he surveyed his team proudly. They set down their coffee cups and stopped their chatting to face him. There was Jake Cummings, his legal adviser, who kept track of upcoming court cases that threatened Second Amendment Rights. Jake was smart as a whip and a sharpshooter. He spent weekends at the shooting range and would be the man you wanted on your side in any shoot-out.

Next to him sat Mike Gunn, an Iraq War veteran who knew firsthand the value of gun skills. He served as legislative liaison and, in the four years he had been on the team, had developed close relationships with many important senators and congressmen.

Susan Britt, his chief of staff, was his jane-of-all-trades. Super organized, she made sure all the loose ends of anything were well tied up. She kept in touch with the regional chapters to keep him up to date on their projects and need for support from national.

Today they also had Kim Webster, a student intern from Georgetown University. Guy had insisted she attend their team meetings. He trusted her to maintain confidentiality and saw she had a bright future in his organization should she choose to follow that route.

"Good morning, everyone." Guy smiled and turned to Susan. "Do we have the agenda ready?"

Susan nodded and clicked the remote in her hand. The agenda flashed on the screen on the wall at the end of the table where they all could view it. Guy felt proud of adding modern technology by having this large screen installed.

"Any additions or corrections to the agenda?" he asked. "Okay, let's start with the legislative report. Mike?"

"I met with two sponsors of the latest legislation on background checks to share the research I had collected on its ineffectiveness."

"Did you meet with them in person or just a staff member?" asked Guy.

"Of course, they tried to foist me off on a staff member, but I persevered. I had to come back three times, but I did finally succeed." Mike shook his head. "Some of those guys are just barricaded against us." He smiled. "But I know Senator Smith has a weakness for Godiva Chocolates, so I think that's what finally got me in."

Guy laughed. "Maybe it will have the hidden benefit of keeping him off the sauce. I don't know if that's scientific fact or just an old boys' tale, but I have always heard it helps."

"I've heard that also, but I don't believe it," said Susan. She was the scientifically inclined health nut of the group. Tall and slim, she could bench-press her own weight, and she wasn't shy about bragging about it around the water cooler.

"Any progress?" prompted Guy.

"Not much, but I tried," Mike continued. "I even shared the UC Davis study from their Violence Prevention Research Program that was inconclusive as to whether California's background-check law did any good."

"Great, I know that study. Done by anti-gun folks and doesn't show what they were looking for a bit." Guy sat back, picked up the fresh cup of coffee his assistant had brought him, and took a big sip. "Ah! She scored my favorite Ethiopian brew again." He set the cup down and signaled his assistant. "More sugar, please, Dolly," he said, then turned back to his team. "But I digress. Go on, Mike."

"Unfortunately, Senator Smith was all too familiar with that study. He blamed it on technology, or rather the lack of technology. Incomplete criminal and mental health records that were available back then affected the results, he claimed."

"When did California pass that law?" asked Guy.

Mike consulted his notes. "It was passed in 1991. The study covered 1981 to 2000. That was awhile ago, I admit, but I still believe we can use it in our lobbying efforts," said Mike. "We just won't mention the dates."

"Yes. Keep at it, Mike. I know there are just a few such studies—thank you, Representative Dickey, for making them illegal—but if the ones that do exist help us, I want us to use them."

"A lot to report from our regional chapters," said Susan.

Guy took a sip of his now very sugary coffee and nodded. "Let's hear it."

"Our people in state offices are working hard to follow the lead of Florida."

"Yes, we can all be proud of what our Florida chapter has accomplished. Marion is an old friend of mine, and she is a bulldog." Guy grinned. "If only we had others like her in every state."

"Well, I'm happy to tell you that she has been coaching her counterparts in at least ten other states in how to get in good with state legislators." Susan clicked the screen to a chart.

Guy held up his hand and turned to their intern. "Kim, do you know what she's talking about?" She shook her head of purple hair and lifted her fingers over her small laptop, ready to take notes. Her bright brown eyes lit up with eagerness. "Fill her in, Susan."

"I'll be glad to." She smiled at the pretty young woman. "Kim, Florida has the most support for gun rights of any state, thanks to our lobbyist, Marion Hammer. I'm sure you've heard about their 'Stand Your Ground' law?"

Kim nodded vigorously. "We studied that last semester. It allows homeowners to protect their property using a gun."

"That's partly right," Susan continued. "It actually allows a person under threat to respond with deadly force from any place they are legally allowed to be—say in the Wal-Mart parking lot, in your car, and, of course, also in your home. And we're talking about the right to self-defense, not just the right to protect your property."

Kim nodded while her fingers flew across her keyboard.

"Tell her about Marion Hammer," said Guy.

Susan nodded her head. "I'm about to. She built relationships with all the Republican legislators in the state and succeeded in getting Florida to pass the first Stand Your Ground law in 2005. But, more than that, not too long ago, she got them to amend the law to change the burden of proof from the homeowner to the prosecutor. This makes it really hard for prosecutors to find a homeowner guilty even if they kill someone. All the homeowner has to show is that he felt afraid and felt threatened when he shot someone he perceived was trying to rob him or attack his family. It's a slam dunk."

Guy puffed up with elation. "And you say we have possibilities brewing for the same law in ten other states?"

"We're working on it."

"I want to see us set a goal of getting Stand Your Ground laws in all fifty states. Aim high, I always say. Nothing is impossible." He paused for emphasis. "And make sure our people remind those running for office that our contributions to their campaigns depend on their vigorous support for our agenda."

Chapter 4

Guy barely made it in time to be last in the line of cars of parents at Parkwood Elementary School that afternoon. He nosed his Lexus behind a silver Prius and checked his watch. School wouldn't be out for ten more minutes and here was a line nearly out into the street. Must be twelve cars in front of him. And he thought he was being so smart to leave the office right after his usual late lunch, beat the rush hour, and be first in line to pick up Little Guy. This was their first outing without the hawk eye of his daughter watching over him for any tiny sign of danger, and Guy thought he was more excited than his grandson.

He had talked to the boy on the phone the night before to find out what they might do. He talked to Laura first, of course, to obey all her rules. She had suggested they go to the library. Who knew they had a special children's section with a children's librarian to help find the best books? He certainly didn't. Another one of the many things he'd missed as a father. He'd learned from Laura that going to the library was one of Little Guy's favorite things to do in all the world. And this library had a kiosk right inside the front door that sold pastries, coffee, juice, and cookies. A good reward, Laura instructed him, for *after* Little Guy had read a few picture books and picked some to check out and bring home. But not before, as the children's section would not let them in with sticky fingers. The boy even had his own library card. Guy was amazed. He had loved to read as a child himself and he really looked forward to encouraging the love of reading in his grandson.

I've got a lot to learn about the helicopter parents in the town, he mused as he sat in his car waiting. *Next time I will aim for arriving thirty minutes before the end of school.* He fiddled with the radio dial in hopes of finding a kid's channel. No luck. *They have TV channels for kids, why not radio stations?* He settled on a classical station, then looked up as he heard the end-of-school bell ring. The line began to inch forward. He peered his eyes ahead as the doors opened and a swarm of kids poured out. He saw the first car door open and two children climb inside. He moved up a space and watched the second car repeat the process with three kids.

Because Laura now worked full time, Little Guy usually stayed for what they called "after school." Guy hoped that when Laura took him to school that morning she had dropped off the note with Little Guy's teacher giving written permission for him to pick up his grandson. He moved up another space, then another. When at long last he got to the front of the line, he scanned the remaining children but saw no sign of the boy. He turned off his engine and climbed out, shading his eyes with his hand against the afternoon sun. The long circular driveway into the front of the school unfortunately faced west straight into the sun. He stepped around the car and under the shade of the sheltered walkway that extended over the sidewalk from the front door to the curb for about fifty feet. He wasn't sure if he needed to go inside. Laura had said not. But where was his grandson? He leaned against the side of his car.

The front door of the school opened, and a tall, black-haired older woman walked out with a boy holding her hand. As they approached, Little Guy spied him at the same time he recognized the boy. Little Guy pulled on the woman's hand and pointed, bouncing ahead. The woman held on and leaned over to say something Guy couldn't hear. Clearly, she was charged with escorting the boy to meet his grandfather.

As Little Guy slowed his eager steps, Guy watched with appreciation. The school obviously was not going to let children climb into any car without proper identification. He smiled and waved. Little Guy waved back vigorously.

"Hi, Granddad!" he hollered. He turned to the woman and said, "That's my Granddad!"

She smiled and waved as well. "Mr. Grant?" she asked as they at long last made it to him.

"Yes, I'm the granddad," he replied. She released the boy's hand. He catapulted himself forward, hugging his granddad around the legs. Guy rubbed the boy's hair. "Hello, Little Guy."

"Mr. Grant, I am Ms. Warwick, Guy's teacher. I understand you have permission to pick him up today?" She gave him a broad smile.

He couldn't help but notice her beauty—dark hair streaked with a few silver hairs, green eyes, a smile that he returned before he even realized it. Her face bore a few lines but shone with a vitality he envied.

"Yes, it's our first solo outing," said Guy. He turned with some reluctance from her beautiful face to address his grandson. "We're going to the library, isn't that right, sport?"

"Yes, we are! Ms. Warwick," crowed Little Guy, grabbing her hand as he held on to Guy's leg with the other, "we are going to read all the books!"

Ms. Warwick laughed. "Reading is fun, isn't it?" He nodded with enthusiasm. "And you are a very good reader, Guy." He shone with pleasure. She turned to his grandfather. "This boy is one of my favorite students of all time. He is so bright, so eager to learn. He's a joy to have in my classroom."

"I'm so glad to hear this," said Guy. "Have you been teaching for a while?" He wasn't sure if he was being too personal and overstepping some invisible line, but he found her so fascinating he couldn't resist.

"Oh, longer than I care to remember. And, I have to say, I have loved every minute. Especially when I have students like your grandson." She squatted down to Little Guy's level. "Handshake, hug, or high five?"

Little Guy did not hesitate. "Hug!" he cried as he threw his arms around his teacher's neck and squeezed. She squeezed him back for a long moment, then slowly unpeeled his arms from around her and stood up.

"Lovely to meet you, Mr. Grant." She extended her hand.

He took it and felt the urge to hug her himself. He quickly let it go. "I can see Little Guy is lucky to have you for his teacher."

"We're both lucky," she replied with a big smile. "Have a fun afternoon reading all the books, Guy. See you tomorrow."

Little Guy grabbed his grandfather's hand. "See you tomorrow, Ms. Warwick." He turned toward the car. "Granddad, do you know the way to the library?" His bright eyes met his grandfather's.

"I certainly do, Little Guy. Let me strap you in and we'll be off."

"You brought my car seat!" he exclaimed as he climbed into the back seat.

"Your mother wouldn't let me go anywhere without it."

He had to admit that he knew the way to the library only because he had looked it up and programmed it into his GPS. He had never actually been to the city's new library. As he drove up the long entrance road, he wondered why not. He didn't read like he once did. At least not for pleasure. He read a lot for work but nothing he needed to go to the public library to find. But surely that was beginning to change.

"I see it, Granddad!" hollered Little Guy from the back seat. "There it is." His little feet beat an excited pattern against the back of the passenger seat in front of him.

Guy's eyes widened as a two-story, red-brick building with glass walls appeared over the rise. Grass and paths and benches with tall trees offered shade on all the sides he could see. A sign that read "Library Park" gave a fitting caption to what he saw. Rather than a sea of asphalt, the parking was in rows beside a grassy median filled with more trees.

Once he got the boy unstrapped from his car seat, Guy had to hold tight to his hand to keep him from running full force to the front door. They passed several adults holding tall stacks of books while leading small children skipping along with smaller stacks. One young father was perched on a bench under a green leafy oak reading to a little girl who had draped herself across his arm to see the pictures on the pages. The wide double doors opened automatically as they approached the entrance. Inside, they found a small cafe area with a few small tables in front of a kiosk stocked with just the treats Laura had told him about.

"When Mommy brings me, she lets me have a snack after I read some books," said Little Guy. "Can we do that too? I mean, after I read?"

Guy squeezed the boy's hand. "Sounds like a plan, but only if I can have a snack too."

Little Guy laughed and squinched up his face as if asking, *Why are you asking me? You're the grown-up!* "Mommy gets herself a snack if she's not on a diet," he confided. "And she hardly ever is on a diet if they have chocolate chip cookies. They're her favorite."

"Mine too," said Guy, patting his belly rolls that wouldn't stay inside his belt.

Little Guy led the way down the hall where they came to a wide opening on the right. A mural of two trunks whose leaves joined overhead on each side made it feel like you were walking into a forest. Behind it were small tables and chairs and an expanse of bookshelves, along with a few cozy nooks with fuzzy beanbag chairs. In the middle, behind a counter, was a young woman whose face lit up when they walked under the trees.

"Hello, Guy," she called to the boy. "Good to see you."

"Hello, Ms. Martin. This is my granddad." He dragged Guy by the hand. "We're going to read a lot of books and then have a snack. Both of us." He grinned up at Guy. "Right, Granddad?"

"Right you are," said Guy. "You must be the librarian I've heard so much about."

"Your grandson is one of our most faithful customers. And quite a good reader for his age."

"I want to see all the new books!" said Little Guy.

"Well, you know where we keep them." She waved toward a display under a large sign that read *New Books*. There were two small tables with chairs and a bright-orange circular rug with large pillows. "Is that where you'd like to start?"

"I want to show my granddad."

"Good idea," she said as she came from behind the counter and escorted them. "We have all the latest Caldecott winners," she said to Guy. "And some Newberry winners also."

Guy nodded, not having a clue what she was talking about, and followed behind as Little Guy skipped ahead.

Picking up a book from the display, Ms. Martin handed it to Little Guy. "Can you read the title?"

Little Guy held the book in both hands and studied the cover. "How . . . Alma . . . Got . . . Her . . . Name." He raised his head to the librarian with a question mark.

"That's right," she said, then turned to Guy. "If you need any help, let me know. Enjoy reading together."

"Want me to read this book to you, Little Guy?" he asked. But the boy had already plopped down on the orange rug and opened the book. "Or perhaps you will read it to me," he said as he lowered himself to his knees, felt and heard a few creaks and crunches, then somehow made it all the way down to sit next to his grandson. He couldn't remember the last time he had sat cross-legged on a rug, and it took him some time to remember how to do it. And he predicted he'd need more time to remember how to get up when that time came.

Little Guy hadn't waited. He was halfway through the short book, reading quietly to himself. When Guy got down next to him, the boy leaned on Guy's thigh and paused his reading briefly to lift his head to his grandfather and say, "We have to read in a whisper in the library so we won't disturb the other readers."

Guy smiled and nodded in agreement. He loved the feel of the boy leaning on him and draped his arm around him. A surge of protective love rose up inside of him. He would never let any harm come to this boy. Never. He listened for a few moments in wonder as the boy sounded out the words and pieced the story together until he closed the back cover. "Good job, son, you are a good reader."

"Thanks," said the boy. "I like this book. Let's read it again. You missed how it starts." In loud whispers, he read it again, this time a bit faster.

"I like this book also," said Guy.

Little Guy thought a minute. "How did I get my name, Granddad? Do you know?"

"I sure do. You are named after me. My name is Guy also."

"I thought so. I thought your name was more than Granddad." The boy turned his eyes to his grandfather's eyes and stared. "My eyes are brown just like yours. Will I look like you when I grow up?"

Guy chuckled. "You'll be much better looking, I hope. But the important thing is that you will look just like yourself."

The boy considered his words a moment. Then he belly-laughed. "I'll have to look like myself because I am myself."

"You certainly are, son," said Guy as he squeezed him into a side hug. "Want me to show you a book I like?"

"Sure."

"I bet they have it here somewhere. It's called *The Cat in the Hat*."

"I know that book," cried Little Guy as he ran off to find it.

Chapter 5

"**W**ell, I'm about to call it a day." It was approaching 5:00 p.m. on Friday. Matt Nichol, LCSW, spoke with some irritation into his phone as he stood with briefcase in hand by his office door. Then he listened, and as he listened, he grew alarmed and then curious. Then he let go of the fantasy of kicking back at home tilting a cool brew and flipping through his junk mail.

"Two days in the hospital and you can't complete an evaluation on him? Really? And what makes you think I can? And why are you discharging him? Need the bed? Give me a break." He listened more. "I'm flattered, but you know I'm not a miracle worker. Okay, send them over. And don't fill that bed because I might just send him right back. And email me the discharge summary first, eh? I'd like to get a little bit prepared."

Returning to his padded rolling office chair, he printed the summary and began to read. *Diagnosis (tentative): suicidal depression with homicidal features.* He skipped to the narrative summary, which usually gave him the real story. *Parents separated six months, mother and 17-year-old son only occupants of the home, father apparently uninvolved. Increasing pattern of outbursts of temper and withdrawal. After returning home from school on Tuesday, he refused to come out of his room, even for dinner. In the morning, mother found him inert and unconscious on the floor of his room with his arm over the body of his dog.* Matt shook his head and whistled. *Mother called 911. Authorities brought him to the hospital. Patient was admitted Wednesday morning. Patient refused to speak or make eye contact or cooperate with testing and evaluation.*

Matt heard the outer door open. He went into his waiting room to find a woman and a young man. Her face was lined and red from crying. She fixed her eyes on him. They began to fill and spill over. The young man, tall but slumped, tensed as she did.

The woman wiped her eyes with her fingers, then extended her hand. "Matthew Nichol?"

"Yes," he said as he grasped her hand. She had a strong grip that communicated she saw him as her lifeline. "You must be Mrs. Carla Schuyler." She nodded. He turned to the young man. "And you must be silent Sam." The young man almost smiled despite himself. "And they couldn't topple you in the hospital?" Matt kept a purposefully serious visage as he observed Sam closely. The boy raised his eyes. Matt saw something there, a strength, maybe even a spark of pride. And a deep well of despair. Matt smiled and waved them toward his office. "Come in, both of you at first. Then, Sam, I plan to kick your mom out and you can tell me how things really are." Matt gave a conspiratorial wink to the boy.

Carla stepped in briskly and sat down on the end of the couch. Sam hesitated. Matt moved forward to herd him in and watched him sit on the couch as far as he could get from his mother. Closing the door, Matt took his chair.

"Mrs. Schuyler, why don't you briefly tell me how you see things and then you may be excused." Matt sat back and waited.

She cast her eyes from Matt to Sam and back to Matt. "I hardly know where to begin. It's just been the two of us since his father left last spring. It's been a big adjustment for both of us." And she uncorked the months of worry and stress and began to pour it all out.

Matt gave her his eyes while he kept Sam in the periphery of his vision. As her tears began to fall with her words, he saw Sam stiffen, then sag. Matt nodded in sympathy for them both. It was a story he'd heard before in slightly other forms, but the injured dog was a new one to him.

"I can't believe he would hurt Bailey," she said. "And of course I'm sure he didn't mean to, well, or want to—it must have been an accident, but it just scared me to death."

Matt nodded and sat up straighter to signal that her turn was almost over. She saw and paused, gathering her last words. *An attuned parent,* Matt noticed.

She turned to her son as she stood up. "Sam, please talk to Mr. Nichol. I love you and I'm so worried about you." Sam didn't meet her eyes or show any signs he had heard. Matt noted the twitching of his right leg that stopped as soon as she stopped speaking.

Matt stood as she left. "Feel free to run an errand or take a walk or just wait in the waiting area. Be back no later than six p.m."

"Okay," she said, sniffling. "I may well take a walk. But, Sam, I'll be back." She reached her hand toward him, then let it fall.

Matt closed the door behind her and sat back down. He waited a few moments to see if Sam would volunteer anything. Over the years he had outwaited many a stubborn teenager, but he wasn't sure about this one.

"Did you hear about the Silent Sam protest in North Carolina?" he asked. Sam shrugged, then gave a weak nod. "Okay, well, then you probably know the authorities were no match for the students. They kept a presence around that statue no matter how often they were told to leave. But they stayed and, finally, the first day of classes this fall, they knocked it over. And it was a big piece of concrete or stone or something very hard to knock over." Matt watched and saw Sam was tracking his words. "The adults were no match for those determined young people. Likewise, I hear all those doctors and nurses were no match for you. I don't really know why they sent you to me because I certainly can't make you open up and talk to me if you don't want to. And I have never been very good at pulling teeth. But I've seen a lot of young people in a lot of pain over a lot of years, and I doubt you can tell me something I haven't heard before. So tell me how you see things, ask me what you want to know about me, tell me how I might help you, or if you think you're beyond help. I'm here, and we've got this time, so go."

Matt sat back, held his hands together in his lap, and waited. Then he sat up. "Oops, I almost forgot the most important thing. I'm not going to tell your mother or anyone what you tell me. This is completely confidential. The only exception is if you told me you were going to kill yourself or someone else, I would have a duty to tell in order to stop you. Get it?"

Sam nodded and examined his hands in his own lap.

There began a long period of silence. Matt waited and as he waited noticed every tick, every twitch, every signal Sam gave. The signals were barely perceptible. A slight squeeze of his hands. Closing his eyes a moment, then opening them with a long sigh. A twitch of his right foot, then his left. Sam's eyes stayed on his hands. Once he raised them and scanned the room until they rested on the clock on the wall. Matt remained silent in deep concentration and slowly growing alarm. He knew that adolescent psychiatric unit well, having worked there when first out of school and consulted there over the years. As part of a teaching hospital, it had lots of interns and trainees and a few savvy staff. But it didn't surprise him at all that they couldn't persuade Sam to open up. Too many, too much, too soon. He needed to assess safety now or send him back to be locked up, but he'd rather not. Sam was tall and lanky and, if he was like most boys, might like to play basketball. When twenty minutes had passed, Matt decided to give it a try.

"Hey, let's go shoot some hoops. It's better than counting the bugs on the rug, eh?" He stood and got his basketball from under his desk. "There's a court just outside that no one uses but me." He began bouncing it on the carpet, then passed it to Sam. Sam caught it and looked up at Matt quizzically. Matt motioned for him to pass it back, which he did. Matt cocked his head toward the door and took a step. Sam shrugged, stood up, and followed.

His office building was next to a small courtyard that did indeed have a basketball goal with about a half-court of playing area. It was surrounded by a high fence and a hedge. No easy way to run off. Matt used it often when working with teens.

Matt passed the ball to Sam and raised his arms to guard him. "Let's play to ten, okay?" Sam nodded and began to dribble. He was fast and nimble and soon got the first basket. "Hey, good job," said Matt. "Two points."

Matt got the ball away on Sam's next dribble and dodged around him. Sam was on him in a flash. *Not so depressed he can't move.* He stooped low and dribbled around him. *Let's see how angry he can* be. Matt passed the ball between both hands and through his legs as he made his way toward the basket. Then he turned around and got to the edge of the court. Sam followed, arms high and wide. Matt shot the ball high and over. It swished through the net. Sam had it before it hit the ground. "You're fast, dude!" said Matt. Sam made a quick goal and laughed. Before Matt could recover, Sam made another goal.

"I've lost count," said Matt. "Is that six to two?"

"Damn right," said Sam.

Matt's eyebrows flew up. He got the ball next and scrambled for another point. But Sam took the ball away and scored again. "You play on your school team?" asked Matt.

"Did." Sam dribbled toward the edge, then back toward the goal. Matt got in his face and hit his arm. "Hey, that's a foul!"

Matt grinned. "You got me." He tossed the ball to Sam.

Sam shook his head as if this was too easy. He dribbled the ball and zinged it in. "I win!" he crowed. He bounced the ball back to Matt. "You did that on purpose, didn't you?" he said.

"Yeah, just wanted to see how sharp you are," said Matt. *And to assess your ability to control your anger,* he thought. "You're plenty sharp. Why did you say you *did* play on your school team? Not anymore?" Matt sat on a bench under a sprawling beech tree.

"Bunch of losers." Sam stood a moment, then sat on the bench as well. Matt saw a black cloud roll in and Sam's mood sink. Sam hung his head and fixed his gaze on the ground.

"Is that part of what's got you down lately?"

"I don't want to talk about it." Sam shut the door and turned the key.

Matt pondered a moment. He didn't feel comfortable letting

the kid go home. He didn't feel great about sending him back to the hospital. He'd have to let the kid choose.

"Got it. You certainly don't have to talk about it right now. I hope you will talk sometime because I believe it will help you. And I'd like to help you. I can see you're a good kid going through some tough shit right now. We all have some shit in life at times, but it doesn't last forever. Especially if you let someone like me help you."

Sam flinched when Matt said "shit" and then smiled just a tiny bit when he said it the second time.

Matt went on. "But as of now I don't know much about you except that you're a good basketball player. I don't know if you're going to leave here and kill yourself or someone else. And that scares me. It's my job not to let that happen." He watched closely as he spoke. Sam showed him a flat face and zero body language. Whatever hole he had retreated to was deep and dark. "So here's the choice: you promise me you won't hurt yourself or someone else until tomorrow when you come back to see me at this same time." He watched Sam's eyebrows lift slightly. "Yeah, I know it's Saturday and you're right, I don't normally work on Saturday, but that's how concerned I am. That's one choice. The other is you go back to the hospital right now."

Fire flashed briefly in Sam's eyes, quickly swallowed up by the black cloud, this time with thunder and lightning barely contained. Matt watched in silence, his alarm growing. Danger flashed inside his mind. He knew if he had to, he could dial 911 and the police would be here in a flash and carry the boy back behind locked doors. He didn't want to do that, but he'd done it before and he could do it again. He didn't see it as the most therapeutic action. The most therapeutic choice was for Sam to return tomorrow and talk to him.

It was up to Sam.

Something in Sam crumpled. Tears begin to pool in his eyes.

Matt's breathing slowed and deepened. Some tension left his shoulders. Still, he waited in silence.

"Okay, tomorrow," whispered Sam, blinking back his tears.

"Okay, now promise. I need to hear you say the words, 'I promise I won't hurt myself or someone else between now and our appointment tomorrow.'"

Sam grimaced. "I promise . . . I won't hurt myself or anyone else . . . between now and then."

Matt smiled and clapped him on the shoulder. "Good. I hate that hospital." He reached in his shirt pocket and handed Sam a card. "Here's my phone number. Call me if you decide you want to talk before then."

Sam stared hard at the card. With a big sigh, he pulled his wallet from his back pocket, inserted the card, and replaced the wallet.

Matt checked his wristwatch. "It's nearly six p.m. I bet your mother is waiting. Let's go find out."

Chapter 6

Guy pulled his car into the first parking space he found. He got out and cast his eyes around. Jake was to meet him here for Saturday afternoon shooting practice. It was Guy's main hobby, one he figured his job required, to walk his talk and keep up his skills as a sharpshooter. He'd invited Jake this time for a bit of feedback, as Jake was a real sharpshooter. Walking around to the back of his Lexus, he flipped open the trunk. Leaning over, he picked up his rifle case. He already had his handgun in the holster under his jacket. He headed for the entrance to the shooting range. Jake was waiting at the door when he got here.

"Hey, boss, I've already checked us in and reserved a spot on the indoor handgun range. I thought you'd want to start there. Should just be a ten minute or so wait. The outdoor range is full, and they estimated an hour wait. This is a popular time."

"It completely slipped off my radar to make a reservation this week; I've been so busy with my grandson. Glad you could join me. I'm sure I will shoot better when I watch your form."

"They don't take reservations." Jake squinted at Guy.

"Oh, right. I have been lost in the granddad zone, I guess."

They walked inside and sat on the bench to wait.

"How is the granddad zone?" asked Jake, taking a swig from his water bottle.

"It's delightful. He's such a great little kid. I intend to make time with him my other hobby as much as possible." Guy nodded to the water bottle. "You were smart; I forgot to bring my water bottle. Again."

Jake grinned and handed him a plastic bottle. "I kinda thought you would. Here, I picked up one in the cafe just now."

"Ah, thanks." Guy unscrewed the top and took a long swallow.

"You plan to bring your grandson out here when he's old enough?"

"I wish. I'm sure his mother won't allow it. My own daughter, one of those anti-gun people."

"Really? Too bad," said Jake. "It's a great sport for a kid, safer than football, I'd wager. I first started as a Boy Scout. I fully intend to bring my kids out when they're older."

"How old are they?"

"My daughter is six and my son is four. I believe kids have to be twelve to come here with their parents. Shooting is not a sport just for boys. And I want Gracia to be able to protect herself when she's older." He chuckled. "That would sure surprise any would-be attackers, to watch her pull out a gun."

Guy laughed. "It sure would. My grandson is the same age as your daughter. I never knew."

"We haven't socialized much outside work until today."

"Does your wife agree with you about teaching them to shoot?"

"I believe I can persuade her. She grew up on a farm, and her dad is a hunter. Right now she's just super protective. Of course, I am too. But they are little."

"What handgun did you bring with you today?" asked Guy.

"My favorite for home protection is my .40 Smith & Wesson. It has some recoil but not more than I can handle. What about you?"

"I brought my 9mm Parabellum. It's smaller, and I enjoy knowing it's used by the Navy Seals. Not that I ever had such lofty ambitions, mind you." Guy smiled.

"Hey, they're signaling. Our wait is over."

Soon they were on the firing range in lanes next to each other. Guy dutifully put on his ear and eye protection, as did Jake. Part of the rules of the club. Guy savored the feel of his gun and was gratified he hit near the bull's-eye with his first shot. The pungent smell of nitroglycerin, sawdust, and graphite filled the air. He glanced over at Jake and saw he hit right in the center of the bull's-eye.

"Watch me once, would you, Jake, and check my form?" asked Guy.

"Sure." Jake walked around the partition and stood a few feet behind Guy but to the side to stay out of the way and get a good look. Guy took his stance and glanced at Jake.

"Good so far," said Jake.

Guy pulled the trigger and hit just off center of the target. "Darn!" he exclaimed.

"Try this," said Jake as he stepped forward. He adjusted Guy's arms up a notch. "Hold your arms straight out and keep them up when you fire. That time you dropped them too quickly, probably anticipating the recoil. Don't worry about it, just let it flow."

Guy aimed his arms straight out and did as Jake suggested. He fired and his arms flew up, but he hit the bull's-eye. "Ah, yes!"

"That's it. You've got it," said Jake. He returned to his side.

As they aimed and fired some more, he began to imagine the

power and protection a schoolteacher or principal would feel having a gun nearby in the case of a school shooter. He had long favored such a solution to the problem of shooters in schools. In fact, they had made a press release advocating just that after the Parkland shooting. It might be time to push the issue again. Maybe an op-ed piece.

When their time was up, they went to the cafe for a soda, relaxing in a padded booth with a plate of fries. Guy squirted ketchup on the fries and popped one in his mouth, wiping the red off his mouth with a paper napkin.

"I sure could use a cool brew about now," said Jake. "I know they don't serve it here, but I think there's a bar one street over."

"It sure seems silly, but guns and alcohol are a bad mix, I know," said Guy. "And I dare not show up at my daughter's house with beer breath if I have a prayer of seeing Little Guy this afternoon."

"Is that your next stop?"

"Yeah, I've been invited to come for dinner. It's not far from here. But let me bounce something off you while we eat our fries."

Jake dribbled more ketchup on the fries. "Bounce away."

Guy leaned forward over the table. "I couldn't help but think we need to push the idea of having teachers trained in how to use guns for protection in the schools. Just standing there feeling that power as I shot, that's what came to mind. What do you think?" He raised his eyebrows and sat back.

Jack shook his head. "I'm for it, but I tell you, there's a lot of opposition. And right now, the law in a lot of states, notably Virginia where we're now sitting, prohibits concealed-carry on school property, among other places. Not sure how we could get around that."

"I'd like us to work on it. Are there any states that allow it?" Guy held a long fry over the plate as he spoke. It dripped red, and he quickly put it in his mouth and in the process smeared the red ketchup all over his face. He grabbed his napkin and wiped his lips, then pulled another from the napkin container on the table.

"Actually, more than you would think—last count twenty-five." Jake took a sip of his coke. He ate a ketchup-coated fry, then licked his fingers. "Florida, as you know, I'm sure, appropriated sixty-seven million dollars to fund a 'school marshals program' to arm teachers in the classroom. This was after the shooting at Marjorie Stoneman Douglas High School."

"Ah, if only every state were like Florida," sighed Guy. "Aren't some individual school districts allowed to make these policies?"

"Maybe. It might be good to try with Alexandria or Fairfax County to see. We live in Alexandria. My wife is active on the PTA. Maybe she knows something."

"What school does your kid attend?" asked Guy, suddenly curious.

"Parkwood Elementary. It's a great school, and she has the best teacher." Jake smiled broadly with pride and pleasure. "She'll be reading before I can blink an eye."

Guy tilted his head. "Is her teacher's name Ms. Warwick?"

"How'd you know?" asked Jake, his eyes wide.

"She's in class with my grandson."

Chapter 7

Sam sat grumbling in the passenger seat as his mother drove him to Matt Nichol's office and parked. He had failed to convince her he could be trusted to drive himself. Something had happened to her when she found him and Bailey that morning. She had suddenly become the strict parent. As if stepping into his dad's shoes. He hated it. Mostly.

He was also horrified to find how badly he had injured his little dog. His back was broken. The doctors at the vet hospital were doing what they could, but it didn't look good. Bailey might never walk again. He might even die. He wanted to blame his father for leaving or Monica for rejecting him. But Sam knew it was all his fault.

Carla turned off the engine. "I'll be right here when you're done." She opened her book and began reading.

He sighed and got out of the car. This guy Matt seemed like a decent enough guy, but Sam sure didn't want to talk to him. Or to anyone. He wanted it all to just go away. If he told him what he was really thinking . . . no way could he do that. He shuffled to the door, taking extra time. He checked his watch: 5:03 p.m. Close enough to on time.

He stepped up the one step onto the small stoop in front of the door and read the sign: Matthew Nichol, Licensed Clinical Social Worker. He sighed again and turned the knob. Matt Nichol stood right inside, not three feet away.

"Hello, Sam, come in," said Matt. "I saw you out the window. Glad you're here." He waved Sam toward his open office door. "I see your mother drove you. She must be very worried."

Sam harrumphed and remained silent.

Once they were seated, Matt asked, "Does this mean you like my office better than the hospital and you're ready to talk to me?"

"If I have to," said Sam, studying his hands in his lap.

"Where would you like to begin?"

Sam shook his head in bewilderment and frowned. "I don't know. Aren't you supposed to ask me questions?"

"I just did."

Sam's frown deepened. He began a monologue inside his mind. *You want me to tell you what a loser I am, how I nearly killed my dog in my sleep? How the girl I like at school thinks I'm not worth shit? How my dad never liked me anyway and took off with some bimbo, breaking my mom's heart? How everything sucks, and I wish I were dead?* Sam looked up at Matt. He gripped his hands tighter. "I don't know what to say."

Matt smiled and nodded toward Sam's hands. "Tell me what your hands are saying. They look pretty tense."

Sam dropped his head and examined his hands. He relaxed the grip they held. He turned them over and laid them open on his thighs.

"They look like they want something," observed Matt.

He harrumphed again. "You speak body language, do you?" He interlaced his fingers and drew his hands together. Holding them up before his chest, he recited, "Here is the church . . . ," he said as he put his index fingers together pointing up and added, ". . . and here is the steeple." He looked up at Matt, shocked to see he was doing the same thing.

"Open up the doors . . . ," said Matt as he opened his hands.

Sam did likewise. "And look at all the people." He gave a wan smile. "I haven't thought of that in a long time."

"Me neither," said Matt, smiling as well. "Where did you learn that?"

"In church. A long time ago." Sam looked into the distance.

"Do you go to church now?"

"My mom goes all the time, she's a regular church mouse. Not me."

"Oh?" said Matt. "When did you stop?"

Sam sniffed. "When I got old enough that she couldn't make me." He pictured that Sunday. She was all dressed to go and called to him. His dad had just left the day before, just packed his bags and left. Of course, not before having a screaming fight with Mom and throwing his glass against the wall so it shattered. He had naturally drunk all the whiskey in it—in the entire bottle, probably. Wouldn't want to waste any. Sam had been unable to sleep that night, had finally dozed off when she started calling. He had locked the door and pulled the covers over his head. She had opened the door—they never stayed locked. He didn't even pull his head out. She must've gone because he slept until noon, and no one was home when he finally got up.

"Did your dad go?"

"Naw, he never went. So why should I? It's a bunch of crap anyway."

"Did you decide that when your dad left?" asked Matt.

Sam's eyes widened. *How did he know?* He couldn't let that pass. "You think you can read my mind?" He sat up straighter and glared.

"Just a guess," said Matt. "I wish I could read minds. Am I right?"

Sam slumped. "Yeah, probably about then."

"But I do know having your dad leave must have been a big event, very upsetting."

Sam felt his eyes fill with tears. *Damn. Stop it, no way am I gonna cry in here.* He took a deep breath, squeezed his eyes tight. "He's an ASSHOLE," he whispered, then punched out the last word.

"I'm sorry," said Matt softly. "That is really an asshole thing to do, leave your family. I don't blame you for losing your faith."

Maybe he can understand. Sam looked up. One tear rolled down his face.

"It's very sad," said Matt, handing Sam a tissue, which he took and balled into his fist. "I bet it makes you mad as well. It would sure make me mad."

"Damn right, it makes me mad." Sam's eyes fired up.

"Might make you lose your temper and want to hit something. Or someone."

Sam nodded. He thought of this guy at school. Now, Rick had a temper. Sam's temper was nothing compared to that guy's. They'd gotten into a fight at school. This guy also liked Monica, said some things about what he planned to do to her, nasty things. Sam told him to shut up, and the guy hit him. Sam exploded and jumped the guy. He never knew he could get that angry. They got pulled apart by the P.E. and science teachers, two big burly guys, and escorted to detention. Separately. But it was like he'd passed some test with Rick. Now Rick kept pursuing him, like he wanted them to be buddies or something. Rick kinda scared him. He wasn't sure, though, if he wasn't more scared of what Rick had unleashed in himself. He didn't know what to do about Rick. But he could never talk about it with Matt. Matt would really think he was crazy then.

"What are you saying with your fist, Sam?" asked Matt.

Startled, Sam realized he was pounding his fist into the palm of his other hand. Had he just zoned out, or what? Now he really was scared. He unfurled his fist and laid his hands on his thighs, palms down, his fingers spread long. "I, uh . . . I dunno. I don't like talking about my dad." He shrugged his shoulders. He saw a few scrapes or scars on his knuckles that must be from his fight with Rick. *Oh jeez, he'll probably see them and ask me.* He quickly turned his hands over.

"I imagine it hurts to talk about him," ventured Matt, tilting his head and watching for Sam's reaction. He had felt reassured that Sam was opening up a bit, but alarm bells sounded when he had just now seemed to dissociate. *This boy has a lot of rage from his father's abandonment and from who knows what else he hasn't told me yet. Our beginning connection is fragile. I need to tread carefully.*

Sam nodded and kept his eyes on Matt's face.

"I'll help you process it all at your own pace," Matt said. "As slow as you need so it's not overwhelming. Does that make sense?"

Sam nodded and kept listening.

"To heal from that loss, we'll need to work it through and find a way you can make sense of it. Kids automatically blame themselves for what parents do or don't do. But you are not to blame. You are not responsible for your father's choices. Get it?" Matt watched Sam's demeanor carefully. He had said "we" on purpose, wanting to communicate the two of them were in this together. He saw a tiny softening. He was relieved. They had the first small signs of forming an alliance.

Chapter 8

Jake stepped into Guy's office on Wednesday morning at nine o'clock. It was a spacious place with a large mahogany desk in front of a wall of windows. There were two padded chairs in front of the desk and a couch against the adjacent wall. Paintings of hunting scenes filled the walls. Guy sat behind his desk, his head bent over a folder full of papers, so engrossed that he seemed oblivious to Jake's arrival. The morning sun shone through scattered clouds in sharp rays that fell over Guy's shoulders from the window behind him as he read and scribbled notes.

Jake cleared his throat. "Boss, you're not going to believe this." He stepped closer.

Guy closed the folder. "What?"

"You know I told you my wife is very involved in the PTA at Gracia's school, where your grandson also goes?"

Guy nodded.

"She told me last night the Alexandria School Board is looking for someone to speak to them at their next meeting about arming teachers."

Guy sat up straighter. "No kidding."

"There's one particular board member, a new member of our organization, who is pushing this. I never knew we had an ally on the board." Jake sat on the edge of the chair, leaning forward in excitement.

Guy rubbed his chin with his fingers. "Very interesting." Then he frowned. "One NRA member on the school board wants someone to speak about arming teachers, and the entire board agreed?"

"That's what she said. Just as we were discussing this issue, here's an opening."

"Are they having someone to speak against it as well?"

"Good question. I don't know. That wouldn't surprise me. But it could be just the opportunity we've been looking for."

Guy checked his watch. "See what you can find out from the school board before we meet. I'll add this item to the agenda."

"Will do, Boss." Jake hurried off.

▷ ⊕ ◁

At 10:00 a.m. sharp, Guy called his team meeting to order. Around the conference table, besides Guy and Jake, were his chief-of-staff Susan Britt, legislative liaison Mike Gunn, and intern Kim Webster.

"Today we will start with a report from Jake on a promising possibility. Jake?"

Jake filled them in. Susan's eyes grew wide. She leaned against the back of her chair and put her hand to her mouth as Jake said, "I just talked to Bob Nolan. He's a member of the NRA and believes as we do that the best defense against a bad person with a gun in our schools is a good person with a gun."

Heads nodded around the table. Jake continued, "As you know, this is a controversial issue, but Mr. Nolan is determined to raise it and is pushing a pilot program to see if one teacher per one hundred students in each school might want to be trained in gun use and gun safety."

Jake paused to let his words sink in. Mike was smiling wide and nodding. Susan's expression became still and sober. Kim wrote furiously on her laptop.

Guy shook his head. "I can't believe you got Nolan on the phone so quickly. That never happens for me."

"He's on a crusade, it seems," said Jake. "He said he was just about to call us. Apparently, the public normally gets three minutes before each board meeting to raise issues. Organizations get five minutes. You have to sign up in advance. But they give priority to parents. Since my daughter attends an Alexandria school, I qualify. I'd be happy to sign up and speak."

Mike spoke up. "We all know that the Commonwealth of Virginia has a law against guns in the schools."

"That's right," said Jake. "And there's a lawsuit pending right now from three counties seeking an exception. The school boards in these counties want to train several employees in each school, give them total psychological evaluations and intensive training in gun use and safety." Jake raised his eyebrows. "All Nolan wants to do is have a pilot program to try out this plan."

Mike went on. "I've talked to the Virginia attorney general on just this issue, and he seems adamantly opposed. I mean, it's a great idea, but I'm not sure how Nolan thinks he can get it approved."

"You should talk to him, Mike," said Jake. "He's mighty persuasive." He frowned, and his stomach clenched in fear they would nix this idea.

Susan spoke next. "I think if Jake is a parent and wants to speak to the Alexandria School Board, we should let him. Who knows, we might get Alexandria to join that lawsuit. But let's help him prepare with numbers and any argument we can think of. Three minutes isn't a long time."

"When does the school board meet?" asked Guy.

"A week from tomorrow, Thursday night," said Jake. He pressed his lips together as drops of sweat rolled down his sides.

"Are we all in agreement that Jake should sign up?" asked Guy.

"Yes!" came the enthusiastic chorus.

Jake grinned and pumped the air with his fists. "Yes!"

"Susan, I want you, Mike, and Jake to do some research and see what you come up with," said Guy. "Drop everything else and show me what you've got first thing tomorrow. This is priority."

▷ ⊕ ◁

Mid-afternoon that same day, the three gathered back in the conference room. Susan led the meeting.

"I admit," she began, "I couldn't find any school anywhere in the US that has armed staff members. School shootings may get a lot of press but, fortunately, they are a rare occurrence. They have school resource officers, SROs, who are allowed to have a firearm, but at most one per school, and in some places one SRO covers several schools." She shook her head.

"I couldn't find any data either," said Jake with a big sigh. "I want to have some numbers, some statistics, to persuade them. There is research on the effectiveness of gun training in improving accuracy, you know, in hitting a target." Leaning his head into his hands, he propped his elbows on the table. "I hope you guys had better luck."

Matt spoke up. "If there's an active shooter, one SRO just doesn't cut it. As a veteran, I think the training needs to focus on incapacitating a shooter as quickly as possible. That takes nerves of steel." He banged his fist on the table.

"Teachers I've had were certainly tough sometimes, but I wouldn't say they had nerves of steel," said Jake, sinking in his chair.

"I know someone will ask about collateral damage," said Susan. "I can just see a nervous teacher shooting a child by mistake. That's the strongest argument I've heard against arming teachers." She sighed.

"That's where good training comes in," said Mike. "And selecting the trainees with the psychological makeup to do the job when it needs to be done. Believe me, the military does it. It can be done."

They worked long past quitting time, sending out for sandwiches at the local deli. When they met with Guy the next morning, they were all bleary-eyed. But their confidence in the rightness of their cause had only grown.

"Good job," said Guy, after reading what they had prepared. "I think I'll attend this meeting as well."

Jake got to the school board meeting forty-five minutes before it started. The meeting location rotated between schools and, by some weird twist of fate, was meeting tonight at his daughter's school, Parkwood Elementary. He walked into the open lobby and followed the signs for the library. Only a few people were there. Guy had yet to arrive, and he found he felt a bit relieved. Having his boss watch him only made him more nervous.

He took a moment to look around. The walls were covered in

shelves of books. Tall stacks of bookshelves stood perpendicular to the walls. In one corner there was a large circular rug surrounded by beanbag chairs. In another corner were small tables and chairs and in another were larger tables and chairs. Furniture grew as the children did, he noted. The large center area was set up with rows of adult-sized chairs in front of the two long tables. The librarians' counter was to the side of the open area. It had a clean smell of furniture polish and new books. Indeed, behind the long tables was a brightly colored display of new books with a baseball-diamond-shaped invitation to read four books for a home run prize. He liked the feel of this place. No wonder his daughter enjoyed reading so much.

"Mr. Cummings?" came a voice from behind him.

Jake turned around and saw a tall man in a gray suit with a blue tie decorated in rifles. His face was a long oval, and his hair was buzzed close to his head. "Yes, that's me," he said.

The man extended his hand. "Bob Nolan. Glad you could make it."

Jake shifted his briefcase to his left hand and extended his right. They shook hands and exchanged pleasantries. Jake sized him up. Nolan had broad shoulders that rippled with muscles and a firm grip. He could have once been a football player, judging by his large frame.

Nolan waved to a couple of chairs behind the back row. "I was hoping I'd get to talk to you a bit. Thanks for agreeing to come early."

"My pleasure," said Jake, taking a seat and setting his brief case on the floor beside him.

Nolan sat down and clasped his hands, resting his arms on his thighs, and leaned toward Jake. "I'm new on the school board, got appointed to replace someone who resigned last year. And, as I told you on the phone, I want to persuade the board to train and arm teachers to protect our children. I know it's a long shot, but that's why I want you and your organization on board."

"We are happy to help. Our records show you are a brand-new member."

"Yes, just joined a month ago. I don't know why it took me so long to join. But I've been a gun enthusiast since my dad took me hunting as a boy. He taught me to shoot and was quite the marksman himself. Once I became an Eagle Scout, I was awarded the merit badge in marksmanship. I think training teachers is the answer to violence in schools." He grinned with the confidence of a true believer.

"Our lobbying team has gathered a powerful list of statistics to prove just that point," said Jake with a satisfied smile. "But you know at this point it's illegal."

"Yeah, well, I'm hoping we can persuade the board to join the lawsuit three school boards have filed. It could happen."

Jake paused a moment to absorb his words. "We were thinking the same thing. Wouldn't that be something."

"It sure would." Bob ran his hand over his nearly naked scalp.

Jake smiled. "As I said, we came prepared with a persuasive data-filled statement."

"That's great. But to be honest, I think stats put people to sleep. I advise you to aim for their emotions. Make them cry at the thought of another young life being snuffed out by some mental guy or kid going crazy with a gun."

Jake considered his words. Three minutes certainly wasn't a long time. The presentation they had prepared seemed really dry to him.

To be honest, the statistics they found were more about the effects of gun training. There were none about arming teachers because it had never been done. He thought of his little girl and felt fierce protectiveness rise up inside him. He could certainly see himself shooting anyone who threatened her. In a heartbeat. *Yes, numbers don't inflame people the way stories do.* "I take your point. But I came with something prepared."

"I understand. Sorry we couldn't get together earlier. Our schedules seemed only to match up tonight." Nolan pulled a piece of paper from inside his jacket. "Here's something I prepared. Take a look and see if you can use it."

Jake unfolded it and began reading. It had the name of a child killed at Sandy Hook, six years old, who wanted to grow up to be a doctor. Then the imagined scenario of that child's teacher with a pistol in her desk drawer, with eight weeks of gun training behind her, aiming the pistol at the shooter's chest and hitting the target. Then another scenario of that child, now grown, entering medical school. Sappy for sure, but he thought it could be effective. He could use his stats about gun training first, or maybe last, or at least some of them, then aim for the heart. He raised his eyes to Nolan, then to the clock on the wall. He had thirty minutes. "This could work," he said. "Let me take what I brought and rewrite with this in mind."

Bob smiled. "I'll make sure you are first on the list to speak. Take a quiet corner."

Jake went to one of the larger tables and sat. He pulled his laptop from his briefcase, opened up his prepared talk, and laid the paper next to it. He dove in.

> ⊕ ◁

Bam! Bam! The sound of the gavel reverberated through the room.

"The meeting will come to order," said Henry Turner, the school board chairman. The audience stopped milling around and took their seats. Jake sat near the front, his hands sweaty and his heartbeat accelerating. There was a full house tonight.

"First as always," said the chairman, "we have the public comment period. Each person who signed up in advance will have three minutes. Not a second more." He nodded to Bob Nolan. "Thanks for taking charge of this task, Bob. Who's first tonight?"

Bob read from the paper in front of him. "Jake Cummings."

Jake took his place at the podium and adjusted the microphone. He cleared his throat and began. "My daughter, Gracia, goes to this school. She is in first grade under the expert tutelage of Ms. Warwick. I want to speak tonight about the epidemic of gun violence in schools today and my proposal that teachers be armed."

There was a murmur from both the audience and the board members.

"I love my daughter and hate the thought of her being harmed in any way for any reason. I count on the school to keep her safe. But we all know the children at other schools have not been safe. Consider a six-year-old boy—I'll call him Daniel—who attended Sandy Hook Elementary School. You all know about the tragic shooting that happened there, but stay with me as we imagine what could have happened instead. He wants to be a doctor when he grows up. He loves reading and science and baseball and his dog, Rusty. Imagine he's in first grade. He comes to school eager to learn. He's smart; he eats it up. Then imagine a disturbed young person comes to school with a rifle in hand, determined to do harm. He bursts into the front door firing away. The office secretary hides behind her desk briefly while she pulls a firearm from a drawer. As the shooter comes into the office and looks around, she aims for his chest and fires. She kills him. She saves everyone in the school. Daniel gets to grow up. He studies hard. Maybe fifteen years later, he enters medical school. Maybe ten more years, he and a group of colleagues find the cure to cancer.

"If we train teachers, send them to eight weeks of training with certified instructors, perhaps this scenario I just described would play out just as I said, with no one but the deranged shooter being harmed. We have in our area master handgun accuracy training programs. If we had a few staff members, maybe one or two or three in each school, who were selected, given complete psychological evaluations to make sure they were up to the challenge, given this excellent training for eight weeks, our children would be safe. With this course, the trainees' skill has been proven, at a distance of zero to six feet from the intended target, to rise from forty-three percent without it to ninety-eight percent accuracy at the completion of the training. At a longer distance, say six to twenty-one feet, accuracy rises from twenty-three percent to ninety-seven percent."

Jake scanned the audience. "I know this proposal is currently illegal. But several school boards in the Commonwealth have filed a lawsuit challenging this illegality. We could join them to make it legal. We can do this. We can keep our children safe. Thank you."

Jake sat back in his seat. A stunned silence filled the room. A few minutes passed before a word was spoken, then waves of murmuring flowed through the audience. The board chair looked pale. He swallowed, then rapped the gavel and nodded to Bob Nolan. "Next speaker?"

Rebecca Olney took the podium and opened a notebook in front of her. She looked hard at the audience, then back at her notes. "My name is Rebecca Olney and I have three children in school, one here, one in middle school and one in high school. I'm a master gardener and I came to speak tonight about an idea to have gardens in every school. I have a long list of volunteer master gardeners willing to help the students plant, tend, and harvest vegetables they grow in these gardens." She drew her short frame up as tall as she could and shook her long auburn tresses. She pressed her lips together and drew her dark eyebrows into a straight line. "That's what I came to say, and I still think it's a good idea. We could feed a lot of hungry kids and more importantly teach them to grow their own small gardens with their parents at home. We do have too many kids going hungry."

Then she closed her eyes. A grimace formed on her face. She wiped a tear from her cheek as she opened her eyes. "But I must spend the rest of my time saying what a terrible, awful, horrible idea the previous speaker has proposed. I will not stand by and see teachers armed. I do not want to see our school, a place for nurturing young minds, turned into a place for a shoot-out. Thank you." She slammed her notebook shut and sat down.

The rest of the evening was a blur in Jake's mind. He glanced once to see his boss in the back row, sitting tall in his seat with his eyes glued to the front. He wasn't eager to hear what he'd say later. He thought he'd done a good enough job, but he had been unprepared for the uproar that followed. Two more speakers left their prepared speeches undelivered. Instead, they spoke in response to his proposal. One agreed with Rebecca Olney, one agreed with him. The chairman had to rap the gavel rapidly and repeatedly to keep order. It seemed a hornet's nest had been opened. The prepared agenda was given at most cursory attention. All Jake could think of was the tall brew he planned to pour himself when he got home.

Cub reporter Neil Simpson felt he had hit a gold mine. When his editor had sent him to cover another boring school board meeting, he had mentally groaned. Of course, being the youngest and newest reporter at the *Alexandria Gazette* (and the cutest, he was sure all the girls said), he had just said, "Yes, sir" and prepared for a dull evening.

But so far, this evening had been far from dull. He had arrived early enough to see a school board member huddled with the man who turned out to be the first speaker. That let him know something different was up. He'd dutifully done his research on the board. They were a pretty diverse group as school boards go. Nine members and two student representatives. Four White, three African American, one Indian, one Asian. More female than male. Of the students, one girl and one boy from different high schools, one a junior and one a senior, already eighteen and eligible to vote but not yet registered. On party affiliation, they were close to evenly split with four Republicans, four Democrats, and one Independent. His editor had been impressed with his thorough research, but Neil was ambitious and had big dreams. The *New York Times*, broadcast news anchor, Pulitzer Prize. As far as he was concerned, the sky was the limit. He was twenty-four and just beginning.

He had covered three other board meetings, and they had all just about put him to sleep. Nothing controversial had been brought up. But this time was different. The room felt electric as the chair struggled to keep control. He began writing this story in his mind even as he listened. The discussion on the issue of arming school personnel was breaking down in some unexpected ways—most of the Republicans were willing to consider it, but some of the Democrats were too. All of the men but none of the women. What surprised him most were the students, who both spoke for studying the issue and then deciding. However, the chair was against it and so was the vice chair, so that might take care of that. What was new to him was the powwow between board member Nolan and Jake Cummings. Something must connect them, and he would find out what.

Chapter 9

Guy Grant studied the website for the Alexandria City Public Schools. It was 8 p.m. Tuesday evening, and he had just gotten home from work. He leaned against the back of the big stuffed office chair in front of his computer desk and looked at a framed photo of Little Guy on a shelf above his computer. Another with him and Little Guy sat next to it. He smiled as he looked at the photos, then cast his eyes around the room. He practically lived in this downstairs den with its dark-brown paneled walls and plush carpet. It also held his television and his favorite recliner. Upstairs he had a kitchen, dining room, and living room, and upstairs from there were three small bedrooms. But he lived here.

With a small table he could pull in front of his recliner, he often ate his meals here—his favorite microwavable dinners and occasional burgers he grilled on the back deck— while he watched the evening news. If his daughter would ever let Little Guy spend the night, he would learn how to cook again. What did kids eat these days? He thought hot dogs and hamburgers would still be popular. Maybe with some prepared potato salad from the neighborhood Safeway. Packaged salad might be good also, who knew. He sighed. He was apparently still on probation with his daughter. He was allowed to come over to see Little Guy when she was home or take him to the library or a Disney movie. But not yet at his house overnight.

He turned his attention back to the school system website. An idea had been brewing inside him ever since he first met his grandson's teacher, Ms. Warwick. She had sparked something inside him that had been sleeping for a long time. It took him a while to admit to himself, but it finally dawned on him: he was attracted to her. She seemed so alive, so vibrant. But he had no idea what to do with the feelings she had awakened. Oh, he had dated some after his divorce. Even had a few wild flings. But as soon as the women showed signs of wanting to get serious, he had shied away. But Ms. Warwick felt different somehow. How, he wasn't sure, but different.

Searching online, he had found out very little about her no matter how hard he tried. Even with all the hoopla about loss of privacy, he couldn't even find out if she was married or divorced or widowed or what. She didn't wear a wedding ring; he had made a point to examine her left hand. Her lined face and graying hair let him know she must be somewhat close to his age. He longed to spend time with her, to get to know her. Volunteering in her classroom seemed the best bet. And a good chance to spend more time with Little Guy. A win-win. He could afford to take off a half-day from work. After all, he worked late so many nights. He probably could take a whole day.

Examining the screen, he found a drop-down menu for schools. He clicked on it, and the long list of schools appeared. Scrolling down to Parkwood Elementary, he selected it. "Volunteer" was one of the choices. He clicked on it. He found a volunteer application form with a warning that background checks would be performed before anyone would be approved as a volunteer. He grimaced. He was the grandfather, for goodness' sake. But in today's world, perverts lurked inside many a family, and they couldn't be too careful, he guessed.

He discovered he could fill out the form online. He bent closer to the screen as he determined what they wanted to know. Just the usual personal information. He filled it out. He only wanted to volunteer in Ms. Warwick's class. Where was a place to indicate that? Maybe he'd just ask her when he picked up Little Guy on Wednesday. He would complete it later. He closed the website without saving what he had filled out on the form and clicked on the solitaire game.

The following Wednesday, Guy parked his car in the visitors' lot and walked into the school. Dark clouds hung low overhead, threatening rain. *A good day for an indoor activity with Little Guy,* he thought. He had permission to take him to the library again, the boy's favorite place. This afternoon was the kids' movie time at the library. Guy had the list at home but had forgotten which one was showing this week. Fortunately, Little Guy always enjoyed them no matter which movie.

He had dressed in his nicest navy suit with his favorite tie and matching handkerchief, both pale blue with a geometric pattern. He couldn't do much with what was left of his hair, but he tried. He had even splashed on some cologne, just a dab. Very out of practice, he wasn't sure what would work to make him more attractive to a woman. Following procedures, he stopped in the office to register. There was a notebook on the counter for visitors and a woman at a desk behind it. He signed his name, glanced at the clock on the wall, and put the time.

"I'm just here to pick up my grandson from Ms. Warwick's class," he told the woman who was watching him.

She raised her eyebrows.

"I've got official permission from my daughter, I promise you. You should have it on file. My name's Grant, Guy Grant."

She scrolled on the screen in front of her. "Yes, I see you. Take a visitor's badge and go on." She smiled as she pointed to the basket on the counter that was full of badges on strings that said *Visitor* in big red letters.

Guy put one around his neck. "Thank you." He smiled back to assure her he was not a child molester.

"Do you know which classroom is Ms. Warwick's?" she asked.

"Yes, room 111. I've been here before." The last time he had come, he had found it much easier to come inside to the classroom to pick up Little Guy rather than to wait outside in the swarm of parents and kids.

She nodded. "I thought I recognized you, Mr. Grant."

He smiled again and headed down the hall. The school was old but clean. He inhaled the familiar smell of cleaning products and markers and sweaty children lingering in the air. Her classroom was at the end just around the corner, past the toilets with silhouettes of puppies and kittens under the words *Boys* and *Girls*. He shook his head. What would they think of next?

He stood in the open door of the classroom. The children were all wiggling in their seats with their backpacks beside them as Ms. Warwick spoke. "Does everyone have their reading log?" Her eyes scanned the class. A few nodded and a few stuffed papers into their backpacks. "Remember, your homework is to spend twenty minutes reading, either with your parents or by yourself. But have your parent sign your log and bring it back tomorrow." She waited a moment. "If you are sure you have everything, I see the first row is sitting very quietly. You may line up at the door." The other children settled into noticeable stillness in response. "I like how the rest of you are sitting now," she said, smiling. "You may all line up." He noticed a few lines around her eyes and deeper creases next to her mouth, but when she smiled, her inner light shone.

Guy stepped inside to the front of the room near her desk to avoid being run over, remaining quiet and hoping she would notice him. Then he decided to make sure. "Hello, Ms. Warwick."

She smiled at him, nodding in acknowledgment, and nodded to Little Guy. "Guy, you may go to your grandfather." Little Guy's face broke into a huge smile. He dragged his backpack across the floor and handed it to Guy, then flung his arms around Guy's legs. Guy bent down to return the hug.

Just then, the bell rang. Ms. Warwick stepped to the door and greeted each child in turn as they left. "Row one, lead the way." Some wanted hugs, some wanted high fives, some needed to be reminded to walk, not run. Guy watched in awe. How she kept this hive of buzzing energy organized was beyond him.

As the other children filed out, Little Guy pulled on his grandfather's arm. "Granddad, let's go."

Guy bent down. "Hold your horses, I want to speak to your teacher about volunteering."

Little Guy's eyes lit up. "You mean here in my classroom?"

"Yes. Would you like that?"

Little Guy nodded vigorously.

When the last child had left, Ms. Warwick turned to Guy and Little Guy. "You're still here. Did you want to talk to me?" she asked.

Guy stepped closer to her. "I want to inquire about volunteering in your classroom. Do you need volunteers?"

"Yes, always," she said. Her face brightened. "I never turn away such an offer."

"I looked at the school system website but couldn't figure out how to request your classroom." He raised his eyebrows in a question. "I can arrange my schedule to come in one afternoon a week or even in the morning."

"That's wonderful!" She radiated her pleasure. Turning to Little Guy, she asked, "What do you say about that? Would you like your grandfather to help out in class?"

Little Guy grabbed his grandfather's arm and jumped up and down. "Yes, I would, Ms. Warwick!"

She laughed. "That would be fun, wouldn't it?" She held up her hand to Little Guy, and he slapped it with his in an enthusiastic high five. Turning back to Guy, she said, "Mr. Grant, we would love to have you." Her brown eyes poured warmth into his. He melted a little.

"How does this work? Can I start next week?"

"If you fill out the volunteer application form, I will keep an eye out for it and make sure you get assigned to this classroom. It may take a few days because they have to do a background check. Let's see, how can I best get in touch with you to set up your first time?"

Guy smiled. This was what he had hoped would happen. He had even written his cell phone number on the back of his card. He pulled it out of his inside pocket and handed it to her. "Here's my cell number. Call me anytime. My phone is always in my pocket."

She took it and read both sides. As she did, he watched in agony. Maybe he shouldn't have used his business card. Maybe she hated the NRA like a lot of people did. Maybe she had read the inflammatory story in the *Alexandria Gazette* after that school board meeting last week with the headline "NRA Infiltrates School Board." At least he hadn't been quoted. Fortunately, his name wasn't even mentioned in that horrible article. But now she knew where he worked. Maybe he should have just written his number on a piece of paper. He thought he saw a shadow cross her face but couldn't be sure. She raised her eyes to his. He could not read her expression. Then it shifted, and she beamed at him.

"I will call you as soon as I hear you're cleared," she said. "It might be as soon as next week, you can never tell." She tucked his card in her pocket.

"Great!" said Guy, feeling relieved.

Little Guy hung on his arm. "Can we go now, Granddad?"

"Yes, I think that's all. Let's go." He tousled the boy's hair.

"Thank you so much for your willingness to volunteer," she said. She extended her hand, and they shook. Her hand felt soft yet firm in his. He felt his heart skip a beat. He had difficulty releasing her touch. "I look forward to having you." She stooped down to Little Guy's level. "Have fun with your grandfather. Hug, handshake, or high five?"

"Hug!" he shouted as he grabbed her around the neck.

She gave him a quick squeeze and stood up. "See you tomorrow."

Little Guy began to pull his grandfather out the door. "See you tomorrow, Ms. Warwick!"

Guy paused in the doorway to get one last glance of her. What did she think of him? He had no idea. She smiled and waved, then turned toward her desk. He gripped Little Guy's hand tighter as the boy bounced down the hall.

Chapter 10

Sam stood at his open locker at the end of the school day and filled his backpack with what he needed for his homework that night. Behind him flowed a heavy current of students packing up and heading out the door. After being bumped a few times by passing students, Sam moved closer to his locker. What a madhouse it was. He had a chemistry test the next day, not his favorite subject, and a calculus test on Monday. He shoved those books into his bag. Nothing in English, so he left that book behind. Notebooks and paper threatened to overflow. Somehow, he got everything in and zipped it up. Then he got bumped again, only this time followed by a voice in his ear.

"Hey, buddy, I've been looking all over for you."

Sam turned in dread to find Rick Green. "What for?" he asked. He'd been avoiding Rick ever since their fight. The guy gave him the creeps.

Rick leaned into his ear, his pungent body odor making Sam wonder if he ever took a shower. His long black hair was dirty and greasy, but Rick had it gelled and slicked it back. Sam felt the urge to pull back, but Rick had him cornered, and he couldn't pull back any further.

"I want to hang out, got an idea I want to bounce off you," said Rick as his hair rubbed against Sam's cheek.

Sam reached his hand to wipe it off. "I can't. I got to go straight home." That was a lie. He had an appointment with Matt Nichol, but he sure wasn't going to tell anybody, especially not this guy.

"Aw, come on, your mama gonna be mad if you don't show?"

Sam felt a flash of anger. He pushed it down. "My mother has nothing to do with it. I got stuff I gotta do. Today's no good."

Rick patted him on the shoulder. "Maybe I'll catch you this weekend. You're my man, Sam. We're a team. Stick with me and we're gonna get famous."

"Maybe I don't want to be famous," said Sam, shouldering his backpack and thinking how strange it was that Rick was pursuing him. The last time they were together they had a big fight. Sam still felt scared and confused by his own rage that had erupted. Whatever Rick had on his mind, Sam didn't know, but he wasn't sure he even wanted to know. He scanned the hall to see how quickly he could escape.

"I guess I'll let you go this time, buddy," said Rick. "But I'll catch you soon, real soon." Rick tilted his head and gave Sam a piercing look with his black eyes. He was shorter than Sam by a few inches but stocky and muscular. Rick turned, walked into the flood of students, and soon disappeared.

Sam took a deep breath and stood still a moment to let Rick get as far away as possible. Then he stepped into the now trickling corridor and headed out. Outside, he cast his eyes around for Rick. No sign of him. Big sigh of relief. Sam found his mother's Civic in the student parking lot, threw his backpack in the passenger seat, and headed out. Parkwood High School stood in a row of schools. Parkwood Middle School was next door and Parkwood Elementary

School was on the other side of the middle school. The high school was the last to finish the school day. By this time, the roads were clear. The clock on the dashboard said 3:30. His appointment was at four and only a few minutes away, which gave him time to get something to drink and a snack maybe.

He stopped at the next convenience store he came to and popped in for a bag of popcorn and a soda. Then he noticed the foot-long hot dogs on the rotisserie. He got one, loaded it with chili and onions, and sat on the bench outside to eat it. What the hell was he going to talk to Matt Nichol about? Matt kept telling him to say whatever was on his mind. What was on his mind right now was his encounter with Rick Green. He had a bad feeling about that guy, like he could do something really bad, and for some strange reason, he wanted to involve Sam. How to steer clear of Rick was turning into a big problem for Sam. The dude was persistent. But he sure didn't want to talk about that. He wanted to forget about it as quickly as he could. What the hell did Rick want? Whatever it was, Sam knew Rick was up to no good. That day when they were sent to detention, he'd overheard the detention teacher, when he caught sight of Rick, say, "Not you again." Sam's stomach knotted with the memory. He shook his head to get rid of it.

Chili began to drip down his chin as Sam took the last bite. He wiped his face with the one thin napkin he had grabbed and, when that didn't get it all, used the back of his hand. These dogs were delicious but sure messy. Holding his hand over his mouth, he exhaled, then inhaled, checking his breath. Yeah, he reeked of onions. Ha, maybe that will get him out of therapy fast today. He checked the time and saw he would be lucky to get there on time.

▷ ⊕ ◁

Matt leaned back in his high-backed stuffed chair and made himself comfortable. Sam sat across from him on the couch, twiddling his thumbs and examining them in minute detail. Matt smiled and waited, taking a deep breath. He sniffed.

"Chili and onions on your hot dog?" he said and grinned.

Sam looked up sheepishly. "You can tell?" His face flushed a bit.

"Yeah, but it's okay. That's my favorite too. I slather those dogs and when I get home, my wife won't kiss me. They're good, but they come with consequences." He laughed. "Like a lot of things in life. Maybe you don't want your mom to kiss you when you get home."

Sam wrinkled up his nose. "Yeah, I guess."

Matt watched him hold back with effort and then give in and chuckle. "I'm all ears, pal, my time is yours." Matt clasped his hands behind his head.

Sam cast his eyes around the room as if looking for a topic. "Umm . . . uh . . ."

"Hard to get started today?"

Sam looked at him with pleading eyes. "Yeah, I guess so. Aren't you going to ask me something?"

Matt put his hands in his lap. "Well, tell me about school, about your mom or your dad, pick one. Start anywhere." He clasped his hands and relaxed. "One door is sometimes as good as another."

Studying Sam's face, Matt saw lines of worry. His first job was to help the young man feel safe. Teens were often so fearful of judgment. He mentally donned his nonjudgmental cap and sat back.

Sam pressed his lower lip up against his top lip. "Hmmm, school is okay." Matt saw something flash on the screen in Sam's mind and watched as he closed his eyes briefly. His face tensed. Whatever it was, Matt couldn't know, but he made a mental note. Sam sat up and looked straight at Matt, the muscles in his face smoother. *Ah, he chose a safer topic.* "My mom, well, she has turned into the strict parent ever since . . . ever since Bailey . . ." Matt saw him shut that door gently.

"She wasn't strict before?" Matt had guessed as much but was curious to know more. And he didn't want to touch the tender topic of Bailey quite yet.

"Naw, she was a real pushover. I could talk her into anything."

"And how is it, having her be more strict?"

"I don't know. Different. At first it made me mad, but then . . ." Sam paused as if lost for words.

"Sometimes you like it?" queried Matt.

"Not like it, really, but sometimes it feels like, well, like she cares more, I don't know." Sam frowned.

"Like you can trust her not to let you get away with . . ." *Murder,* he thought, then changed his mind. "With too much?" He watched Sam's reactions carefully. *A kid who nearly killed his dog doesn't need to hear "murder."* Sam's face remained placid. "She's got better boundaries now?"

"I guess," said Sam. "I know this sounds weird, 'cause I'm a teenager and all." He raised his eyes to Matt.

"Go on."

"I guess I like knowing where she stands. Like she's strong . . ."

Sam swallowed.

"And can take care of you? If you need it?" Matt considered his next words. "Like you respect her more?"

"Yes, that's it. I used to think she was a doormat. She was with Dad for sure. But now she's . . . I didn't respect her much watching her let Dad walk all over her."

Matt stood at a crossroad. He could ask about Sam's father. He decided not to yet. Better to stick with the mother for now. "But you respect her now?"

A dawning awareness washed over Sam's face. "Yeah, I guess I do. He put her through hell and she . . ."

"She could have fallen apart, but she didn't?"

"Yeah, she didn't, she got stronger."

Matt felt pleased. Maybe they were getting somewhere. "She's showing you the map."

Sam looked up with questions in his eyes.

"The map through hard times to growing stronger." Matt saw Sam take this in, digest it, and take nourishment from it.

"I never thought of it that way," Sam said quietly.

Matt wondered if Sam was ready to talk about Bailey. He knew this was a vulnerable subject. He waited to see what Sam would say next. They sat in silence for a while. Matt decided it might be worth the risk.

"You said she got more strict after Bailey was injured?"

Sam's eyes grew soft. "Yeah, that seemed to do it. She loves Bailey."

"And I know that makes two of you who love him." Matt saw his eyes fill.

"I sure do. He is really my dog."

"I know that was painful for you. Are you up for talking about that?"

"Yeah, I guess. All I remember was that I had a nightmare and woke up thrashing and seeing Bailey . . ." He couldn't go on. His screwed up his face in a vain attempt to contain the tears that flowed down his cheeks.

Matt watched in growing concern. "What are you experiencing right now, Sam?"

Sam sobbed, then pulled himself together. "I felt so helpless. I didn't know what to do." He looked down and shook his head. "I knew my mom wouldn't know either. I did nothing. I went back to sleep."

Matt found this part of the story disturbing. A helpless kid believing the one a kid is supposed to turn to is also helpless. "From what you've said, your mom is no longer helpless."

Sam wiped his eyes with a tissue and nodded.

"If you could do it over knowing what you now know about your mom, what would you do?"

Sam lightened a bit. "I would wake her up."

"Yes, I bet you would. It might not have made a difference in Bailey's condition, but you would have had help."

Sam's face softened. "Yeah, I would have."

Matt wanted to know more about the dream. "What did you dream?" Matt tiptoed into the water with Sam.

"About a girl at school. I like her, but she doesn't like me." Sam sunk in his seat.

"Ouch. That must hurt. I'm sorry."

"Yeah, well, it happens."

"Tell me what you remember of the dream, just as you dreamed it, using present tense." Matt saw Sam frown. "Sometimes this can reveal the message of the dream."

"Okay. I'm at school and see this girl, Monica, but she doesn't see me. I stand in front of her. She pushes me away. I slap her." Sam paused, his eyes tightly closed.

"And what is the mood? How are you feeling?"

"Hurt, rejected, angry." Matt watched Sam's face turn red and his breathing turn fast and shallow. "She hits me, I hit her. I explode. I wake up kicking and punching and hearing Bailey yowling."

Matt was afraid he'd gone too far. "Sam, look at me." Sam opened his eyes. "Take a deep breath." Sam did. "It was a bad dream, a very bad dream." Sam nodded. The muscles in his face became smooth and relaxed. Matt decided to continue. "How does the mood of this dream relate to your waking life?"

"What do you mean?"

"What happened, say between you and Monica, that felt the same?" Matt studied Sam's face. The boy closed his eyes. This could mean an image had popped up inside Sam, one he was deciding whether to reveal.

"I asked her to the fall dance. She laughed." Sam winced. "She didn't even bother to say no."

"Ouch! That must have hurt like hell." Matt remembered his first crush. He was in high school, maybe fifteen. She was a cheerleader, slender and curvaceous, with flowing chestnut hair. Every time she did a flip on the sidelines of a game, his heart did a flip. He never got up the nerve to approach her. "You were brave to ask her.

I used to hate having to do that when I was your age. At least you tried."

Sam snorted. "Yeah, I tried. And she laughed in my face."

"Yes, she was certainly rude in her response. I'm not sure you aren't better off."

"Maybe."

He saw Sam slump and thought he'd better find a positive focus before their time was up. He'd have to take a guess.

"How about Bailey? Where is he now?"

"He's finally at home. And the vet thinks he's going to recover, but it will take some time." Sam raised his head and gave a wan smile.

Matt gave a wide smile. "Good news! I bet you feel relieved."

"Yeah, relieved is right. And I thought he would be mad at me for hurting him, but he still loves me." Sam brightened as he spoke.

"I bet you're taking good care of him."

"I try. He loves me to pet him and scratch behind his ears. He's in a kind of back brace and on pain meds. I give them to him inside a pill pocket. He thinks they're treats." Sam smiled.

"It sounds like you're taking very good care of him."

Sam looked down. "I sure want to. After what I did . . ." His eyes drifted away. His face fell.

"I hope you realize it was an accident. You certainly wouldn't hurt him deliberately."

"Not deliberately, no, but I did hurt him." Sam's look dared Matt to tell the truth.

He spoke with firmness. "You did, it was an accident, you regret it, and now you're doing whatever you can to make it up to him."

Matt paused for emphasis. "Sometimes that's the best we humans can do."

Sam nodded. The corners of his mouth turned up a tiny bit.

"You've worked hard today, Sam. I'm proud of you. Good job."

"Thanks."

Matt stood and extended his hand. Sam reached his hand out in return. His face looked soft and open as they shook hands. "See you next week."

Sam's face tightened. "I guess."

Once Sam left, Matt sat back and gave a big sigh. He knew Sam had more secrets to spill. He would have to move very carefully. But he felt amazed by how far they'd gotten today. Knowing teenagers, though, it could all be washed away in a split second by something that happened between sessions. They were far from the top of the mountain now, and there could be an avalanche ahead.

Chapter 11

Sam lay on his bed on Saturday afternoon with his calculus book on his lap. He leaned against a pile of pillows and stared blankly at the page. It was a beautiful fall day, and he would rather be out playing a pickup basketball game or something, but here he was, trying to study. He had a big test on Monday. He had a B-plus going into the test and he wanted an A. The chemistry test he'd had the day before had gone better than he expected. Of course, he had stayed up half the night cramming. College applications were due by the end of the year, and these grades mattered.

Ping! went his phone. He picked it up and grimaced when he saw a text from Rick. Sighing, he opened it. It read, *On my way to your house, K?*

His stomach knotted. *No. Gotta study.* How did Rick even know where he lived?

Take a break. Got plans to make.

Not now. Can't.

Be there in 10.

Sam slammed his phone down and swung his legs over the side of the bed. What was wrong with this guy? He galloped down the stairs in search of his mother. There she was, curled up on her big stuffed chair by the window with a book in her hand, completely absorbed.

"Mom!" he said, alarm in his voice.

Startled, she looked up. "What's wrong?" she asked.

"This guy is on his way over here. He's a real creep and I . . ."

"Don't want to see him? Who is he?"

"Rick Green, the guy I got into a fight with at school last week." Boy, was he glad she had grown a backbone. "I told him I needed to study, but he didn't listen. Can you?"

She sat up and set her book on the end table. "Want me to send him away?" She stood up in her warrior stance, as if she held a sword and shield.

"Yes, please." Sam gave a big sigh of relief.

"I'll take care of him, don't worry. Go back to your studies."

Sam returned to his room but left his door cracked just enough to hear what was about to happen downstairs. He smiled as he imagined Rick coming to the door and his warrior mother greeting him.

Sure enough, in close to ten minutes, the doorbell rang. Sam heard Rick's voice, sounding polite and ingratiating. "Hello, ma'am, is Sam home?"

"He's busy and can't come out today."

Sam cursed as he heard Rick's reply: "We're supposed to study together for the test we've got Monday, ma'am. He's expecting me."

Damn you, dude! Liar, liar! He prayed for his mother to be firm.

"I don't think so. Goodbye," she said as she closed the door.

Sam pumped his fist in victory. *Thanks, Mom! You're the best.* He listened out the window until he heard Rick's car drive away.

A few minutes later, his mother appeared at his door. "What was that all about? What does he want with you? And how did he find out where we live? What a manipulator . . . and, I agree, a creep."

"I don't know, honest, Mom. I don't know what he wants with me. I don't know how he got our address. I try to stay away from him."

She came in and sat on the edge of the bed. "Good." She examined him closely. "He seems like nothing but trouble."

"Thanks for getting rid of him, Mom." He threw his arms around her and squeezed her hard. She hugged him back.

"Anytime, Sam, anytime." She drew back and studied his face a moment, her hands on his shoulders. He thought for a moment she was going to kiss him. He thought maybe he'd like that. Then he thought maybe he wouldn't. She let go. She glanced at the cover of his calculus book. "How's it going? Wish I could offer to help, but I never even had calculus when I was in high school."

"It's going good. I like it. Our teacher is awesome." Sam paused. "I think I might even pull off an A."

"Great! Good for college applications." She smiled and stood up. "I'm thinking of grilling burgers tonight. How's that sound?"

"Super." He returned to his textbook.

"Okay, burgers it is," she said as she left him to his calculus.

Ping! went his phone. It was Rick. *Hey, man, gotta show you my arsenal. Gonna take out more than anyone ever has.*

Sam turned his phone off.

Chapter 12

Guy Grant had just pulled into his driveway and opened the car door when his cell phone buzzed in his shirt pocket. It was Monday at 7 p.m. and he was just getting home from work. Feeling a bit annoyed, he got it out on the second ring. It had been a long day and his ear was sore from talking on the phone off and on all day. He considered ignoring it. He was hungry and tired and had a beer waiting for him. *But you never know, it could be important.* He'd been trying to get up with the Virginia attorney general, who seemed to be avoiding his calls.

"Hello?" he said.

"Hello, Mr. Grant, do you have a moment?" The voice sounded familiar and nothing like the Virginia attorney general.

"Ms. Warwick?" His hands felt clammy, and his heart raced as he waited to hear her response.

"You recognized my voice." Bells of laughter rang in his ears. "Yes, it's Kate Warwick."

"Good to hear from you," said Guy, trying to hide how excited he felt. "I am free to talk."

"You passed the background check and have been cleared to volunteer in my classroom. I'm calling to set up a schedule."

"Great!" He smiled. He had never doubted he would pass the background check, really, so why did he feel so relieved? A surge of warmth flooded his body. "When do you need my help? I can come anytime."

"Really? I thought you were the head of the NRA–ILA?" She spoke with a teasing tone. "You mean the boss can take off whenever he pleases?"

He barely could contain his gasp of surprise. Then he remembered: it said clearly on the business card he had given her that he was the head of the National Rifle Association Institute for Legislative Action. Of course, she knew what his job was, and she did not sound horrified as he had feared. Could it be, she sounded playful?

Regaining his composure, he chuckled. "Well, within limits. An afternoon time would be easiest, but I could arrange a morning if you need me." He paused. "Not Wednesday morning."

"How about you start Wednesday afternoon this week?" she said. "Don't you usually pick up your grandson that day?"

"Yes, I do. That would be perfect. What time would you like me to arrive?"

"Can you get here at 1:00 p.m.?"

Guy made a quick calculation in his mind. He could start the weekly team meeting at nine thirty and be ready to leave at noon, grab a burger from a drive-through, and get there close to then if he ate in the car. Or he could change the meeting to Mondays. Start the week off right. "I can make it work."

"Wonderful. See you at one on Wednesday. Have a nice evening."

And she was gone. He sat in the car, one leg out the door, unable to move. Romantic fantasies began to rise up inside him. He shook his head. *Stop it, just stop it,* he told himself. He grabbed his briefcase and got out of the car. He ran through the inventory of dinner possibilities in his mind as he unlocked his front door and walked in. Leaving his briefcase just inside the door, he dropped his coat on a dining room chair as he made his way into the kitchen. Only when the cold blast hit his face did he realize he was standing in front of the open freezer. Shaking himself alert, he rummaged through the choices of frozen microwaveable dinners and selected Marie Callender's Meatloaf.

Chapter 13

"**I** think I aced my calculus test on Monday." Sam began his session with Matt for the first time without being prompted. They sat across from each other as usual. Sam had a lot on his mind and knew he had to talk about something. He'd start with the good news and see how he felt about the other stuff. Keep to the surface where it was safe. The black hole yawned inside him, darkness waiting to suck him down. Monica and his father rejecting him made him feel like shit. He thought maybe if he didn't talk about it, it would go away.

Matt smiled and nodded. "Good for you."

"Yeah, my mom says it's good for college admissions. She's always talking about college."

"Is she? What are your thoughts about college?"

"I want to go. Not sure where or what I want to study, but we visited a few places last spring." Sam remembered going with his mom over spring break. He couldn't remember where his dad was, just that he didn't go with them. But that was typical then and now, just the way it was.

"What schools are you interested in?"

"Virginia, maybe, or William and Mary. I want to go away. American and GWU are too close." Sam paused, considering what to say. "Mom wants me to go in-state. She says it's cheaper." He worried some about leaving his mom, now all alone, but he wasn't sure he should worry. With his dad gone, he worried about how college would be paid for, especially after she said he had to go in-state. He stared off into space and zoned out.

Matt noticed. "What are you thinking right now?"

Sam blinked and sat up. He might have known Matt would catch him. He still wondered if Matt could read his thoughts. Surely not. But he sure could read his body language. He'd better be careful. But this time, he decided to tell him, even though his stomach knotted up some.

"Just wondering a bit how my mom will do after I'm gone from home." He studied Matt's expression. *Two can do this reading body language game,* he thought. Matt's face looked warm and calm. Sam relaxed.

"It is a big transition for both of you," said Matt. "How do you think she'll do?"

"She has talked about it. She says she'll miss me, but she won't miss my big clodhopper shoes all over the living room." Sam laughed.

Matt chuckled. "Yes, I bet. She'll just have her own mess to deal with."

Sam had to correct him. "My mom is the neatest person I know. I've never seen her make any mess—she just cleans up other people's." He thought about the mess his dad would leave. Coat on the couch, books and papers piled up on the dining room table. Right after his dad left, she went into high gear picking up and straightening and cleaning every room until it was super tidy. He looked at Matt and saw he was waiting. He'd better say something before the thought police radar got turned on. He could mention his dad's mess, but, no, he didn't want to talk about that asshole. "My mother can't stand one single piece of junk mail to lie around for more than one day. She keeps the house super clean and tidy."

"How is that for you?" asked Matt.

Sam thought a minute. "Pretty good, I guess. Especially because she lets me keep my room the way I like it. She told me, once I got about thirteen or fourteen, that she was no longer going to clean my room, and I was in charge of how neat it was."

"An enlightened mother, choosing her battles," said Matt. "And what did you do then?"

Sam smiled, remembering. "I let it get real messy at first, but then, whenever I had friends over, there was no room to sit. I started cleaning before anyone came over, and then I found I liked it clean and tidy."

"So you take after your mother?"

"I'm not the neat freak she is, but I do like some order." Sam thought about how neat his room had been on Saturday when Rick had threatened to come over. At that thought, the black hole yawned inside him and began to pull at him. Dark figures jeered, now with Rick added to Monica and his father, shadowy shapes threatening to suck him down into the pit where he'd be lost forever. He'd been trying his best to forget Rick and had succeeded in staying away from him at school. He wasn't sure Rick had even been at school the last few days. His stomach tensed and he began to lose his balance when he thought of Rick's last text to him, that weird stuff about an arsenal and all. He had pushed it out of his mind. But it had popped up in a dream—really a nightmare—that very night, where Rick came over and shot him and his mom and he'd fallen, fallen, into endless darkness. He'd woken up in a sweat. He shook himself to dispel the images in his mind. They clung like tar.

He wondered if he should tell it all to Matt. No, it was too weird. But he'd had trouble sleeping ever since, with Rick running around inside his dreams and the black cloud looming. He watched Matt and knew he was waiting for him to speak. He'd better say something quick before Matt guessed about the whole crazy black hole Rick thing. Maybe it showed on his face. He'd give him a tiny bit.

"My room is pretty messy now," Sam said.

"Oh?" said Matt, raising his eyebrows with curiosity and studying him with new intensity.

"I've had a lot of tests and been studying all the time. But the tests are over now, so I'll clean it up, maybe tonight." Sam stared hard at Matt's face, trying to read it. Hoping he wouldn't ask any more about what had been going on that his room had gotten messy. Maybe he *should* tell him about the whole Rick thing. No, Matt would just think Sam was crazy. Or he'd jump on it and do something and everyone at school would find out Sam was in therapy and think Sam was crazy. He fidgeted in his seat, stretched his arm over the back of the couch and stretched back until his spine popped. Matt's face showed nothing bad. "Am I glad those tests are over," said Sam.

Chapter 14

Sam's mother had already left for work. Sam was packing up his backpack and about to head out the door when the doorbell rang. It was Halloween. When he opened the door to find Rick dressed in a long black robe with a hood pulled nearly over his face and his hand holding a sickle, he just thought Rick was starting early on the evening festivities. At least he hoped that's what it was.

"Hey, dude, I got a robe for you. Let's go," Rick said.

Sam stared at him. He had not spoken to Rick in days and had turned the other way whenever he saw Rick headed his way. He had received multiple texts that he hadn't opened.

"What are you talking about?" said Sam.

"You know, I texted you. Get in the car." Rick's face grew red and angry.

"I'm not going anywhere with you, dude. Goodbye," said Sam. He slammed the door. He ignored the crescendo of knocks and doorbell rings and went out the back door. When he drove around the house and onto the road, Rick was standing in the front yard waving his sickle at him, screaming and jumping up and down. Sam kept going but saw Rick throw the sickle into the back seat and get into his car. In his rearview mirror, Sam saw with alarm that Rick was gunning his motor and, with squealing tires, catching up to him. After making a few extra turns, Sam lost him. At school, he parked as close as he could to the bustle of students and teachers at the front entrance and hurried inside. Much to his relief, he saw no sign of Rick.

Sitting in his first period class, he couldn't concentrate. Mr. Hancock was discussing *Julius Caesar,* something about Brutus and the Ides of March, but he wasn't listening. *Maybe I should have read the texts.* He thought of his phone in his pocket, turned off as required in school. He dared not look now. *Maybe I should have told someone. But who and what? Rick dressed up as the Grim Reaper?*

He raised his head as his teacher spoke about the death of Caesar and the killers dipping their hands in his blood.

"You'll see as we read further that a lot of people will die before this play ends—a bloodbath is coming," said the teacher. "Consider what lessons we can take from this."

Sam shuddered and his stomach knotted up as the image of Rick in his black robe rose up inside his mind. A black hole opened up and began to pull him down. He looked down at his feet. They were planted firmly on the floor beneath his desk. He shook his head and focused on the solid top of his desk, on his hands gripped together on top of it. He took a deep breath. Now, however, he began to feel nauseated. That big stack of blueberry pancakes his mom had made felt heavy inside him. He looked up at the teacher in desperation. If he threw up in class, he would never get over the embarrassment. He sat paralyzed, swallowing hard to push the bile back down.

"Sam, you look a little green around the gills," said Mr. Hancock, his forehead furrowing in concern. "Do you need to be excused to go see the nurse?"

Sam could only nod, his hand clamped tightly over his mouth.

"You're excused. There's a wicked intestinal bug going around. I'd just as soon you not share it." Mr. Hancock waved a hall pass at him.

Sam didn't pause to take it or his backpack from under his desk. He bolted out the door and barely made it to the boys' room. There he heaved every last bit of his breakfast into the sink. Splashing cold water on his face, he felt a rumbling in his innards. Cursing, he jerked his jeans down and got on the toilet just before the other end of him gushed. Leaning his head in his hands, he stayed put for long enough to feel totally empty inside. Then he put himself back together as well as he could and shuffled down the hall to the nurse's office. She took one look at him, waved him to the small bed, and picked up the phone to call his mother.

Guy Grant walked into Ms. Warwick's classroom Halloween morning to help with the class party. Since he had changed his team meeting to Mondays, he had started volunteering on these mornings. He was dressed in a black priest's cassock with matching sash. She wore a witch's outfit, with a long black skirt, black long-sleeved blouse, and a tall, pointed hat. When Ms. Warwick had suggested he also come in a costume, he had been at a loss. She had suggested the choice of costume and directed him to the nearby shopping mall with its costume store open just for the month of October. He hoped this meant she thought of him as a good person. He had been volunteering for several weeks and he had never had so much fun. The kids were eager to learn and loved him. They gave him hugs, called him "sir," and beamed with any praise he gave them.

Ms. Warwick had just gotten the children settled in their desks with a Halloween-related worksheet. She laughed when she saw Guy. "Welcome, Father," she said. Turning to the class, she said, "Children, say good morning to Father Grant. He is here to help us this morning."

"Good morning, Father Grant," they said in unison, a few giggles escaping from some.

"If anyone would like Father Grant's help with your worksheet, please raise your hand." Several hands went up. "When we finish, we'll have a story, a ghost story." She smiled at Guy. "I have just the perfect story for you to read if you're willing."

"I'd be delighted," he said. He gave her a big smile and wondered when he would ever get up his courage to invite her out, for coffee, for dinner, something. He had done his best to be the best classroom volunteer she had ever seen, hoping to meet her where he knew her heart was. But he had not yet found an opening to suggest a social get-together outside of class. He had barely had a chance to share any personal information. She had made a brief passing reference to a husband, now deceased. Ah, music to his ears. He bided his time, waiting and hoping.

He made his way among the rows of desks filled with goblins, fairies, angels, devils, spacemen, and an array of characters from movies and books. Little Guy's hand shot up, but Guy stopped first at Gracia's desk. He had explained to Little Guy many times that he was there to help all the children and could not help him first every time. Little Guy remembered these instructions better some days than others. He wore a wizard's costume and waved a wand made of soft Styrofoam in his hand. Guy knew that Halloween was his favorite holiday. Every time Guy had seen him, he'd been talking nonstop about his costume and the party at school.

Guy paused to tousle his hair. "Let me help Gracia, Little Guy, then I'll get to you."

With a long face, Little Guy brought down his arm. "Okay, Granddad."

Guy squatted next to Gracia's desk and looked at her worksheet. He had learned in his weeks volunteering that if he bent over every time, his back would complain loudly. Of course, his knees squeaked if he squatted long. Being with the children was delightful and it also showed him his age.

"How can I help you, Gracia?" Her sheet looked complete and correct to him. He had developed a special relationship with this little girl, knowing she was his coworker's daughter. She was dressed all in white, with angels' wings made of coat hangers and white stockings. *Her daddy's little angel*, Guy thought. She was smart and quick and extremely polite. And she liked attention.

"Did I get them all right, Mr. . . . I mean, Father?" She smiled at him, and his heart melted.

"Let me see." He took a few moments to study her sheet. "Brilliant!" he crowed. "Yes, they are all correct. Now, can you read the words to me?"

She sat up straight. "Sure, they're easy. *Witch, wizard, angel, devil, goblin, fairy, pirate, ghost, werewolf, vampire.* See, easy."

"Good job, Gracia," said Guy. "Smart girl."

She wrinkled up her nose. "These are so tame, so easy. I wish we'd had harder ones, like *Tyrannosaurus rex.*" She smiled at him proudly.

"That's a big word," said Guy.

"Everyone knows that word," she said.

Guy smiled and moved on to Little Guy, who had been hanging on to every word and was busy trying to write *Tie-ran-oh-sir* . . . on the bottom of his paper.

"Want me to show you how to spell it?" asked Guy.

Little Guy nodded and handed Guy his pencil. Guy began to write *Ty* . . .

"Oh, I thought so," said Little Guy. "It's a funny spelling. I forgot." He watched intently as Guy finished the word, then reached for the pencil. "I can do it now." He leaned over in concentration and wrote *Ty-ran-no-saur-us.*

"Good job," said Guy. He examined his work. "And I see you have gotten the worksheet all right too."

Little Guy beamed at his grandfather. "Thank you, Father Grant," he said.

"Boys and girls," said Ms. Warwick. "If you have finished your worksheets, put them on my desk and come to your assigned seats in the story circle." She waved toward a circle of small chairs on the rug in the back corner of the classroom. "When you are all sitting in silence, Father Grant will read the story."

Like a flock of little birds flapping their wings, the children scurried their papers to her desk and hurried to their assigned seats in one of the chairs or on the rug in front of the chairs. They quieted and raised their eyes in expectation toward the lone adult-sized chair in front of the semicircle where Guy took his seat. As always, he felt amazed at her skill at corralling twenty-five children in such an orderly chaos in such a short time. She handed him the book *Big*

Pumpkin. He wasn't familiar with it, but that was nothing new. His knowledge of children's literature was limited to his time with Little Guy in the public library. He hadn't yet seen one that portrayed safe gun use and wondered if he needed to write one. He opened the book to the side so he could read and they could see the pictures.

"Big Pumpkin," he began. The children fidgeted and craned their necks to see the picture.

The intercom came on with a loud crackle and a strange, gravelly voice said, "Heh heh heh, it's the Grim Reaper and he's coming to get you! Heh heh heh." Then the intercom clicked off.

Guy caught Ms. Warwick's eye. Was this some kind of Halloween prank? He held up the book to ask if he should continue reading. She shook her head in confusion. He saw fear on her face. The children began to wiggle where they sat. She held up her hand to still them. They all listened intently. The silence was eerie. A feeling of doom filled Guy.

Then they heard the pop of something like firecrackers. Guy felt a current of alarm run through him. This wasn't firecrackers—he knew this sound. It was gunfire. He stood up and took a step toward Ms. Warwick.

She spoke sharply. "We will now lock and secure the classroom. Boys and girls, to your cubbies."

A thud of footsteps echoed in the hall, coming around the corner as if from the front office. Their classroom would be next. Terror rose up on every child's face.

Ms. Warwick ran toward the door as Guy began to shepherd the children to the side of the room. She pushed the door to close it, but before she could lock it, a force on the other side thrust it open, knocking her against the wall. A figure in black ran into the class-room wielding something long that he pointed at them. Guy knew well what it was. Before he could move, he heard a pop and felt fire in his thigh. He tumbled to the floor, striking his head on the edge of a desk, and losing consciousness.

He awoke to a scene of devastation. His thigh throbbed in pain. Propping himself on an elbow, he saw a pool of blood under it. Feeling his head swim, he unwound his sash and used it to tie a tourniquet around his leg. Holding onto consciousness with sheer force of will, he looked around. There were piles of little bodies and oceans of blood. He'd never seen so much blood. And the smell! Pungent and pervasive, metallic and slightly sweet, mixed with gun smoke, the smell of death. *Little Guy!* He felt panic rise inside him as he scanned the room. He didn't see his grandson. He gasped as he recognized Gracia, lying face up on top of at least three bodies. *Ms. Warwick!* He twisted his body toward the door where he had last seen her. His thigh screamed at him with pain. He passed out.

When he next opened his eyes, he was on a stretcher bouncing in the back of an ambulance whose siren was blaring. Leaning over him, a man in an EMS uniform said, "You're awake." Guy started to say something but found his voice wouldn't work. The EMS guy shushed him. "We're on the way to the hospital. Save your energy."

He closed his eyes again, not wanting to see this new reality. He opened them as he was lifted out of the ambulance and wheeled through automatic doors that led into a space smelling of antiseptic and buzzing with activity. He heard strained voices over him, sometimes speaking vague reassurances to him but mostly giving orders to each other as they poked and prodded and bandaged and rolled him. Sharp pain, a needle piercing his arm, and he was out again.

He woke in a bed with a curtain separating him from the next bed, dressed in a hospital gown. His bandaged thigh throbbed with a dull ache. A thin sheet covered him. He heard urgent voices broadcasting calls for various doctors and shouting codes. At the foot of his bed, he saw people in white coats and green scrubs walk hurriedly back and forth in the hall. One of them walked by, then stopped.

Picking up a clipboard from the bottom of his bed, a tall woman in green scrubs with short brown hair stepped up to his bedside. "Hello, Mr. Grant, I'm Dr. Wesley. You're in the Alexandria Hospital Emergency Department waiting to be moved to your room." She spoke fast, her words clipped.

Guy cleared his throat, trying to speak. Dr. Wesley pressed a button that moved the top of his bed up enough so she could offer him a straw in a cup. He realized he was very thirsty. Gratefully, he took a long sip of the exquisitely delicious water and swallowed. This helped.

"What happened?" he asked, raising his eyes to Dr. Wesley's face.

"There was a shooting at Parkwood Elementary. We don't have much detailed information." She lowered her eyes to the clipboard. "You were very lucky. You were shot in the thigh. The bullet passed right through you, missing the main artery and the bone. You should recover fully."

Guy gave a slight nod and took another long sip. Tears welled in his eyes. "My grandson? Guy Ivey?"

"I'm sorry, Mr. Grant, but I don't know. The injured are still arriving for triage." She glanced at his chart. "Next of kin?"

"Laura Ivey, my daughter."

Dr. Wesley wrote it down. "Do you want us to notify her?"

"Oh, yes, please," said Guy.

"Someone will take you to your room when it's ready, Mr. Grant." She replaced the clipboard and moved on to the next cubicle.

He strained his ears to hear who lay next to him, hoping against hope that someone he cared about had survived this nightmare, while gradually becoming aware of a cacophony of sounds—moaning, weeping, and screaming from all around him near and far. He heard running footsteps, rolling gurneys, voices on the intercom calling for doctors, the sounds of an overwhelmed hospital. The reality of the extent of this disaster began to hit him. The desire to know about Little Guy, about Ms. Warwick, burned like a flame inside him. Then his energy dissipated, and he wasn't sure he could bear to know. He closed his eyes.

Sam woke to find himself in his bed, his mother sitting in a chair next to him.

"Mom?" he said.

She wrinkled her brow as she examined him. "You gave me quite a scare. I barely got you home and to the bathroom before you threw up. Thank God you weren't at school. I got you home just in time."

She put her face in her hands.

Fuzzy images began to come into focus inside his mind. He remembered lying in the nurse's office on the small bed while she tried to track down his mother. She had given him sips of water that he promptly threw up. When his mother got him home, he had thrown up again. Then he had collapsed on his bed and passed out.

He squirmed and tried to sit up, leaning on his elbows. "What time is it?" He searched for the clock.

"Nearly 10:00 a.m." She began to speak, then stopped herself. He studied her face. She was pale and held her hands together.

"What happened, Mom?" Exhausted, he leaned back into the pile of pillows behind his head. He felt drained of energy.

She gave a big sigh and shook her head. "Let's get you feeling better. Would you like some broth? Or maybe ginger ale. That can settle your stomach."

"Ginger ale, I guess." That sounded more appealing than broth. He was more awake now, and it came back to him. The weird costume Rick wore, sitting in class in a fog, then the blackness and the sickness. The rest was a blur. He looked at his mother for a clue.

She got up. "Ginger ale coming right up," she said and left.

With her gone, he felt suddenly bereft. The blackness hovered over him like an alien spacecraft covering the sun. He closed his eyes. His stomach rumbled, and he felt a twinge of hunger. The image of Rick in his black robe holding his sickle popped into his mind. He shuddered. Whatever had happened, it couldn't be good.

She returned with a tall glass full of ice and ginger ale with a straw. He took it eagerly. Pulling the cool liquid deep into his throat, he felt it slide down into his stomach's embrace. It tasted delicious.

He took another sip, then another. His mother stood waiting.

"I feel better now, Mom." He raised his eyebrows. "Something bad happened, didn't it? Why did you say you got me out just in time?" He set the glass on the bedside table.

She sighed, sat on the edge of his bed, and studied him carefully. "You do look better. There were some school shootings, that's all I know so far. The news just broke while you were sleeping."

"What?" he cried. He grabbed her arm.

She nodded, and for a moment they just looked at each other. She shook her head. "It apparently started at the elementary school soon after school started."

"Go on," said Sam, feeling a tightness in his chest. He took a deep breath.

"Then at the high school right after I picked you up."

His face grew pale. "The high school? There was a shooting at the high school?" He thought of Rick in his black robe.

"Yes, we just missed it." Her face looked tense and worried. She took his hand and squeezed. "We were lucky. Very lucky." Tears began to fill her eyes.

"Oh, Mom." He leaned over and embraced her. They held each other for a few heartbeats. Sam leaned back. "Who?"

"They have someone in custody but haven't released the name yet," she said. "It really just happened. Maybe an hour ago. They're still looking for other shooters. The schools are on lockdown."

Sam sighed, thinking he knew who at least one of them might be. He couldn't bear to say it, though. His stomach knotted with nerves, or was it hunger? It rumbled. Maybe he'd better eat something, build his strength up again, fill the emptiness inside that now felt vast.

That's what Matt, his therapist, would say—good self-care, he always preached. There wasn't much else he could do now anyway. And who knew what lay ahead?

"Maybe I would like some broth now," he said.

"Good." His mother walked slowly down the stairs.

▷ ⊕ ◁

It was nearly lunchtime when a nurse finally moved Guy into his hospital room.

"You're here overnight for tests," said Nurse Rosemary, as she inserted an IV. "Precautions." She was short and round with rosy cheeks, gray hair, and an efficient manner.

"What's that for?" he asked.

"Your heart," she said, taping the IV apparatus on his arm. "Dr. Schwartz is concerned about your irregular heart rhythm and high blood pressure."

"Dr. Schwartz?" he asked. Had he met this doctor? He had no memory of it if he had.

She nodded as if he knew Dr. Schwartz. "You have had a traumatic experience, and for a man of your age and given your recent cardiac events, he wants to check all the systems."

Guy felt insulted—a man of his age, indeed. But emotion was quickly replaced by a twinge of fear. "Can you tell me any more about what happened? How is my grandson, Guy Ivey? How about the teacher, Ms. Warwick?"

Nurse Rosemary made eye contact for the first time. She sighed. "All we now know is there were shootings at Parkwood Elementary,

Parkwood Middle School, and Parkwood High School. There were multiple injuries and fatalities." She picked up the clipboard by the bed and studied it a moment. "Your next of kin is listed as Laura Ivey. She has been notified and will be in to see you." Nurse Rosemary replaced the clipboard at the foot of his bed. "You need to rest now. Dr. Schwartz will be in later." She padded from the room, closing the door.

Guy lay back, stunned. Three schools? How could this be? Rest? He could not rest until he found out if his grandson was safe. The image of Gracia lying lifeless over a pile of small bodies flashed on the screen of his mind. The blood and mayhem and other bodies he could not identify, the moaning he heard faintly—it all came back to him in a rush. He closed his eyes, but that just brought the scene further into focus. His body tensed as if he had been struck by lightning. He opened his eyes and scanned the room. Wasn't there a television? Yes, high on the wall. He rolled to get out of the bed to turn it on. Pain shot through his leg, and he lay back.

Wasn't there a remote somewhere? He felt beside his body in the covers, then pulled the cord to find the plastic rectangle with the call button. He pressed it and waited, then pressed it again. The rolling table beside his bed just held a box of tissues, a pitcher, and a glass with a straw. He had to get the TV turned on. Undoubtedly, reporters were crawling all over those schools with nonstop coverage. He grabbed the plastic rectangle with the call button and pressed it repeatedly. Nothing.

After an eternity, Nurse Rosemary returned to his room. "What do you need?" she asked. Her dark brows arched. He could tell she tolerated no nonsense.

"Is there a remote or some way to turn on the TV?" he asked. "I want to see the news. I have to find out about my grandson."

She picked up the clipboard and read. "Unfortunately, that TV doesn't work."

His jaw dropped. "It doesn't work?"

She shook her head. "Don't ask me. I just work here. Your blood pressure is dangerously high. The blood pressure medicine hasn't had time to work yet. But I can give you something to calm you." She disappeared and soon returned with a syringe.

"No, bring me a newspaper!" he cried.

"You don't want to stroke out on us, do you?" she asked. She arched her brows at him again.

"Okay," he said.

She administered the medication through the IV. *An experienced nurse*, he noted as he felt whatever it was enter his system. He began to feel woozy and sleepy. He lay back against the pillows and was out.

▷ ⊕ ◁

"Dad?" He felt a hand on his arm and opened his eyes to see Laura leaning over him. Her eyes were bloodshot, her lids swollen, her face pale as a sheet. She sat on the edge of the bed.

"Laura." Looking at her face, his eyes began to fill with tears. "Little Guy?"

She closed her eyes tightly and shook her head. Tears ran from the corners of her eyes. Then she brought her hands to her face and sobbed.

He grabbed her arm. "He was killed?" She nodded silently. His own tears began to fall, and he reached to embrace her. She leaned into his arms and sobbed harder. Then with considerable effort, she stopped crying and sat up.

"Are you okay?" she asked, wiping her eyes with her fingers. "They told me you were there and were shot."

"Yes, but I'll recover. I'm sorry, my memory is fuzzy."

"The nurse at the desk said something about stroke risk. And irregular heartbeat?"

"Yeah, yeah. They're checking for everything. I'm okay, really." He handed her a tissue from the box on the table next to his bed and took one for himself. "But no one will tell me anything. Except that all three schools were hit."

She wiped her eyes and blew her nose. "That's about all I know. Most of his class were killed."

"His teacher?" Guy asked, dreading the answer.

She choked back the tears that kept coming. "Honestly, after I heard, after they told me . . ." She paused to collect herself. "After I knew Little Guy was dead, I stopped listening."

"Was Tom with you?" He put his hand on her arm.

"I got to the school before he did." She looked off into space. "I must have fainted or something. Tom had to take me home. I couldn't drive."

"Where is Tom?" asked Guy, casting his eyes toward the door.

"He wouldn't leave Little Guy. Maybe by now he's at the funeral home, making arrangements." She dissolved into weeping, then stopped herself. "When I was able to drive, I came here. Sorry I couldn't come sooner."

Only then did Guy notice through the window that the sun was lower in the sky. "What time is it?"

"I really don't know." She consulted her wristwatch. "Three fifteen."

"What's happening out there? I have no idea."

"The hospital seems overwhelmed. I was lucky someone could tell me what room you're in." She raised her eyes to his. "I'm glad you're okay. I really want to go be with my son and my husband."

"Of course." He squeezed her arm. "Go."

Once she was gone, the reality began to hit him and pull him down. He closed his eyes and held Little Guy's image close to him. *Gone, his precious grandson was gone.* Tears ran down his face. He didn't try to stop them.

▷ ⊕ ◁

Sam slept into the late afternoon, then woke with a start when his mother sat on the edge of his bed. He blinked his eyes and studied her face. He saw worry and something else. Fear coursed through his veins and propelled him to a sitting position. It was nearly four o'clock.

"Tell me," he said, taking her hands in his. "Just tell me."

She took a deep breath and sat up straight. "There's no easy way to say this, but you seem like you feel better."

"Yes, I do, tell me." He stared at her and squeezed her hands.

"The shootings were at all three schools." Anguish knotted her brows and twisted her features. "The elementary, then the middle school, then the high school. They are still counting the dead and injured. They have released the name of one of the shooters. They are still looking for others."

Sam's face fell. "Who?"

His mother pressed her lips together. "Rick Green."

"Damn. Shit. Fuck." He shook his head and looked down at their hands clasped together. He considered apologizing for his language until he saw his mother's expression.

"Yes, damn shit fuck is right." She studied his face. "You know him. Did you have any idea he was planning something like this, Sam?"

"No! I haven't talked to him! Hell, no!" Then he relented. "He did come by here this morning wanting me to go with him, but I refused."

"He was here?" Her mouth fell open. "He wanted you to go with him? Why on earth?"

"I have no idea." Sam furrowed his brow as he studied her face.

She pressed her lips together and raised her eyebrows. She withdrew her hand from his. "What did he say, Sam? Tell me the truth."

Sam raised his voice. "I am telling you the truth! I can't stand the guy."

Carla said nothing.

"Mom, what is wrong with you? You know I would never do anything like this." He paused. "I know I hurt Bailey, but that was an accident. An accident!"

Carla's face relaxed. "I know. I know. I'm sorry. I just . . . I'm just so shocked. It's so horrible what he did." She reached for his hand. He let her take it. "What did he say when he came here?"

"Not much. I slammed the door in his face and got away as fast as I could."

"Of course you did." Relief washed over her face.

Sam's brow furrowed. "I can't stand the creep, Mom, you know that."

She nodded. A few tears slid down her cheek. She let them fall. They both sat in a stunned silence. His stomach gurgled loud enough for her to hear. "You sound hungry."

He nodded. He was ravenous and also scared to eat much. "Got any bananas?"

"Yes. Be right back." And she was gone.

He sat still for a moment, absorbing the news. Then he remembered the texts he hadn't read. Grabbing his phone, he saw there were many. He opened one.

We're going to be famous, dude! Break all the kill records!

Black guilt knotted his stomach as he read. He read another.

You and me, pal. Grim reapers!

He felt sick and ran to the bathroom, but he had nothing to throw up. He rinsed his mouth and drank some water. When he got back to his room, his mother was there with a tray that held two pieces of toast and a banana, plus a small cup of applesauce.

"I'm cooking some rice just in case," she said. "I needed something to do."

"Thanks." He sat on the edge of his bed and bit into the buttery crunch of whole-wheat toast. Feeling it go down and land, he waited to see if it would stay. Yes. In short order, the toast and banana were gone. He leaned against his pillows, picked up his phone, then put it down again.

Downstairs he heard his mother rustling about in the kitchen. Then the doorbell rang. He listened to the sharp sound of deep male voices. He heard his mother say emphatically, "No, we have no guns in the house. Yes, I'll get him," as she ascended the stairs.

"Sam," she said with a trembling voice. "The police are here to talk to you."

Chapter 15

Sam stood on wobbly legs and made his way downstairs. Two police officers stood inside the front door. One had a weathered face and gray hair; the other one, younger, had brown hair and a clean-shaven face. They both bore serious expressions. Sam had no idea what he was supposed to do. They didn't make him wonder for long.

"Are you Sam Schuyler?" asked the older one.

"Yes, sir," said Sam.

"We'd like to ask you a few questions," he continued. "May we sit down?" He nodded to Sam's mother.

"Of course," she answered, waving them to the couch and matching chairs in the living room.

They sat on the couch. Sam and his mother sat on the chairs on either end of the couch facing each other. The younger officer pulled a small notebook out of his shirt pocket.

"I am Detective O'Riley, and this is Officer Parton," said the older man. "We are investigating the shooting at the schools today. We have a suspect in custody. On his phone he has numerous texts to your phone," he said, giving Sam a hard look. "We want to know why."

Sam swallowed and glanced at his mother. "Sam had nothing to do with this shooting," she said. "He got sick at school, and I picked him up before any shooting began. I was with him."

"Yes, ma'am, we're just here to collect information," said O'Riley. Turning to Sam, he said, "Please answer the question, son."

Sam's maternal grandfather had been a defense attorney. He turned to his mother with raised eyebrows. Something passed between them.

She nodded to her son before she addressed the officers. "Is my son a suspect?"

O'Riley sighed and turned to her. "Ma'am, this shooting happened this morning, a matter of hours ago. A great number of students and teachers have been killed or injured. We're at the beginning of our investigation. We're just trying to learn everything we can."

The younger man spoke, his voice tight with anger. "At this point, everyone is a suspect." O'Riley gave him a sharp look. Parton hung his head.

Carla turned to Sam. "Don't say anything, Sam." Then she turned back to the officers. "I do not want my son to answer any more questions without a lawyer present."

Alarms bells went off inside Sam's mind. His stomach clenched, and the black cloud hovered closer above him. He swallowed hard as he felt the toast and banana inside him rumble. He cast his eyes toward the downstairs bathroom and wondered if he needed to make a dash. He swallowed again and felt everything settle into its proper place. He took a deep breath. With his innards quiet, his mind woke up in a panic.

Why hadn't he told someone about Rick? Why hadn't he read the texts when they had first arrived days before and done something? Now he was a suspect. Now his mom had to spend money on a lawyer. His thoughts began to spiral out of control. His college money would be spent on legal fees. He'd be convicted as an accomplice and spend the rest of his life in prison, even though he was innocent. His mind raced down that road, seeing himself as an old man, bent over and walking with a cane. Then he heard Matt's voice saying, "Don't get ahead of your headlights. One step at a time." He felt a longing to talk to his therapist. Deep in this disaster, he jumped when the detective spoke.

"In that case," said O'Riley, "we will continue this conversation at the police station with your lawyer present." He consulted his watch. "Son, we're taking you with us."

"Are you arresting him?" asked Carla.

"No, ma'am, we're detaining him until we can get the information we need." He nodded to Officer Parton, who brought out handcuffs. "We have a job to do. People have been killed."

Sam's face whitened. He'd never ever done anything against the law. He'd never been arrested. Shame weighed him down. What would his friends think?

Carla stood up. "Cuffs are not necessary, Officers."

Sam stood up. He wanted to tell his story. A flash of anger filled him. He wanted to see Rick fry. "I'll come," he said.

"Your cooperation works in your favor, son," said O'Riley. To Parton, he added, "We won't cuff him." He and Parton, cufflinks back on his belt, stood and took Sam's arms on either side.

"I'll be there as soon as I can, Sam. With a lawyer." Carla kissed his cheek and released him to them.

▷ ⊕ ◁

Sam sat at a metal table in the interview room at police headquarters. Julian Parker, attorney, sat next to him. This room reminded Sam of every TV crime show he had ever seen. Instead of a bare light bulb hanging over the table, however, there was a fixture in the ceiling with a couple of uncovered fluorescent tubes, the only light in the room. They had once had a translucent white plastic cover over them, shards of which stuck to the ends of the fixture. Sam wondered how the cover could have been broken. He shuddered, imagining what fierce interrogations must have occurred in this room. With no windows and a low ceiling, the place felt like a cave.

He folded his hands in front of him on the table and watched the door. Julian saw him and patted his arm.

"They do this routinely before they question suspects. Make them wait, hoping to get them rattled." Julian smiled at Sam. "Remember, you are not a suspect. You are here to help the investigation. Just tell the truth."

Sam had met Julian Parker barely ten minutes before, just enough time to spill his story rapid-fire as they sat at this table. Julian had short, kinky dark hair, olive skin, and brown eyes that sparkled in a kind face. Bushy dark brows sat under deep furrows in his forehead, and smile lines framed his mouth. He seemed tough and experienced. He sat ramrod straight. Sam felt like slouching, or even laying his head on the table, but sat straight also. He imagined his grandfather had found this lawyer, but he hadn't gotten more than a few moments with his mother. She had whispered in his ear, "He's supposed to be the best," before Julian had arrived and he'd been escorted in here. His mother tried to walk in but had been told she had to wait outside in one of the hard plastic chairs lining the hall.

Julian had arrived after Sam had sat alone for an agonizing thirty minutes. It was now nearly 6:00 p.m.

The door creaked open. Detective O'Riley and his sidekick Officer Parton came in, taking their seats across the table. O'Riley laid a folder on the table.

Julian extended his hand to both men. "Julian Parker. I represent Mr. Schuyler." His smile radiated confidence.

"Yes, Mr. Parker, I believe we may have met before. Many times," said O'Riley.

"Yes, we have," said Julian.

"Your reputation precedes you," said O'Riley. "I assure you I am only asking questions of your client that are necessary."

"We are here to aid in your investigation, certainly," said Julian.

"This is shaping up to be the worst school shooting in the nation, with three schools hit. They are still adding up the casualties, but they number over fifty so far, including killed and injured."

Sam grimaced. He could not understand how Rick was still alive. When the police had arrived, surely they would have shot him dead. Over fifty? He shuddered.

"Well, let's begin," said O'Riley. He turned toward Sam. "Son, we want to know about the texts from the suspect's phone to your phone. What is your relationship with Rick Green?"

Sam glanced at Julian, who nodded. "We have no relationship," he said. "I didn't even read those texts."

O'Riley looked puzzled. "There were over a dozen texts over several days and you didn't read them?"

"No, sir," said Sam. "I wanted nothing to do with Rick Green. He creeped me out. Big time."

"You didn't read them, huh?" O'Riley spat his words. "Twelve texts to your phone. You would have had to leave your phone unopened not to see them. You didn't block his number. I know you kids. You always have your nose glued to your phones." He sat back with a wicked smile. "You know what I think?" He narrowed his eyes. Parton joined him in staring hard at Sam. "I think you and Rick planned this shooting together."

Sam blanched. "No, I had nothing to do with any of this. Like I said, I didn't read those texts. I didn't want to read them."

"Tell the truth," said O'Riley, his eyes blazing as he leaned toward Sam. "We found another black robe in the suspect's car. He sent multiple texts to your phone outlining his plan to kill many people, to massacre students, teachers, and staff at three schools." Now he was shouting. "This is clear evidence of your complicity. Admit it, you two planned this horror together. Who else was involved? We know you know! Tell us the truth!"

"I hardly know Rick. He's not a friend of mine. He gives me the creeps. I am telling the truth!" shouted Sam.

Julian Parker placed a restraining hand on Sam's arm. He stared back at O'Riley. "Stop harassing my client or this interview ends now!" He spoke at a low volume but punched his words.

O'Riley took a deep breath, cast his eyes down, and visibly contained himself. Half to himself, he muttered, "Too many people have died today." He opened his folder. "According to school records, you and Rick got into a fight and were sent to detention together. Tell me about that."

Sam again glanced at Julian, who nodded. "He said some nasty things about a friend of mine, a girl. I hit him," Sam said, then sat back. "He deserved it."

"You were in school detention together." O'Riley raised his voice a few decibels, staring daggers at Sam, then slowed his words and stretched them out. "Lots. Of time. To plan. This crime."

Sam trembled. Julian laid his arm over the back of Sam's chair. Sam sat up a tiny bit straighter. "We were not alone in detention. They kept us apart. I didn't even speak to him. After that, I stayed far away from him."

Julian leaned over and whispered "Tell them everything about Rick, Sam."

Sam nodded. "For some crazy reason, he started following me around." Sam took a deep breath, then spit out his words. "He was stalking me. He kept telling me he was going to make us both famous. I had no idea what he meant."

"He didn't tell you *how* he was going to make you famous?" O'Riley frowned, clearly skeptical and growing red in the face.

"No! Like I said, I wanted nothing to do with him. You can even ask my mom—she sent him away one time when he came by my house. She thought he was creepy too."

O'Riley took some notes. "We will indeed ask her about that." He narrowed his eyes. "Don't tell us there's nothing else."

Sam looked at Julian, who nodded. "He came by my house this morning. I did *not* know he was coming."

O'Riley raised his eyebrows. "Continue."

"He was dressed in this long black robe, like the Grim Reaper, you know."

O'Riley nodded. "Yes, we know," he said through gritted teeth.

"I told him to get lost and slammed the door in his face."

"What did he say before you slammed the door?" O'Riley leaned forward.

"I barely remember. He said something about wanting me to go with him. I had no idea what he was going to do. He freaked me out. I slammed the door and went out the back door and drove to school. I was scared. He yelled like he was furious, and he followed me. I managed to lose him and never saw him again." Sam felt drops of perspiration run down his sides from his damp underarms. "I went to class. Then I got sick. My mom had to come take me home. I wasn't even at school when it happened." Sam paused, feeling he might get sick again. He took a few slow breaths and recovered.

O'Riley stared at him through narrowed eyes. "You know lying to impede an investigation is a crime, don't you?"

"I'm telling the truth!" Sam shouted.

"Okay, let's say that you are. Why didn't you tell someone?"

Sam felt he was on trial. Tears filled his eyes and spilled over. He put his hands to his face. "God, I wish I had. I wish I had." He began to sob.

Julian put a protective arm over Sam's shoulders. He stared at O'Riley. "This interview is over, gentlemen."

"For now," said O'Riley.

Officer Parton spoke for the first time. "Yeah, for now."

"Your blood pressure has come down and your heart rhythm has stabilized," said Dr. Schwartz as he removed his stethoscope from Guy's chest. "The medication seems to be working. I'm going to keep you on it." The doctor was short and barrel-chested with a bald head. His face bore the lines of age and long hours in the hospital. Fatigue radiated from him.

It was late Thursday morning. After Laura had left Wednesday afternoon, Guy had spent a restless evening trying to absorb her news. *Little Guy is dead. My precious grandson is gone.* The tape ran on endless repeat through his mind. He went through an entire box of tissues weeping and blowing his nose. He refused the dinner tray of what they claimed was food. His appetite and energy felt gone for good. Around 9:00 p.m., the head nurse came in with extra medication, this time in the form of pills. He didn't care what it was. If they had given him the entire bottle, he would have swallowed them all. He took them and slept through the night. He felt hungover and did eat a piece of toast, but just to make the nurse happy so she would leave him alone. Now this doctor was poking him and referencing a future that no longer existed.

Guy said nothing and stared off into space.

"The staff reports your mood has plummeted since your daughter's visit, that your grandson was killed in the shooting." Dr. Schwartz's clear blue eyes rested gently on Guy's face.

Guy nodded. Seeing the doctor's expression, tears welled in his eyes. He continued to stare off into nothing, the nothing that lay ahead of him.

"Medically there is no reason to keep you. The nurse will remove the IV when she has a moment," said the doctor. "But psychologically . . . I know your heart is broken."

These words pierced Guy's heart. This doctor was not only a medical person, he was a kind person. He blinked and considered moving his eyes toward the doctor, but it just took too much effort.

"I am ordering a psych consult before I release you. The psychiatrist on call will get to you as soon as possible. I'm afraid there are a lot of patients needing a psych consult today."

Guy said nothing. He gave a deep sigh.

Dr. Schwartz wrinkled his brow. "Are you tracking what I'm saying?"

Guy finally turned his head to meet the doctor's eyes. Slowly, he nodded.

"Do you have any questions?" he asked.

Guy paused. He had lots of questions. How was he going to live without his grandson? Why would he want to live without his grandson? The image of Jake's adorable little girl Gracia lying face up and inert on a bloody pile of children's bodies bored into his mind. Surely, she had died too. How could he face Jake? How could he sit at the conference table with him and his staff at work? How could he do anything? He had been there but hadn't been able to keep them safe. Wouldn't he be better off dead? *Psych consult, huh. What good would that do?* He had no questions Dr. Schwartz could answer. He shook his head and closed his eyes against the light.

▷ ⊕ ◁

After Dr. Schwartz left, Guy finally got to read the newspapers. His cell phone was dead, and he had no charger, so it was useless for feeding his hunger for information. Guy read a long account in the *Washington Post*, then another in the *Alexandria Gazette*, and watched a TV that actually worked in the waiting area at the end of the hall. It was packed with family members of patients, but when they saw him rolling in his wheelchair, trailing his IV on a rolling stand, someone moved a chair over to give him room. No one spoke. They sat in a stunned silence watching local news stations and cable news stations. Each report had a piece of the story, and over time, they had what seemed like the full story. Guy inhaled every news report, did nothing but follow the endless coverage of endless speculation by journalists, the press conferences by the police, and the endless offers of "thoughts and prayers" from all sorts of elected officials. The entire world seemed to be in shock.

The shooter (or shooters—they hadn't determined how many) had started at the elementary school, where they shot and killed the office staff, allowing access to the intercom. Then they had gone to two classrooms and riddled each with bullets. Someone had called the police, who arrived within ten minutes, but by then the shooter had moved on to the adjacent middle school. There, they repeated the assault, starting with the front office and this time shooting into only one classroom, the one closest to the office. The police arrived quickly, but the shooter or shooters had already gone on to the nearby high school. School officials were in the process of locking down the school. But not before the shooters got to the gymnasium where two P.E. classes were being held: a volleyball court full of girls at one end and a basketball court full of boys at the other. The one school resource officer at the high school had been useless, hiding behind a door outside. With a long-range AR-15, the shooter mowed them all down from a safe distance. Then he walked outside with his arms in the air, and the police took him into custody. He wanted to get caught. Guy knew most shooters either shot themselves or were shot by the police. But not this guy.

Tears welled up, followed by a surge of anger, as he thought about Little Guy. If he got his hands on this guy, he would rip him apart with his bare hands. He deserved to be tortured and to die slowly. Very slowly.

Watching and reading became repetitious for Guy, but he couldn't stop himself. Through the waiting-room window, he heard the press clamoring outside the hospital, making him dread his eventual release. He was grateful none had been allowed inside the hospital. He saw his boss, NRA President Pierre LeChien, on TV bemoaning the lack of armed staff at these schools.

Guy wiped away tears as he rolled back to his room dragging his IV. The classroom scene rose up inside his mind. If he'd been armed, he could have saved them all. He could have saved his grandson, but he'd failed. Guilt mingled with grief flooded him. He climbed into bed, gratefully swallowed the pills Nurse Rosemary brought him, and closed his eyes. In a deep stupor of grief, he fell into a dreamless sleep, not caring if the psychiatrist came or if he got released. Nothing mattered.

Early Friday morning, Nurse Rosemary removed the IV and stood over him until he ate a few bites of breakfast. He ate the toast to get rid of her, refusing the eggs and juice. Not only had he no appetite for food, he could no longer stomach the news. He sunk into his bed and into a vast emptiness.

Sunday afternoon, Guy opened his eyes to find a tall, wiry man with wild silver hair and a face like Albert Einstein standing at the foot of his bed. Guy blinked. He felt he'd been at the end of a long, dark tunnel and was now walking very slowly toward this man who exuded authority. Their eyes met. Guy felt he was being dissected through his eyes, cut open with his gaze, and laid bare on the bed. He couldn't speak.

Finally, the spell was broken. He cleared his throat. "You must be the shrink," he said.

Einstein-face smiled. "I'm Kenneth Mehlman." He motioned to the chair by the bed. "May I sit down?"

"Sure," said Guy.

Dr. Mehlman sat and scooted the chair closer to the bed. "I'm sorry I couldn't get to you yesterday, but we're pretty much over-whelmed. I know you've lost your grandson in the shooting. I'm so sorry for your loss."

Guy studied Dr. Mehlman's face. It was full of lines—frown lines on his forehead, crow's feet by his eyes, deep lines from his nose to the corners of his mouth. This man was obviously very experienced and just as obviously comfortable with silence. Dr. Mehlman said nothing more and waited. Guy hadn't had a psych consult before. He had thought he'd be interviewed extensively, asked a lot of personal questions, and that anything he said could be held against him and give reason for him to be locked in the psych ward. He had not expected to feel safe. But he did.

He wasn't sure what he was supposed to say. What did he want to say? Then words popped out.

"I was there, I was volunteering in my grandson's classroom. I got shot. I don't remember much." He wasn't aware he had started weeping until Dr. Mehlman handed him a tissue. He dabbed his eyes. "Thank you," he said. He looked at Dr. Mehlman's face and saw strength, sadness, kindness. "I don't know what I'm going to do. I never thought . . ." He lapsed into silence.

"You're in shock. It will take you a while to process this terrible event. Be gentle with yourself."

Guy did feel shock, shock to hear these words. *Be gentle with myself?* He couldn't remember ever being given this advice. Nor could he remember ever being gentle with himself.

Dr. Mehlman nodded. "I can write you prescriptions, something to keep your mood from sinking too low, something to help you sleep." Dr. Mehlman held up his prescription pad. "But the best thing is to pull those you love close to you and cherish them. Talk about your feelings. Listen to theirs."

Guy thought of Laura and Tom. She had stopped by only once. He had tried to call her on the phone in his room but had just gotten her voice mail. He couldn't imagine what they were going through. He didn't think he even knew how to talk to them. He had to try. He nodded.

Dr. Mehlman scribbled on his pad. "Here is something to help you sleep. Take it for the next week, then we'll see if you need an antidepressant . . ." He paused. "I will see if I can work you in to see me after a week, but it may be two weeks." He sighed. "I am suddenly very busy and so are all my colleagues. But I'll do my best."

Guy nodded. Medication for sleep he welcomed, but an antidepressant? That was foreign territory.

"I have to ask you one more thing," said Dr. Mehlman. "Have

you felt like hurting yourself? Now or at any time in the past?"

Guy zoned out, found himself back in the long, dark tunnel. He didn't know how to answer. Yes, maybe, no? "Not really," he said.

"Not really?" Dr. Mehlman leaned his head toward him.

"No," Guy whispered. Then he realized he'd better make eye contact if he didn't want to be locked up. He looked directly into the shrink's eyes and spoke loud and clear. "No, I mean no."

Dr. Mehlman tilted his head and raised his eyebrows. When Guy said nothing else, he said, "If that changes, call me at once." He handed Guy a business card. "That's my office number and cell number. Someone is available at those numbers twenty-four-seven."

Chapter 16

Saturday morning, when Guy was finally discharged from the hospital, he was surprised to see his son-in-law appear to drive him home. Nurse Rosemary was reviewing the discharge instructions in his room when Tom walked in. Guy, dressed in his street clothes, sat in the chair next to his bed, a wheelchair next to him.

"Oh, Tom," said Guy, his voice catching. He reached his hand toward him, but Tom didn't respond. "Where's Laura?"

"I'm here to take you home," was all Tom said. His face was drawn and sallow, his usual erect posture slumped. He barely made eye contact with Guy.

Nurse Rosemary quickly finished. She handed him two bottles of pills, a sheaf of papers, and a plastic bag with the rest of his belongings and left.

"Well, let's get you home," said Tom. He stepped behind the wheelchair and held the handles.

"Tom," said Guy, searching Tom's face before he transferred from chair to wheelchair. "How's Laura doing? How are you doing?" His voice broke. "I can't believe Little Guy is gone." He felt tears well up. He choked them back.

"How do you think we're doing?" said Tom with an edge to his voice.

Guy wasn't sure what to say. Tom had always been quiet when

he'd visited them. The focus had always been on Little Guy, who bounced and jumped and pulled on Guy's hand. He couldn't remember ever being alone with his son-in-law. He felt he needed to say something. But what?

"I'm still in shock," he said. "I imagine you and Laura are also. It's unfathomable, awful, horrible."

"You got that right," said Tom. He moved the wheelchair slightly. "You got everything?"

"Yeah, I think so."

"Let's get going."

Guy grabbed the arms of the wheelchair and somehow got settled with minimal discomfort. He could walk but hadn't done as much as they wanted him to, even with the crutches, which he now tucked beside him in the wheelchair. They stuck up over his head. Tom pushed them down, the tips on the footrests. He pictured walking from his kitchen to his den to his bedroom. All stairs. He dreaded it.

Tom rolled him down the hall to the elevators. There were several people waiting—someone else in a wheelchair, a few with long faces, a few in green scrubs. When the doors opened, they squeezed in. A heavy silence filled the elevator as it descended to the ground floor.

When they got to the bottom, Guy remembered the crowd of press that had been outside for days. He stiffened in anticipation. Tom rolled him outside and left him at the curb while he went to get the car. Immediately, reporters swarmed him, sticking microphones and cameras into his face. He had experience dealing with the press for his job, but not like this. He felt he was a piece of carrion being attacked by vultures.

He shook his head. "No comment. No comment. No comment,"

he repeated like a mantra.

Some journalists backed off, but others kept coming. A young reporter pushed through the others and asked the question he had most dreaded. This guy had done his homework.

"Guy Grant, as head of the NRA Institute for Legislative Action and in the aftermath of yet another school shooting, do you still endorse the NRA's policy recommending that school staff should be armed?"

Guy reeled as if shot. How did this guy find out who he was? He stared at this young man, holding a notepad and pencil, leaning forward, eager. He scanned the drive for Tom's car, longing to be rescued. The crowd around him reacted. Some stared at him, some murmured to those around them: "He's NRA." The crowd moved away, stared daggers at him. Other reporters moved closer.

"I understand you were injured in the shooting," said the young reporter. "Why were you at the school?"

Guy couldn't breathe; he felt disarmed, naked. He wanted to disappear into Tom's car, into his home. How did this kid find all this out? He sat speechless, gaping at the reporter. Others shoved microphones in his face and spoke over each other in their hurry to ask their questions. It all merged into an aggressive tidal wave of sound. He closed his eyes.

The reporter saw an opening and took it. "Here's my card. I'm Neil Simpson. I have a few questions. Perhaps we can talk later."

Guy felt invaded, felt a fire light inside him. His eyes flew open. "No comment!" he shouted. "No comment!" Where was Tom? He looked around in growing agitation.

Neil Simpson slipped his card into Guy's shirt pocket and stepped back. Just then, Tom pulled up next to the curb. Relief washed over

Guy. But Tom seemed to be moving in slow motion. He opened his car door, stepped out, closed it, walked around to where Guy sat, opened the back door, and helped Guy into the back seat with his crutches. Then he closed the door, walked around to the driver's side, got in, and drove off. All this without saying a word. Tom's silence unnerved Guy.

"Jeez, the press were driving me mad. Glad you rescued me. Thanks," said Guy.

"I'm sure you know how to handle them, given what you do for a living," Tom said with ice in his voice.

Guy said nothing for the remainder of the drive. His mind buzzed, his heart ached, his thigh throbbed. He understood exactly why Tom was being so cold to him and why Laura had stayed away. He knew how Laura felt about the NRA. He expected Tom felt the same way. Was he now going to lose them as well as his grandson? Awash in tremendous guilt, he closed his eyes in a vain attempt to hold back the tears that streamed down his face.

What did he think about the NRA's policy? He wasn't sure anymore. Everything felt different now without Little Guy. He longed to see his daughter, to give her a big hug, to weep with her over Little Guy's death. Her absence felt like a poison dart that was now seeping under his skin, into his bloodstream, into his heart.

▷ ⊕ ◁

"I thought they were going to arrest me," said Sam as he sat with Matt Nichol. It was Saturday afternoon, but Matt had agreed to see him. "But my lawyer convinced the police to interview my teacher, the nurse, and my mom before doing that."

Matt kept his eyes on Sam's face and shook his head. He knew how tough that detective could be, how eager to find another shooter. Sam was not the first of his young clients who'd had to deal with Detective O'Riley. The man could cross the line with undue pressure when interviewing a suspect. He'd never been accused of soliciting a false confession. Yet. And now the entire community was reeling. The police felt enormous pressure to solve this horrible crime, and they could project it onto any possible subject.

"That sounds really rough," Matt said. "I'm sorry." He nodded toward the basket on the table next to Sam's chair. It contained hand-sized basketballs, footballs, even a small stuffed monkey. All good for stress relief. There was also a plastic sphere sitting next to the basket with intricate pieces that allowed it to open up into a bigger sphere. It was called a Hoberman Mini Sphere, and Matt used it to demonstrate the concept of minimizer-maximizer, holding things in and letting things out, and the need to be able to do one or the other depending on the circumstances.

"Boy, am I glad to be here instead of there." Sam grabbed a rubber ball from the basket and worked it over fiercely with his grip. "If Mom hadn't gotten me this high-powered lawyer, Julian Parker, I'd be sitting behind bars now, I bet."

"Your mother is a smart lady."

"She sure is," said Sam. He picked it up the mini sphere, extended it to its full size, and began to pour out the whole story. Matt listened, riveted. He had followed this story closely in the news. They had not yet found another shooter. This suspect denied anyone else helped him. Listening now to Sam, Matt felt sure Sam was innocent. How

Rick Green was able to cause so much damage by himself astounded Matt. But so far, they hadn't found anyone else. Maybe Rick was the only shooter.

As he listened, Matt assessed Sam's mental and emotional state. They'd been working together a relatively short time and it had taken Sam a while to open up. Sam's words were clear, no pressured speech or rumination evident. He was traumatized but clearly not paralyzed. Matt felt the boy now trusted him some and knew he needed a safe place more than ever. His father was still missing in action, which was a hard enough loss, but to have been accused of being Rick Green's accomplice would traumatize someone much more stable than Sam. He did seem stronger than when he first came in. But he was still depressed. Matt wanted to help Sam stand up for himself, especially with Detective O'Riley.

"I know they're going to want to haul me in for further questions. But I don't know much more." Sam paused after finishing his long story. "That's about it." The relief of telling showed on his face.

"I know Julian Parker," said Matt. "You're in good hands there. O'Riley can be tough but so can Parker." Matt decided to switch to a tender topic. "Have you heard if any of your close friends got hurt?"

Sam's face fell. "I talked to some over the weekend. Monica, that girl I liked, got killed. So did her sister. They were both in P.E., playing volleyball in the gym." Tears began to fill his eyes. He reached for a tissue and dropped his head.

"I'm so sorry," said Matt.

"That hit me so hard, I didn't want to hear any more. I just quit answering my phone. Or reading texts." He raised his eyes to Matt. "I keep feeling it's my fault. I should have read those texts Rick sent."

Matt's curiosity was aroused. "Have you read them now?"

Sam nodded.

"What did they say?"

"Stuff like, *We're gonna be famous. I got guns. We can kill every-one. You and me. Together.*" Sam kept his eyes on Matt's face. "You see what I mean? Crazy stuff."

Matt felt a pang of horror, of regret that he hadn't been able to help Sam open up to him about Rick earlier. "Real crazy."

Sam put his head in his hands and began to sob. "I should have read them. I should have told someone. Those texts couldn't have been any clearer. I wish to God I had done something to stop him."

Matt rolled his chair closer and put a gentle hand on Sam's arm. Slowly, Sam collected himself and stopped his tears. Matt handed him a tissue. Sam wiped his eyes and took a deep breath. With a question on his face, he looked at Matt.

"It's not your fault. Rick is the shooter. Not you. Remember that." Matt spoke firmly.

Sam lifted his tear-stained face. "I know that, but I wish I had told someone."

"Let's look at that a moment. If you could do it over, what would you do differently?"

Sam thought a moment. "I would have read those texts. I would have at least told my mom. She would have known what to do then." He raised his eyes to Matt's eyes. "I wish I'd told you."

"I wish you had too," said Matt. "Any idea why you didn't?"

He shook his head. "I don't know, really."

"That's okay," said Matt. "We haven't known each other very long. And it's hard to know what might have happened had you told your mother or me."

"God, I wish I had." Sam pressed his lips together. "I just wanted to hide my head under a blanket or something. All I thought of was staying away from Rick. If I didn't think about it, about him, it would go away. He would go away." He sighed. "I think I do that a lot. Avoid."

Matt nodded, giving his full attention. His intuition told him a pivotal moment was at hand.

"My dad ran away. Even with all the news about this horror, we haven't heard a word from him. Unless he's living under a rock, he has to have heard about it. He's a jerk, off chasing some dream, of I don't know what, with some other woman." Sam shook his head. "I don't know what he could be thinking. My mom is awesome. I sure don't want to follow his example. I think avoiding is like running away."

Matt stayed quiet, listening. But listening with full energy.

"I want to learn to stop avoiding. I want to step up. I want to do something. But what?" Sam paused. "I don't know what."

"Not yet," said Matt.

"Not yet," echoed Sam.

Then they sat in silence for a while. Matt observed him carefully and silently as well. Sam's face grew long and somber. "There's a candlelight vigil tonight at school," he said. "You know, to remember the victims. Thoughts and prayers and all that."

Matt nodded. "You going?"

"Yeah, I think so." Sam clasped his hands. He drew his fingers to his lips and bowed his head. He closed his eyes a moment before opening them and lifting his head. "I keep thinking, what if I had told someone? Could I have stopped it?" He looked open-eyed at

Matt. "I feel guilty. I'm scared to go and face everyone. But I want to go, I have to go."

"You don't have to, but it might be good for you to go. To find out no one blames you. Except you."

Sam paused to take this in. "You really think so?"

"Yes, I do. Just like I know you don't have to follow your father's bad example. You can make your own choices."

Sam frowned. "I'm going to be eighteen in the spring. I'll be legally an adult."

"Yes, you will."

"I want to do something. But what? I don't know what. I'm sick of thoughts and prayers."

"Yeah, me too. You have insight. You have energy," said Matt. "Stay with that question as you process this tragedy."

Sam turned inward and his eyes glazed over. "There's got to be something."

"Sounds like a new goal for you is to avoid avoiding, as we say."

"Avoid avoiding, yes, that covers it," Sam said.

"Are there other goals you want to set for what lies ahead?"

Sam sat silent for a while. Then he sat up and spoke: "I need to learn how not to fall apart with that detective. He scares me as much as Rick scares me. And I'm wondering if I really had that stomach bug or if it was nerves."

"Hmm," said Matt. "Could be a little of both. But probably a twenty-four-hour bug encouraged by the stress you've been under. How's your stomach now?"

"It seems fine. I'm eating like normal."

"Good. What are your thoughts about how you can hold it

together under O'Riley's pressure?"

"It seemed like he wanted me to yell. I'm amazed I didn't yell more." He smiled. "I think I did better than I thought I did."

Matt smiled. "Sounds that way from what you said."

"I did find stopping to take deep breaths helped me. A lot."

"Good strategy."

"And having Mr. Parker there helped a lot. He advised me when to answer and how to answer."

"Good."

"Yes, I guess that's what a lawyer is for."

"Yes, and you let him help you." Matt was pleased at Sam's insights. He summed up. "Ask for and accept help, one of the basic rules."

Sam nodded.

"And one more important one." Matt pointed to a sign he had on his shelf. It read: "Notice: Make sure brain is in gear before engaging mouth."

Sam smiled.

Chapter 17

Guy sat at his kitchen table, the *Washington Post* and *Alexandria Gazette* open in front of him, his bandaged leg propped on a chair. Tom had just left after giving him a few perfunctory parting words like a greeting card that basically said, "Get well soon." Obligatory and trite. Tom's frostiness hung in the air. As did Laura's absence and Little Guy's ghost. He could almost see the boy bouncing around the kitchen, getting into everything. Guy sighed. He blinked and saw a lonely room. A cookie jar full of oatmeal raisin cookies that Guy had chosen over the chocolate chip ones, thinking them a bit healthier, would never again have a tiny hand opening it. Little Guy would never again climb up on a chair, lift the lid, grab a cookie, and *then* ask Guy if he could have one. Guy smiled through his aching heart.

He turned back to the papers. A list of those who had died had finally been published in the papers. He searched for Kate Warwick's name but could not find it. Was the list complete? He had no idea. Did she survive? Had she been in the hospital near him? The need to know burned inside him. He picked up his phone to call her, but his hand trembled too much for him to dial. He put it down. He couldn't bear to learn of another death. He scoured his memory of that day to no avail. His last memory of her was of her announcing to the class they would lock and secure the classroom. Then what? She must have gone to the door to lock it.

His mind was fuzzy. The next image he had was of the shooter and then being shot and falling into blackness. The effort to recall pierced his heart. Tears burst into his eyes. He shook his head. *Oh, Little Guy.* An image of Gracia lying dead on a pile of bodies flashed on the screen of his mind. His hand went to his heart. *Oh, Jake. What must you be going through now? I should call you, see how you're doing.* He couldn't right then imagine what he could say.

Guy put his head in his hands and wept. He felt immobilized. After a moment, he wiped his eyes with his fingers and looked around for a box of tissues. He spotted one on the kitchen counter. He used his hands to move his leg off the chair. Where were his crutches? Leaning against the kitchen door, just out of reach, where Tom had left them. Leaning one hand on the table and one on the chair, he pushed himself to standing. Taking a shaky step, he got the crutches and reached his hands through to grab the hand holders. *How did they tell me to do this?* He tried to remember. *Slowly.* He knew that much.

He decided he wanted a glass of water and hobbled to the cabinet and sink. He found one clean glass that he filled from the tap and made his way back to the table. *Whoosh*, he exhaled a loud sigh of relief as he lowered himself back into his seat and set the glass in front of him on the table. He took a few sips and realized how thirsty he was. He downed half and set it down. *Save some for later.* He glanced toward the kitchen sink, which now seemed a football field away. There sat the box of tissues he hadn't gotten.

The doorbell rang. The front door was two football fields away. Grumbling, he hoisted himself back up, grabbed the crutches, and began the long journey to answer the door.

"I'm coming! I'm coming!" he hollered as he made his way from the kitchen through the small hall into the living room to the front door. He peered through the decorative windows that fanned across the top of the door. Two men in police uniforms stood there, one holding a folder.

With a sigh, Guy opened the door. He knew the police would want to talk to him eventually. "Yes?" he said.

"Good morning," said one. "I'm Detective O'Riley, and this is Officer Parton. Are you Guy Grant?"

"Yes, sorry I was so slow to answer the door," said Guy. "As you see, I don't move very fast now. What can I do for you?"

"You are one of the survivors of the Parkwood Schools shooting. We're here to get a statement. I'm sorry we didn't get to you while you were still in the hospital. May we come in?" asked O'Riley.

"I guess so. Follow me." Guy turned around and hobbled to the living room, where he lowered himself into his recliner, pulling the lever on the side to lift the footrest under his feet. He leaned the crutches against the side table. They promptly fell to the floor. Guy cursed.

The police followed and stood at attention.

"Sit down, sit down," said Guy, waving them to the couch.

They sat. "As I said," began O'Riley, "we had many people to talk to in the hospital. We were planning to talk to you this morning, but you got discharged before we could. We just want to hear whatever you can tell us that will help in our investigation of this horrible crime."

Guy felt his stomach tighten at the thought of reliving the shooting again. Then he wondered, *Maybe they can tell me about Ms. Warwick.*

"I was volunteering in Ms. Warwick's first grade class where my grandson was a student." His voice cracked, and he paused, feeling tears threatening. He wished he had his water glass. He cleared his throat. "Would one of you please get my water glass from the kitchen table for me?"

"Of course," said O'Riley. "Parton, get the gentleman his water, please."

"Yes, sir," said Parton as he got up and stepped past O'Riley and Guy. He stood in the living room door, casting his eyes around the small hall.

"Keep going," said Guy. "It's the next room."

"Oh, yes," said Parton. "Want me to refill it?"

"That would be wonderful," said Guy. "And fetch that box of tissues, too, while you're at it."

"Yes, sir," said Parton from the kitchen. They heard water running and Parton rustling around. Then he was back with a full glass of water and a box of tissues. "Here you go."

"Thanks," said Guy. He set the tissues on the end table next to his recliner and drank another half glass before setting it down as well. *Jeez, do I now need to pee?* Considering what it would take to traverse the distance to the half-bath off the hall, he decided to wait. The last thing he wanted was to have the police either help him get there or watch him struggle. "Where was I?"

"In the classroom," prompted O'Riley. "Volunteering."

"I'm afraid I don't remember much. We were in the process of locking and securing the classroom when the shooter came in. I was shot," he said and waved toward his thigh. "I fell and passed out. That's about it."

"What led to the decision to lock the classroom?" asked O'Riley.

Guy stared off into space, trying and not wanting to remember. "I was reading the children a story. We heard a voice on the intercom, then gunshots and footsteps. As you know, we were too late." With effort, he stifled his tears. "My grandson was killed." He grabbed a tissue and dabbed at his eyes.

"We are so sorry. I'm sorry to keep asking questions, but we must find out all we can."

"I know. You're just doing your job." Guy balled up his tissue in his fist and nodded. "I will help you if I can."

"Thank you," said O'Riley. "Can you tell us what the voice on the intercom said?"

"It was strange. He said he was the Grim Reaper and was coming to get us. We—Ms. Warwick and myself—we . . . then we heard shots and footsteps, and you know the rest."

"Did the shooter say anything? Was there anyone with him?" O'Riley continued.

"No, nothing. It happened so fast. I didn't see anyone else."

"Did he seem to be aiming at anyone in particular or just spraying bullets?"

"I don't know. As I said, I got hit and passed out, I'm sorry." Guy gave a big sigh.

"I don't know what happened to Ms. Warwick." He looked at them, pleading. "Can you tell me?"

O'Riley turned to Parton. "Do we have the list?"

Parton opened a folder and riffled through papers. He handed a paper to O'Riley, who examined it front and back.

"At this point, I'm afraid our list is incomplete. But I don't see her name here."

Guy sighed in relief as he absorbed the words. *The list is incomplete.* His face sank. "Can you find out for me?"

"We will eventually have a list of everyone who was present in each school and the names of all those killed and injured. I'm afraid we don't have it yet. It's a very long list." The lines in O'Riley's face deepened. "I'm sorry, Mr. Grant. I wish I could tell you, but I can't."

Guy closed his eyes a moment. An image of Ms. Warwick's face floated inside him. Her radiant smile, her bright eyes. He opened his eyes and sighed. "I really want to know what happened to her. She was a wonderful teacher."

O'Riley pressed his lips together and turned to Parton. "Make a note to find out and tell Mr. Grant."

"Yes, sir," said Parton as he scribbled on the paper.

"Can you describe the shooter, Mr. Grant?" asked O'Riley.

"Not very well," said Guy. "A guy about medium height in a long black robe with a hood covering most of his face. Pointing an assault rifle. That's all I can tell you."

"That's about what we've gotten from everyone we've interviewed," said O'Riley.

"Listen, all the news reports say you have someone in custody. They even said he was a student at the high school and that he confessed. They said his name was Rick Green." Guy pressed his lips into a thin line. "Do I remember correctly?"

"Yes. We're just covering all the bases."

"And they say he acted alone. How is that possible?" Guy raised his voice.

"That's what we're in the process of investigating," said O'Riley, adopting a professional manner like pulling a cloak around his shoulders. "Is there anything else you remember that might help us?"

"I don't think so." Guy hung his head, drained.

"Well, then, we won't trouble you any further," O'Riley said and stood. Parton followed suit. "Thank you for your time." He handed Guy a card. "If you think of anything else, please call me at one of the numbers on my card, office and mobile. Don't hesitate."

"Okay," said Guy. He held the card like a lifeline. "Just do your job. Find justice for all these children and their wonderful teachers." He wiped away another tear.

"We'll do our best. We wish you a speedy recovery. Have a good rest of your day. Don't get up. We'll see ourselves out." O'Riley picked up the crutches and leaned them against the recliner where Guy could easily reach them.

"Thanks," said Guy. He watched them close the door behind them before he dissolved into tears. When spent, he grabbed a fistful of tissues and blew his nose multiple times. Used tissues littered the floor. *Now I really do have to pee.* He sighed as he cast his eyes toward the door to the hall and contemplated the long journey that lay before him.

▷ ⊕ ◁

When Sam and his mother arrived at the candlelight vigil, they found the school parking lot already full. It was a crisp, cool night, clear with a million stars blanketing the sky. Uniformed police officers stood along the street and toward the school buildings, guarding and directing traffic. TV camera crews and reporters stood by their trucks outside the line of police. One officer at the head of the line waved Sam and his mother toward a spot on the street. They parked and followed signs to the football field, apparently the only place large enough to hold the crowd. Sam cast his eyes around to find any of his friends, but in the swarm of people, it took him awhile. At the gate to the field, he saw two students he recognized as members of the student council holding buckets of candles. Next to them stood a large lit candle on a tall stand, guttering in the breeze. Holding the ones they had brought from home, Sam and his mother paused to light the candles as they had seen others before them do.

Inside the stadium was a sea of parents and students with tear-stained faces, hands gripping candles. The lights flickered and shimmered as the crowd shifted to allow them to join. They were arranged in concentric circles that became untidy the further from the center. In the middle of the field was a platform and on it a circle of large candles on tall holders. A few people sat on chairs. Sam wasn't close enough to identify them. They slowly made their way through the crowd, weaving steadily toward the inner circle around the platform. When he could see them, he saw mostly students. The mayor, chief of police, and superintendent of schools were the only adults on the stage. Then Sam remembered: the high school principal had been in the gym and had been shot, as had many staff members of the elementary and middle schools.

Someone called his name. Sam turned to see his buddy Mark Gregson waving him over. Sam turned to his mother, who urged him on. She'd found Mark's mother, Gail, a good friend of hers. Sam wove his way through the tearful faces to Mark, who somehow had made it into the inner circle in front of the platform. They embraced. Mark had been the one who had called him first after the shooting. They'd been in first-period class together when Sam got sick. As Mark had told him, halfway through class, the school went on lockdown. When the bell had rung for second period, the shooting was finished, and police were loading Rick Green into the paddy wagon. They'd stayed on lockdown for another two hours as the police scoured the building. It took Mark another hour to get home through the bottleneck of emergency crews, news trucks, and hopeful parents who had come to pick up their hopefully surviving children.

On the platform, a young woman stood holding a guitar. Sam recognized her as Sarah, Monica's best friend. Tall and slim, she had long black hair tied into a braid that draped over her shoulder. Sarah stepped up to a microphone on a stand and began to play and then sing "May the Circle Be Unbroken." Slowly, the crowd joined in. Their voices merged and swelled as Sarah switched to "Amazing Grace." Then she sang the high school's alma mater, and even more of the crowd sang along.

When she finished, she set her guitar into its case at her feet and remained at the microphone.

The crowd became still, waiting. She stood in silence with head bowed for long enough for Sam to wonder if she was going to say anything. He looked at Mark, who shrugged his shoulders. Sarah raised her head and dabbed her eyes with a tissue in her hand. Then she picked the microphone off the stand and gazed up at the stars before she faced the crowd.

"My name is Sarah Hunter. I lost my best friend on Wednesday," she began. "Monica and I had been friends since kindergarten—which is amazing with all the military and government people moving in and out of this area. I can count on the fingers of one hand the kids I've known all through elementary, middle, and high school. We had both been accepted to the same college, William and Mary, on early decision and planned to room together. She got her acceptance letter on Monday. I got mine on Tuesday. We were so excited!" Sarah's voice cracked, and she paused.

Sam caught a sob in his throat when he heard Monica's name. His heart beat wildly, and he put a hand to his face. Mark patted his shoulder. He was one of the few friends who knew Sam had been infatuated with Monica. Now she was gone. Sam raised his eyes to listen, as if he could retain a piece of Monica through Sarah's words.

Someone handed Sarah a bottle of water. She took a swallow and handed it back. "The last time I saw her was just before first period Wednesday when she went off to P.E. class and I went to algebra." She took a moment to turn her head from right to left over the crowd. "I know each of you has a similar story. Maybe you lost a friend, a favorite teacher, maybe you lost several people you loved. Maybe you're here as a parent and lost your child. This vigil is for all three schools, and seeing the size of this crowd, I know we all lost a lot of loved ones. I know we all have a lot of tears to shed. I know I do." She pressed her lips into a firm line. "Then I want to do something. I'm *going* to do something." She nodded, then handed the microphone to the tall, thin, dark-skinned boy standing next to her and took her seat.

He stood holding the microphone in silence for a moment. Sam recognized Derek Cline, the school track star who was also in every Advanced Placement class the school offered. Athletic and brilliant, Derek was in AP Physics and AP Calculus with Sam. His dad was retired military and his mother taught middle school history. Sam felt a jolt. Had Derek's mother been shot? He didn't know.

"Hello, everyone," began Derek. "I'm Derek Cline. This is a sad night for us all. My mother teaches, um, taught history at the middle school. She got shot in the head and is still in the hospital ICU, the Intensive Care Unit. She survived, but she still might die. If she lives, we don't know if she will ever be the same. I know I won't." He glanced back at Sarah, then back at the audience. "I should feel really lucky I was in first period French on Wednesday, but I don't. Perhaps like me, all of you standing here maybe do feel both lucky to be alive but devastated at losing someone special." There was a murmuring of affirmation from the crowd. "Like Sarah, I want, um, I will be crying over my mother for a long time. And grieving the loss of others I care about. But I don't want to stop there. I want to do something." His voice rose with anger. "There have been too many of these school shootings. I want this one to be the last one. Something needs to be done. If you feel the same, join me in the high school cafeteria immediately after the conclusion of this vigil."

A couple others on the stage spoke, sharing their personal losses and the invitation to action. The adults on stage also spoke briefly, assuring the crowd that school safety was their top priority and they'd be reviewing policies and making changes. There was a palpable feeling of grief and anguish and anger building in the crowd. Then there was an open mic time. A microphone was passed around.

Sam stood trembling. One part of him shuddered in shame that Rick had come to his house Friday morning and he had done noth-ing. Another part wanted to speak into the microphone and tell this story and ask to be forgiven for not speaking up. He stood immobilized between these two voices in his head. The microphone passed within three feet of him as students shared their grief and anguish and, increasingly, their anger. He stood paralyzed and afraid. If he spoke, what would the crowd do to him? Tear him limb from limb? *No, don't be ridiculous, remember what Matt said. It's not your fault.* In the end, the shame won. He remained silent.

Then a young woman he didn't recognize took the mic. She was petite with long brunette hair that fell over her face like a curtain until she tucked it behind her ears. She shook as she held the mic and had difficulty keeping it still and at her mouth as she spoke.

"My name is Annette," she said. "I graduated last year. I go to the community college but live at home. I feel horrible about this." She broke into sobs and couldn't speak. A girl next to her put an arm around her shoulder and whispered to her. Annette nodded and went on. "I know I bear some responsibility for this tragedy. I knew Rick was really messed up and had been for years. Ever since . . ." She stopped. Another sob caught in her throat. Her friend squeezed her shoulder. A deep hush fell over the crowd. Annette took a deep breath before she collected herself. "I talked to him Wednesday morning. To Rick. He was full of crazy talk that made no sense. I had been begging our mom to get him some help. I was the only one home with him that morning. I wish I had called someone, but I didn't. I never thought he would do any of the crazy things he talked about. You see, Rick is my brother."

Chapter 18

Sam stood frozen as he absorbed Annette's words. The vigil concluded. Like a huge, coiled cobra, the crowd began to unfurl. Mark grabbed Sam's arm and pulled him along beside him. When they got outside the football field, Mark led Sam to a nearby picnic table and pushed him down where they could sit together. Only then did Sam rouse from his stupor.

He turned to Mark. "What happened to that family? What was she referring to that messed Rick up so bad?"

"Don't you remember?" said Mark. "I think it was three or four years ago. Their dad shot their mom and then himself. It was supposed to be one of those murder-suicides, but the mom lived. Just barely. She was in the hospital for a long time. Now she's in a wheelchair, paralyzed from the waist down. She works at the convenience store on King Street."

"That's them? I heard about it back then but forgot who it was. Jeez, that's so messed up. No wonder Rick is crazy." Sam scratched his head.

The thinning crowd moved past them, and a line of mostly students headed for the cafeteria.

"Want to go check out this meeting?" asked Mark.

"Sure. Let's go."

Sam pulled his phone from his pocket, but before he could text his mom for her permission, she and Gail walked over. He got her blessing.

Inside the cafeteria, people were pulling chairs into a circle. It was a small group, maybe thirty, mostly students with a few parents. Sam looked to see who he recognized. He saw Annette Green and led Mark to sit by her. Her friend sat close on the other side of her. He felt a strange bond with Annette.

"Annette, thanks for what you shared," Sam said. "It took courage, real courage."

She gave him a tearful smile. "I just wish I had done something before . . ."

"Yeah, I know how you feel. Rick stopped by my house that morning." Sam felt relief to tell her.

"What?" She was wide-eyed.

"Yeah, he wanted me to go with him. I had no idea what for. I thought he was nuts." He studied her reaction. "I told him to get lost."

"He did? You did?" She sat with her mouth hanging open.

"Yeah, and I got sick at school—that stomach bug—and came home before Rick got there. I guess I'm lucky I got so sick. I didn't even know what happened until my mom told me after seeing it on the news."

Annette listened, riveted.

"I feel guilty like you do," said Sam. "That I didn't tell someone. But I had no idea he was going to do what he did."

"Wow. I thought I was the only one he talked to." She put her hand over his and squeezed. "I'm so glad you told me. I've been feeling so alone. So guilty." She returned her hand to her lap.

Sam's heart fluttered, and his throat felt suddenly dry. He stroked the place on his hand she had touched. He smiled at her, feeling himself drawn into her deep blue eyes. She met his gaze, then withdrew behind the curtain of her long brown hair. There was a rustling on the other side of her.

"I'm Elaine," said her friend, leaning over to shake Sam's hand. She had a head of blond curls that bounced as she spoke and dimples on both cheeks. Sam took her hand gratefully, then felt Mark jostle his shoulder against Sam's.

"And this is Mark," said Sam, releasing her hand as Mark extended his.

"Aren't you in first period English with us?" Mark asked.

"I think so," said Elaine, tilting her head as she considered the question. "Hancock's class? Yeah, I remember seeing you all there now that I think of it."

"Hey, they want to get started," said Annette, lifting her head and tucking her hair behind her ears. She turned to face the center of the circle. The rest of them did likewise. Derek and Sarah shepherded the outliers to join the circle. Chairs and tables were moved to make room for a larger circle. Soon there were nearly forty of them.

"Hello, everyone," said Derek. "Thanks for coming. I'm hoping maybe we can make something good come out of this."

"Yes," echoed Sarah. "I've never tried to do anything in response to something so horrible, but then, I've never experienced anything so horrible." There was a murmur of assent from the circle. "I've asked my mom who's a social worker to help facilitate this meeting because she's done that a lot. Mom?"

A tall, slim woman stood up next to Sarah. She was an older version of Sarah, with similar features and dark hair that fell in waves to her shoulders. A few gray strands were sprinkled through it. Her face bore deep laugh lines around her mouth and even deeper worry lines on her forehead.

"Yes, I'm Priscilla Hunter and I work for the mental health center where I run support groups. I want to assure you that I'm not here to lead, just to help you all talk. We're all stunned by this tragedy. But this happened at your schools, and this is your meeting. How does that sound?"

A few words of agreement were tossed out. "Yes." "Great." "Let's go."

"Okay, I'm going to suggest that we begin with a few moments of silence and then go around the circle in turn and either speak or pass. I'm borrowing this method from our Quaker tradition and have seen it work well. It doesn't matter who starts. Everyone will get a turn if they want one. When we've gone around the circle, we will open it up for discussion. Does this make sense?" She cast her eyes around the group. One by one, they all nodded. "Okay, then let's settle into a brief period of silence." She sat down and closed her eyes.

Sam stirred around in his chair to find a comfortable position, putting his feet flat on the floor, and closed his eyes. He was aware of a similar rustling around the circle as others also settled in. At first, the stillness felt strange, but after a while it began to feel comforting. They were joined in their grief and in their desire to take some sort of action. He had no idea what to expect. He had always been more of a follower than a leader. Inside, he watched thoughts and images drift across the screen of his mind, buzzing. Then the buzzing flew away, like a bunch of bees going elsewhere, and a new calmness spread through him. He thought of Rick and the horror his father had brought on their family. Had Rick gotten help? He felt less afraid of Rick now and more sorry for him. Rick had gone nuts and followed in his dad's footsteps, but tenfold. Crazy, just crazy.

As he sat, Sam wondered who would break the silence. He felt surprised when a column of words rose up inside him, and he found himself speaking.

"I want to do something because I didn't do anything before this shooting happened," Sam said while keeping his eyes closed. "Rick had been after me, ever since we got into a fight at school. He scared me, and I stayed away from him. But he came by my house Wednesday morning." Sam opened his eyes to see all eyes on him. "He wanted me to join him in I-didn't-know-what, but I knew it couldn't be good. I got away from him. I wish I had done something, but I didn't know what to do. I don't know what to do now, but I want to do something. I want to hear what you guys think." He passed his eyes around the circle, then closed them again.

Annette sat on his left. She shook as she spoke, and her words tumbled out in a rush. "I want to do something, but first I want to understand why this happened. My brother was very disturbed. He needed help, but I couldn't make him get help. My mother, as most of you know, is in a wheelchair because my father shot her."

Annette's voice cracked, and for a moment she couldn't speak. Elaine held her hand and gave her a tissue. Annette dabbed her eyes, took a deep breath, and continued. "Our house was full of guns. All kinds. Dad took Rick out to learn to shoot when he was only ten. After Dad was gone and Mother recovered, she got rid of all our guns. We thought. But I guess Rick hid one somewhere. I want to learn what we can do to keep guns out of the hands of disturbed people like my brother." She looked at Elaine and sighed.

Elaine spoke next. "I want to educate myself about what the gun laws are. I don't even know. We never had guns at home. My father always said he'd never have guns in the house because too many toddlers get shot by accident. I never knew anyone with guns until I got to know Annette's family. And that sure taught me that some people should never have guns. Maybe we could study the issue and find some experts to come speak to us."

"Remember Parkland?" asked Derek. "Let's organize another march. I'm connected with some of the Parkland kids on Twitter. They can advise us. We can't have too many marches. Let's march until they pass stronger gun laws. We can't quit." He slammed his fist into his other hand.

Everyone in the circle spoke; no one passed. Some told stories of those they had lost, some cried, some raised their voices in anger, some had ideas of things to do. There was a gradual crescendo from tears to anger to action. In the general discussion, a few threads emerged. A study committee was formed, a march committee, a letter-to-the-editor writing committee. A next meeting was set for the following weekend. Sam walked out feeling uplifted and exhilarated.

Chapter 19

Guy lay in bed Monday morning wondering why he should get up. Since he'd gotten home Saturday afternoon, he had done nothing but sleep. Thanks to Dr. Mehlman's miracle drugs, he had slept and slept. Part of him wanted to keep sleeping. Another part felt the rumble of hunger. A ray of sunshine pierced the half-closed blinds of the window next to his bed and lit up the pile of clothes on the rug. Undressing the night he had gotten home had been hard enough. Putting his clothes away had seemed too much effort. A cup of coffee would help now. But did he even have any coffee? Dinner the first night had been a frozen pizza he'd found in the freezer. He hadn't really checked his supplies. Did the local coffee shop deliver? He had no idea.

He felt groggy from the medicine and fixed his mind on coffee. His full bladder was what finally got him up. Once he had emptied it, he figured he might as well proceed downstairs to see what the kitchen held. In his scruffy green plaid robe, he grabbed his crutches and hobbled slowly, slowly, one step at a time, *tap tap tap*, leaning against the wall, down, down, down to the bottom of the stairs.

Peeking out the windows in the door, he saw the *Washington Post* on the front stoop, two days' worth. He wanted them. He unlocked the heavy door and swung it open—to find a hand picking up the newspapers and extending them toward him. Guy lifted his eyes to find the hand attached to the pushy young reporter he had met at the hospital. Guy blinked and frowned. He took the papers wordlessly and began to turn back inside.

"Good morning, Mr. Grant," said the reporter. "Neil Simpson. I see I might have arrived a bit early."

"You can say that again," grumbled Guy. "What damn time is it anyway?"

"It's nearly half past nine."

"I haven't even had my coffee yet. I have no comment." He turned further inside and began to push the door closed.

Neil Simpson held up a cardboard container with two large cups wedged inside. "Neither have I, actually. Mocha latte or black?" He moved onto the threshold, blocking the door with his body from closing completely. He lifted a bag. "Cinnamon scones?"

Guy stuttered. "Wh—wh—huh?" Then he grabbed the bag. "Mocha latte, to be sure. But come back later. Much later."

Neil handed him a large cup. "I just have a few questions. But let me help you get this latte inside, and I'll come back later. How does that sound?"

Guy squinted. He examined the bag of scones he had in one hand, the cup of latte in the other, and the papers tucked under one arm. He realized there was no way he could carry them all to the kitchen table while using crutches. Ah, but then he saw the small table inside the door. He set the cup and papers on it. If this reporter came inside, he'd never leave.

"I can manage," Guy said. "Thank you for bringing me breakfast. I don't have anything to say." The last thing Guy wanted was to give this kid an interview, but he now felt obligated by the coffee and scones. They radiated warmth from inside the bag. His mouth began to water. The aroma of the mocha latte enticed him. He wanted to enjoy them while they were still warm. He glared at Neil. "I thank you, but don't you dare come back before noon."

"Noon it is." Neil grinned and left.

Guy slammed the door and hobbled with the bag of scones to the kitchen, then hobbled back for the latte and hobbled again for the newspapers. He gave a big sigh when he finally sat down and took a big sip of latte and a big bite of scone. *Damn that reporter, but damn this tastes good.* He spread the newspapers open over the table and began to read, thinking how he could be somewhere else before noon. Or perhaps even bar the door.

Kate Warwick woke up in bed not sure where she was or what day it was. She looked around the room where she found herself. The hard thing over her face was the first clue that she was in the hospital. She knew what it was, but her mind felt too fuzzy to call up the word. *Ah, oxygen mask.* She heard the beeping and whirring sounds of machines near her bed. Consciousness slowly returned. An IV was in her arm. A tube in her nose irritated her. A sheet and thin hospital blanket covered her body. Metal rails framed the bed. A blood pressure cuff squeezed her arm slowly tighter, then released. She blinked and turned her head toward the diffused light that came through a window. On the other side of her bed, a curtain separated her from other beds.

"Ah, you're awake." A woman in a nurse's uniform appeared at her side, smiling at her. The nurse removed the oxygen mask. "The doctor said as soon as you woke up, I could remove these things. You don't need this nasogastric tube anymore. This may feel weird, but it'll be quick." She pulled the tube out.

Kate winced as a long tube came out of her nose. She closed her eyes briefly. Then she opened her eyes wide and looked at the nurse. "Where . . . wh . . . " She tried to speak.

"You're in the ICU at Alexandria Hospital," said the nurse.

Kate frowned in response. "Wha . . ." She tried again.

"You had a bad head injury. The doctors had no choice but to put you in a medically induced coma to minimize the swelling and inflammation of your brain." The nurse patted Kate's arm. "That you have awakened on your own is a good sign. And, by the way, I'm Betty, your nurse today."

Kate stared at the nurse, trying to absorb what she was saying. She felt she had been far away in another world. Maybe she had been. Images of strange scenes had swirled inside her mind, of her floating and falling, of children crying. And one vivid image of the Grim Reaper holding a gun rather than a sickle. Nightmares, surely nightmares. Could she talk? She tried again. "Wah . . . der."

Nurse Betty responded as if she understood. "Would you like water?" Kate nodded. In a moment, another whirring sound and the head of her bed rose until she was reclining, halfway to sitting up. "Here you are."

A cup with a straw bent at the top reached her lips. Kate sipped the refreshing liquid and felt it move slowly down inside her. She reached for the nurse's hand that held the cup. She swallowed several more times before she leaned back and released the straw.

"Thank you," she managed.

Nurse Betty placed the cup on the bedside table and examined the machines beside the bed. The blood pressure cuff tightened again, then released. She gave Kate a long look. "Your vital signs seem good. Do you feel up to a visitor? Your daughter has been waiting."

"Oh, yes!" said Kate. Emma's face appeared in her mind. Her long brown hair, her bright blue eyes like her father's, her slender frame. She smiled.

"Just a short visit, mind you," said Betty. "You still need to rest. I'll get her."

As Kate waited, she breathed slowly and deeply, grateful that she could. She had only a vague sense of why she was there. Head injury, the nurse had said. She turned her attention to her head. It hurt, yes, but not too badly. What had happened? The image of the Grim Reaper popped back into her mind. That was quite a nightmare. Or was it?

"Mother, oh, Mother." Emma held Kate's hand as she stood beside the bed. "I'm so glad you're awake. What a relief!"

The nurse pushed a chair close to the bed for Emma. "Just a short visit, remember. I'll be back soon," the nurse said as she left them.

"Okay, thank you," said Emma, turning toward her mother. She sat down and raised Kate's hand to her mouth for a kiss. "How do you feel?" she asked, still holding Kate's hand.

"I feel like Rip Van Winkle, just waking up." Kate smiled. "I hope I wasn't out as long as he was."

Emma laughed. "Rip Van Winkle? Not at all, more like five days. I'm relieved, you sound just like yourself. Ha ha, Rip Van Winkle."

"The nurse said they induced a coma, that I had a head injury." Kate peered into Emma's blue eyes, hoping for a clue.

"You apparently hit your head on the metal edge of your white board, the sharp edge of the tray that holds the markers, as you fell." Emma stopped. She tilted her head, thinking. "Do you even remember what I'm referring to?"

"I'm not completely clear-headed yet," said Kate. "I had such terrible nightmares while I was out. Something involving a Grim Reaper."

Emma's shoulders slumped. "Oh, Mother, it wasn't a nightmare. I'm afraid it was real."

Kate's eyebrows went up in alarm. "What do you mean?"

Emma sighed. "There was a school shooting. Someone dressed as the Grim Reaper shot up your school, your classroom."

Kate's mouth fell open. She covered it with her hand in horror. "A shooting? My children?" The sounds of children's cries she had heard in what she'd thought was a dream filled her mind.

"I'm sorry, Mother. All gone." She reached both hands and clasped her mother's arms.

"All gone. You mean dead?"

Emma nodded, tears filling her eyes.

Kate stared at her daughter as tears coursed down her cheeks. Slowly, her memory began to focus. It remained spotty but clear enough to fill her with the horror.

"Every one of my students were killed?" Kate held her breath, waiting. "This can't be true."

"Mother, oh Mother, I know, but it's true." Emma's tears began to flow.

Kate closed her eyes as her grief overtook her. Sobs racked her frame. Emma squeezed her hands, put her head down on the bed, and sobbed with her. When they were both spent, Emma sat up and waited for her mother to speak.

"What about my volunteer?" Kate asked, fearing the answer.

"You had a volunteer there also?"

Kate exhaled slowly. "Yes, Mr. Grant, the grandfather of one of the children." Tears welled in her eyes. Kate let them flow. "A boy named Guy after his grandfather."

Emma handed her a tissue from the box on the bedside table. Kate took it wordlessly and stared off into space. Emma took both her mother's hands in hers.

"That little boy so loved having his grandfather in the class-room." Kate closed her eyes and wept quietly a moment. Then she collected herself and opened her eyes at her daughter. "I can't believe something so horrible . . ."

"Yes," said Emma. "It was horrible. But, Mother, I'm just so grateful you weren't shot, that you're alive. I don't want you to get too worked up, too tired." Now Emma was weeping. "When I first heard the news, I thought . . ." She turned her tear-stained face to Kate. "I love you, Mother."

"I love you too, Emma." Kate squeezed her daughter's hands and choked back her own tears. "I'm okay, really, don't worry. I'm going to be okay."

Just then the nurse appeared. "Oh, no, is it already time to go?" asked Emma.

"I'm afraid so," said the nurse.

"When can I visit again?" asked Emma.

"Go get yourself some lunch and come back in a few hours," said the nurse. Then with a twinkle she said, "I'm going to see how your mother does on our delicious hospital food."

Emma kissed her mother on the forehead and left. "See you after lunch."

Kate watched her leave and turned to the nurse. "Delicious hospital food? Is that even possible?" She felt relieved to have something else to think about for a second.

"Yes," said the nurse. "And the special for you today, I'm sure, will be Jell-O and broth."

"I'm not really hungry," said Kate. She felt a wave of grief wash over her. "Can I have a newspaper with lunch?"

"I'll ask. But be careful; there's no good news."

▷ ⊕ ◁

Guy searched through his refrigerator and cabinets, taking inventory of what supplies he had. Some sliced ham that smelled questionable, some bread that might be okay if he toasted it, some mustard and mayonnaise, frozen pizzas, and microwavable dinners. The milk was sour. There was an almost empty bag of ground coffee. He started a list with milk and coffee. He soon added eggs and cereal. He hoped he remembered correctly that the local Safeway delivered. Otherwise, he'd have to call Laura. If she would answer the phone. He had tried several times after he got home with no luck. He wanted to find out when they were having a funeral for Little Guy. Surely, they would tell him. Or maybe they were too overcome with grief to even plan one yet.

As he worked, he kept a close eye on the kitchen clock. How could it already be eleven thirty? That nosy reporter would be here before he knew it. What was he going to do? All the doors were securely locked, he had made sure of that. He scanned the kitchen. The back door led to a small deck with a few patio chairs and table. Then the garage at the end of the driveway. Could he hide in there? When had he last been in there? He couldn't remember. It was full of junk, he knew that much. Broken patio chairs, lawn mower, old computers, boxes of old magazines. No room for a car. Then he saw the door that led downstairs to the den. Could he navigate the stairs with his crutches? Possibly. There he had his favorite recliner and a television.

Ah, yes. He would go down where he couldn't even hear the front doorbell. He found a can of Coke, an unopened bag of potato chips, and an old bag of Oreos. There was a jar of salsa, which by some miracle had nothing in it growing hair or teaching its young. He even found a can of Coors in the back of the fridge, along with a jar of olives and a block of cheese with just a bit of green growing on it. He picked up his phone and charger. On second thought, he muted it and left it upstairs. It had rung constantly. He hadn't answered because no calls were from anyone he wanted to talk with. It took him several trips up and down the stairs to get everything down. Placing his snacks on the small table next to his recliner, he leaned back, panting, and chuckled to himself.

Whee, I'm free! Ha ha, I'll have the beer. Wait, didn't they tell me no alcohol with my pain meds? Oh, what the hell, I'll have it anyway. Opening the salsa, he grabbed a potato chip, wishing he had tortilla chips but hesitating to climb back up the stairs to look, and scooped up a big pile of extra-hot salsa. It was indeed still hot. He popped open the beer and downed half of it to ease the fire in his mouth, then scooped up more salsa. Before long, the beer and chips and a lot of the salsa were gone. He enjoyed a few cookies and olives. Then he leaned as far back as he could in his recliner and, full and depleted, fell asleep.

When he woke up, it was nearly 2:00 p.m. He sat the recliner up and listened. A blessed silence filled the space as far as his ears would reach. He chortled in satisfaction, imagining the reporter coming, ringing the doorbell over and over, and finally leaving. Then his bladder began to speak to him loudly. Sighing, he grabbed his crutches and began the long climb to the half-bath at the top of the stairs. When he had completed his bathroom mission, he hobbled into the kitchen. The sun shone through the window, and the blue sky beckoned. Checking the thermometer on the wall, he saw it was unseasonably warm. He opened the kitchen door and was about to step onto the deck when he spied the dreaded reporter sitting there.

Before he could get back inside, Neil Simpson was standing in front of him.

"Hello, Mr. Grant. I'm happy to see you," said Neil. "I love your deck. Shall we talk here or in your kitchen? It looks very comfortable also."

"How about we don't talk at all?" grumbled Guy, moving to close the door.

Neil was quick on his feet, which were now making it impossible to close the door. "Perhaps you'd rather talk to the TV reporters."

Guy shrunk back in horror. "I would not!"

"If I am forced to leave, I will have no choice but to tell them where you live. Right now, no one knows where you live. They'll find you in time, I'm sure, but if you agree to give me an interview, I can delay it for you."

"What?" said Guy, incredulous. "How?"

"I have my ways," said Neil. "What do you say?"

Guy leaned on the door frame and pondered his choices. He had done his best to keep his address and phone unlisted. But he was familiar enough with the news media to realize they would find him eventually. They were probably pounding down the door of NRA headquarters right now. He doubted anyone would let them in, if anyone was even there. Could it be possible that he hadn't even checked in with work? Impossible to believe, but he hadn't. He looked at this young reporter. Neil waited calmly, his soft young face so apparently innocent. Clean-shaven, his brown hair neatly trimmed. Guy had vast experience dealing with the press. He felt he could make this interview exactly what he wanted: short and sweet. And maybe he could get this guy to help him.

"Okay," said Guy. "Come in the kitchen."

"Great!" exclaimed Neil, following Guy inside.

Guy seated himself at the table and propped his injured leg on a chair. "Before we begin, could you do something for me? Bring up my snacks from my den?"

"Sure," said Neil. "Point me the way."

Guy did, and soon Neil had returned with an armful of bags and bottles. Guy pointed to the counter where Neil set them down. "Thanks."

"Anything else before we begin the interview?"

"Bring me a glass of water."

Neil retrieved a glass from the dish drain, filled it from the tap, and brought it to Guy. Sitting in an empty chair, Neil pulled out his notebook and pen and his own phone. "Mind if I record our conversation?"

"Yes, I do mind," said Guy, eyeing the phone in Neil's hand.

"Recording just helps me quote you correctly. It's so easy to mis-hear what people say." Neil raised his eyebrows in a question.

Guy thought for a moment. He certainly didn't want to be misquoted. That had happened plenty of times in his career, and it had been an irritating distraction, taking valuable time to try to straighten things out and keep their message in line with the NRA talking points. He strained his memory to call up their talking points. They were fuzzy at best. With Little Guy gone, everything felt starkly changed.

"I guess you can. But I just want to say up front that I am just out of the hospital, and this will be the shortest interview on record." Guy nodded for emphasis. "I am still recovering from my injuries."

"I understand totally," said Neil. "Let's begin, and I'll be out of here quickly."

Butterflies began to fill Guy as he watched the reporter pull out and unfold a sheet of questions. His usual confidence facing the media melted. Instead, he felt like a sick old grandfather with no legacy, no heirs, and nothing but death waiting. Ironic that the shooter had dressed as Death. Guy might be alive, but the shooter had certainly taken his life when he took his grandson.

"First off, please tell me how you happened to be at Parkwood Elementary School when this horrific event occurred?" Neil paused with his pencil aimed toward his notebook and watched Guy.

Guy looked down and clasped his hands together tightly. *He's starting with a softball question. Okay, I can answer this one.* He raised his head and began. "I was volunteering in my grandson's classroom." He swallowed and looked down again. His fingers hugged his hands.

"And how long had you been volunteering?"

Guy sighed. "Just a few weeks, maybe four or five." *It was so much fun,* he thought as images of eager, smiling young faces clamoring for his attention rose up inside his mind, faces he would never see again. Tears rose up. He fought them down. He turned his gaze away from the reporter to the trees and grass and plants in the backyard. He took a deep breath.

Neil consulted his list and raised his eyes to Guy's face. "Can you describe what happened that horrible day?" He waited, his eyebrows lifted.

The reporter's dark brown eyes flowed toward Guy in a kind of soft sympathy that Guy found surprising and disarming. One part of him relaxed and felt the floodgates open to pour it all out. Another part cautioned him to remember this guy was a reporter going after a story, the lowest kind of human. The two parts warred inside him, carrying on such a ruckus Guy was sure Neil could hear it. But Neil sat still and quiet, waiting. Just as he had waited while Guy, oblivious, had slept downstairs. Guy flicked his eyes around the room and realized he wanted to pour it all out—wanted to desperately. Maybe he needed to call Dr. Mehlman, someone to whom he was supposed to uncork all his feelings. He wished it were Dr. Mehlman sitting before him. But it wasn't. He had to say something, at least to get this kid to go away. But what?

Guy faced Neil. "It's hard to talk about. I'd rather not."

"I understand completely," said Neil. "Is there anything you can tell me now that will help people understand anything about this horrible, horrible, horrible event?"

Guy returned his gaze to the outdoors, to the sun and green leaves, to life. *I know what this guy wants me to say. He wants me to say what I think about the NRA talking points. About arming teachers, about the right to keep and bear arms, all that stuff. But that's not what I want to talk about. I want to talk about Little Guy and how special he was, how smart and cute and how much I miss him. And I can't tell him that. I can't. I won't. I must.*

"My grandson died. That's all I know. There's nothing else." Guy let anger replace his tears. "I want you to leave now." He closed his eyes and put his head in his hands.

When he opened them again, Neil was gone. Guy scanned the table for Dr. Mehlman's card. Picking it up, he studied it for a long time. *Call anytime,* he remembered being told. He dialed.

Chapter 20

"Mike, the boss got shot! In this horrible school shooting." Susan Britt, Guy's chief of staff, pushed the *Washington Post* across the nearly empty conference table where she sat with Mike Gunn, legislative assistant. "Now I know why I haven't been able to reach him," she said. She grabbed a tissue to blot back tears she couldn't control.

Mike picked it up. "What?" He scanned the headline. "NRA Chief Lobbyist Injured in School Shooting." He lifted his head, wide-eyed, to her. "He was there that morning?"

"Yes, to help with the class Halloween celebration. Remember, he was volunteering every Wednesday morning. Read the article." With shaking hands, she poured herself another cup of coffee, her third that morning, from the carafe on the table. "I'm getting sick of this."

Mike frowned as he read on. "I know how you feel." They sat in silence for a few moments. "Apparently, one reporter got to talk to him." He raised his head. "You never got him to answer his phone all these days and a reporter got to him? Unbelievable."

"Isn't it?" She shook her head. "Maybe he'll answer now. I'm sure he's seen this headline."

She downed her coffee and poured another. "I know I'm not supposed to say this, I mean, I do work for the NRA, but another shooting? It's too much." She reached for a donut.

Mike absorbed the news with half a donut in his mouth. "Mr. Grant got shot. Unbelievable."

She gave Mike an incredulous look. "It almost eclipses the mid-term election results. Or maybe the shooting caused the results. As they say, the October surprise. Can you believe, all down the ballot, the gun control candidates won? Amazing."

"I know, unbelievable," said Mike. "I was up late following it but fell asleep before all the results were in." He read further. "Wow. Nobody I voted for won. I'll be damned." He raised his eyes to Susan as he thought a moment. "I can't believe I'm saying this, but maybe we're on the wrong side."

She drew her lips into a fine line. "All those children killed, I hate it, I really do." She pushed her chair back. "Let's go to him. Like now. I want to make sure he's okay."

"If we can get past the reporters and TV crews on the street. Have you looked down at the front of our building? There's a mob."

"I parked under the building. We can drive past them. Nothing else I want to do here. And I'm tired of trying to deflect the reporters all wanting a statement from us." She stood up. "Hell, let's just go. Are you coming?"

Mike stood up also. "Sure, I'll go with you."

Guy shuddered as he read the *Washington Post*. He had talked to that young whippersnapper barely five minutes, and yet he had become the breaking news story. He had barely retrieved the newspaper from the front stoop when TV camera crews and dozens of reporters showed up. He had retreated down to his den to hide. He marveled at how this reporter had made a front-page story out of such a short interview. Well, very little of the article was about him. Most of it was about his position at the NRA. Big news—NRA guy felled in a school shooting, lost his beloved grandson.

And the mid-term election. He smacked himself on the head. He had forgotten to vote. The first time in his entire life he hadn't voted. How could this be? What was happening to him? Had getting shot and losing his grandson caused him to lose his grip on reality? A pang of guilt struck him. Susan had called him repeatedly, and he had not picked up the phone. Once he got home from the hospital and charged his phone, he could have answered. He hadn't even answered his home phone. He should at least let them know he was alive. And Jake, oh Jake. He really should call Jake and offer his condolences. A lightning bolt of more guilt hit him hard. He had been there, helpless to protect Gracia or Little Guy. What could he say to Jake? "I'm sorry" felt woefully inadequate.

Sitting up in his recliner, he picked up his phone. He stared at it as he tried to build up his courage to use it. To call Jake. To call the office. He bent over with nausea as he thought of returning to work. Hell, what was wrong with him? *Do something, you idiot, don't just sit here.* He dialed Laura. It rang and rang, until finally, she answered.

"Hello, Dad." Her voice sounded thin and clipped.

Guy felt tears rise up, and with them, feelings of sorrow and emptiness. "Hi, sweetie, good to hear your voice. How are you?"

All he heard were her sobs. He waited. He didn't know what to say and was afraid to say the wrong thing. "Oh, sweetie, oh Laura, I'm so sorry, so sad. I miss him so much!" he managed finally.

"Dad," she said softly. "Dad, you were there. What happened?" She began to cry again. "I just . . . you and your damn NRA! I wish it had been you and not Little Guy." She spit her words, then stopped to blow her nose. "That's why I haven't answered your calls. I'm just . . . I don't know how to go on without my son."

Guy felt stunned and speechless. Was he to blame? Was the NRA to blame? His mind became a buzzing hive of guilt and grief, his stomach clenched, his lower back twinged in pain. He felt faint and leaned back. He wanted to say something. He didn't want her to hang up on him now that she'd finally answered.

"I don't know how to go on either," he said. "I miss him, too, honey." He began to cry. "I wish it had been me. Really, I do."

Laura snuffled and sighed. Sounding calmer, she said, "I don't know if I really meant that, Dad. It's just so hard, so hard . . ."

"I know." Did he dare ask more? "Have you decided on a service for Little Guy, Laura? I really want to help."

"Yes . . . no, I don't know. Reverend Clifford has been here with us almost every day. He's been a comfort. We'll do something." She broke down again. "I'm just not ready to put my baby in the ground."

Guy's tears began to fall again. "Of course, I understand."

"I'd better go," she said.

"When you decide, please let me know, Laura." He spoke softly, his voice trembling.

"My baby can't be gone." Her voice was a whisper, as if she were talking to herself. Then there was an edge in it. "You and your damn NRA." She hung up.

Guy starred off into space. He let his phone fall onto his lap. A black vortex swirled around him and pulled him down, threatening to suck him into oblivion. His whole life, his long career, what did they add up to now? A big cipher. He sank lower and lower and realized he didn't care if he died then and there. Leaning his recliner all the way back, he closed his eyes.

He must have dozed off, for a racket from upstairs startled him. He saw on the clock that half an hour had passed. Those damn reporters! Will they never quit? He heard the doorbell ring over and over, the sound he usually couldn't hear from where he was. Then his phone rang. He picked it up and saw the name: Susan Britt. This time he decided to answer her.

"Boss, we're here," she said when he answered his phone. "Come let us in. We've come around to the back door to escape the media. But they're likely to follow us. Let us in!" She sounded frantic.

Guy knew he couldn't get up there before the reporters did. "Susan, just to the right of the door is a flowerpot," he said. "Underneath you'll find a loose brick. Lift it up and there's a key. Come in and lock the door behind you. I'm downstairs in my den."

He sat up and was about to navigate with his crutches to stand up when he heard a clatter from upstairs, then voices shouting and a door slamming. Footsteps pounded down the stairs. Susan and Mike soon stood before him, panting. Guy was momentarily speechless.

"Got any chairs?" asked Mike as he scanned the room. He pulled a couple of desk chairs in front of Guy, not too close, then heaved himself down on one. Susan took the other.

"How are you, Boss?" asked Susan, reaching to pat his knee. "We just found out you were injured. And, wow, what a scene outside your house."

"Yeah, we got inside just as those vampires rounded the corner of the house," said Mike. "How long have they been here?"

Guy found his voice. "Just this morning, since that damn breaking news article."

"Yeah, that's what got us to come." Susan shook her head. "But tell us, how are you?"

Guy studied them and considered how much to share. He felt drained from all his tears. He had never broken down in front of them before and wasn't sure he wanted to now. But he didn't think he could say much without doing so. He decided he'd start simple.

"I got shot, but not badly," he said.

"I've been trying to reach you," said Susan.

"Yeah, I know, I'm sorry. I was in the hospital a few days." He paused, gathering his words.

"You were in your grandson's classroom when it happened?" She tilted her head toward him.

Guy sighed and looked down. "Yes." He felt a wave of sadness wash over him. "Yes."

Susan and Mike exchanged glances and waited. When Guy remained silent, she said, "The press has been pestering us for a statement. I've put them off and referred them to the head office. But I wanted to consult you. But maybe you're not up to it . . ."

Guy kept his head down. He said nothing.

"Is there anything you want to say?" asked Mike. Susan shot him a sharp look.

Guy had a lot he wanted to say but not to the press. Despite his best efforts, a few tears escaped and rolled down his cheeks. He wiped them away with his fingers and raised his head. He had to say it, but saying it felt like stabbing himself with knives.

"Your grandson was killed?" asked Susan, preempting him.

Guy gave her a grateful smile and nodded.

"We're so sorry, Boss," she said.

"It's gotta be tough," said Mike.

Guy swallowed and cleared his throat. "Have you . . . have you talked to Jake?"

"Yes," said Susan. "His daughter was killed, I guess you know." Guy nodded. "He's, um, not good, as you would expect. I told him to take all the time he needed and not come to work until he was ready. I hope that's okay."

Guy nodded again. "Sure. That's good of you. I haven't talked to him yet." He began to tear up and paused. "I'm not in such great shape myself."

They nodded. "What can we do for you, Boss?" she asked.

"Yeah, anything?" echoed Mike.

Guy's phone rang. He held it up. "Thank goodness. I've got to take this. Hello?"

Susan and Mike turned away discretely as if they couldn't hear every word.

"Anytime. Yes. Right now? Put me down. Thanks." Guy hung up. "Here's something you can do—give me a ride to the doctor. I just got worked in." He didn't tell them it was Dr. Mehlman's office.

"Of course," said Mike.

Chapter 21

Bailey greeted him with smiles and wags when Sam opened his crate. His back was held tightly by a brace, but he could still climb into Sam's lap, and if Sam leaned over, give him slurpy kisses. The vet had advised Sam that daily walks were the best thing he could do to help Bailey. Sam vowed not to miss a day, no matter how he felt.

Sam clicked the leash on Bailey's collar and led him down the stairs to the front door. "You're my best friend, Bailey." Sam squatted and rubbed behind the dog's ears. "I'm so glad you're doing better. And so glad you seem to still love me after what I did." Sam choked up. "I'm so, so sorry I hurt you, sweet puppy."

Bailey sat down, tilting his head to listen.

"I know you're not a puppy anymore, and you probably don't like me calling you one, but you'll always be my sweet puppy." Sam wiped a tear from his cheek. "I feel I can tell you anything."

Bailey looked at the door and whimpered.

Sam stood and opened the door. "I know, too much talk, not enough walk."

Bailey could walk a bit further and a bit faster each day. Today he pulled ahead on the sidewalk before he found a place to stick his nose and smell. Sam imagined Bailey found messages from all sorts of animals. He let the dog dig his nose into the leaves and grass for as long as he wanted.

Sam slumped as he waited, then said, "It's been a rough few days, Bailey." Bailey lifted his head and sniffed Sam's feet. "Yeah, you can probably smell it on me."

Bailey pulled on the leash, and they moved on. Sam enjoyed these walks too. His mood lifted as they went. When Bailey found the right spot and left a pile, Sam leaned over with the poop bag and smiled. "Good boy, Bailey, good boy." Mission accomplished, they headed home.

Sam found his mother standing over something on the stove.

"Hi, Mom," he said. He fed Bailey, then sat at the kitchen table. He put his head in his hands and ran his fingers through his hair.

"Hungry?" she asked. "Pork chops, potatoes, and green beans coming up." She turned and washed him with her eyes. "How're you doing?"

"Okay. I've been better."

"Yeah, we all have," she said. "You going to the organizing meeting? Mark called while you were out and said they moved it to tonight. He's coming by to get you."

Sam sighed. He thought of Annette. She could probably understand how he felt, being Rick's sister. The load of guilt he still felt weighed him down. His feet felt embedded in concrete, his shoulders stooped as if carrying a boulder. He remembered how elated he'd felt after the Monday night meeting. Everyone coming together, making plans to do something. The black cloud around him had lifted. Now it was back.

"I don't know," he said. He would like to see Annette again, but going anywhere tonight felt like swimming upstream. "I'm not sure I'm up for it."

"Oh?" said his mother. She set a plate of steaming food in front of him and took her place with her own steaming plate. She took his hands across the table and bowed her head. "Be present at our table, Lord, be here and everywhere adored, these mercies bless and grant that we may feast in paradise with thee. Amen."

Sam dutifully closed his eyes and listened but did not join in as he'd done since he was old enough to talk. He just wasn't sure he believed anymore. So many bad things had happened with his father leaving and now this school shooting. How could a so-called loving God let stuff like this happen? He had tried praying but got no answer. It just made the black cloud sink deeper over him. Maybe there was no God.

"Amen," he added, not wanting to give his mother too much distress by his silence. Lifting her head, she examined him with raised eyebrows but said nothing. He cut a piece of pork chop and put it in his mouth.

"It might do you good to go, Son," she said. She passed him a basket. "Corn bread?"

The black cloud pressed lower. He thought of Mark and the meeting and sighed. He plucked out a warm piece of corn bread and slathered it with butter.

"Maybe you'll feel more like it once you've eaten. As your grand-mother used to say, a hot meal can warm up more than your insides."

Sam smiled. He barely remembered his grandmother, who died when he was small, but his mother had tutored him on many of her favorite sayings. According to his mother, his grandmother believed many things could be cured by a warm meal, a hot bath, and a good night's sleep. As he felt the warm food reach his stomach, he wondered if maybe she had a point. His mood went up as his belly filled. Maybe he would go.

Dr. Mehlman's office was small but cozy. Guy had expected something fancy but instead, when Susan and Mike dropped him off, he found a small building that looked like a garden apartment. He was relieved to find the sign outside just read, "Kenneth Mehlman, MD." He was embarrassed for his staff to know he was seeing a psychiatrist. He knew that was silly, but he did have his pride. He assured them he would get a taxi or an Uber or something for the ride home and sent them on their way. The reporters outside his house had finally left, so he didn't feel he'd need an escort to get back inside.

He stood outside a moment watching them drive away, surprised by how nervous he felt. He breathed a big sigh and stepped inside. Beads of sweat ran down his sides. A sudden urge to turn around and run gripped him. Being on crutches helped him squelch it, barely. A receptionist behind a big desk to the left gave him a big smile.

"Mr. Grant? You're here to see Dr. Mehlman?" she said. He nodded. "Take a seat and make yourself comfortable. I'll let him know you're here." She waved toward a small waiting area to his right.

"Thank you," he said as he sat on the ladder-back chair next to the couch. He held onto his crutches and peered at the door off a small hall with a sign on the door he could barely read: "Kenneth Mehlman, MD, Psychiatry." The couch looked more comfortable, but he couldn't imagine he could sink into it and get up again easily. He sure hoped he wouldn't have to sit there long.

He didn't. The door opened, and Dr. Mehlman appeared.

"Nice to see you, Mr. Grant," he said as he took the few steps toward Guy. "Please come in." Dr. Mehlman waited with arm extended to help Guy stand, but Guy was on his feet in a moment, glad he didn't need help.

He hobbled into the small office and straight to a chair with arms and a firm seat that would allow easy elevation. There was also a love seat arranged beside the chair in front of a desk. Its cushions looked deep and plush. He could imagine sinking in and never coming up. He didn't want to spend the night here.

Once Guy was seated, he let go of his crutches, letting them clatter to the floor. Dr. Mehlman closed the door and took his place in a high-back office chair with wheels. He turned warm eyes to Guy and waited. Guy examined the large tomes on a floor-to-ceiling bookcase against the wall and felt somehow reassured. This man was at least well educated. Guy cleared his throat, unsure where to start.

"How are you doing?" asked the doctor.

Guy felt grateful to be prompted. Maybe this could be just a conversation. But where to start? He raised his eyes to Dr. Mehlman. "I don't know." He closed his eyes briefly. Then he decided. To tell the truth, the whole truth, nothing but the truth. He opened his eyes. "Yes, I do. I'm doing terrible, horrible." And he began to pour it out. The bottle uncorked. He surprised himself by how much he shared. His grief, his regrets, down to the last drop, he told it all.

Dr. Mehlman gave him his full attention, as if he had all day and all week to listen, offering only an occasional "Hmm" and "Go on" as Guy spoke. When Guy finally finished, he waited, eager to hear what the good doctor would say and fearful at the same time. *You need to be locked up, yes, it is hopeless, yes, your life is over.* These were Guy's conclusions, but he wasn't the authority here, Dr. Mehlman was. Guy studied the doctor's face. Warm and inscrutable. He had no idea what he'd say.

Dr. Mehlman nodded and, with a serious face, gave his summary. "You've had a very traumatic experience and a terrible loss in the death of your grandson. It sounds like you feel both in the dark and in the limelight and you don't enjoy either."

Guy's mouth fell open. For a moment, he sat speechless, his throat dry. The knot in his stomach loosened. "Yes, exactly."

"And you don't know where to go from here. Is that right?" Dr. Mehlman paused.

"Yes, yes, oh yes," said Guy. A sense of relief poured over him. His eyes filled with grateful tears.

"You've always been a leader, been someone in charge, and now you feel lost. A new experience for you."

Guy sat in a stunned silence. How this man had taken his jumble of words, his incoherent outpourings, and made sense of it amazed him. He now saw before him a guide with an aura of wisdom shining around him. "Can you help me?" he asked, hoping he didn't sound as desperate and pitiful as he felt.

Dr. Mehlman smiled. "Yes, I think so. But first, let's reframe it. You have before you an opportunity for transformation. Such an opportunity often comes when one falls into a strange and deep darkness . . ."

Guy hung on his every word. Then he smiled. "And I thought you were going to give me some more medication."

"If it turns out you need some chemical support, I'll provide it. But I see that as a last resort." Dr. Mehlman shifted in his seat, crossing and recrossing his legs, then leaned forward, his arms on his thighs. "What I'd like you to ponder is what this traumatic and tragic experience has to teach you about what is most important to you in your life. That will light your way, our way, on the road forward. Does this make sense?"

Guy nodded, the wheels in his mind starting to turn. "When do we start?"

"We've already started."

The school cafeteria was brimming with people when Sam and Mark arrived, maybe twice the number from Saturday night. Due to the ongoing investigation, the school was closed, but someone had gotten special permission to use the cafeteria for this meeting. Sam scanned the crowd for Annette. The chairs were in large circles with three rows. They found seats in the third row. Sam finally spied Annette in the front row with Elaine. He smiled at her but couldn't tell if she saw him.

"Thank you all for coming," said Derek from the inner circle. "I see the word has spread." He turned to Sarah beside him. "Good job, Sarah, getting the word out."

She smiled. "It's easy if you know how to use social media. I know you've been busy too."

"Yes, we have permits for a march and rally on the National Mall on the first Saturday in December. That will give us nearly a month to get the details organized: speakers, musicians, signs, and all that." He grinned. "We're going to make a lot of noise and do our best to get the attention of lawmakers."

"And we're going to rely on all of you to help," Sarah said. "And to be the main speakers." She paused. "We may have offers from celebrities, but we want this to be our rally." She waved her arm around the room. "Don't worry if you aren't in the debate club. Anyone who wants to speak, can speak."

After some discussion, they divided into working groups. Groups for speakers, publicity, arrangements, sign making, and training in nonviolent direct action. As the crowd stood and milled around into different corners of the room, Sam kept his eyes peeled for where Annette chose to go. He had no idea what he wanted to do except talk to her again. He couldn't imagine being a speaker, and he knew nothing about publicity and arrangements. He could help make signs, he supposed, but he didn't even know what nonviolent direct action meant. In the crowd he lost track of Mark, but he was able to keep his eye on Annette and followed her into a corner of the room. Moving quickly, he pulled up a chair next to her. She smiled when she saw him.

She leaned over and whispered, "Hello."

"Hi," he said. His heartbeat quickened. "Good to see you again."

"So you're interested in speaking?" she asked.

"What? No!" He felt chagrined. "Is this the speakers' group?"

She laughed. "If you don't want to speak, why did you come over here?"

Sam blushed. "I . . . um . . . I don't know. I just wanted to say hello to you."

"That's nice," she said. "But you know we both have a story to tell." She raised her eyebrows and leveled her eyes at him.

Sam sat in awe of her. He couldn't imagine how she could even think about speaking when it was her own brother who had done this terrible thing. "You are much braver than I am."

"Hmm," she said. "I'm not brave at all—I'm terrified." He believed her because she trembled as she spoke. A lone tear rose in the corner of her eye and rolled down her cheek. She ignored it and gathered herself up. "But I don't want to let that define me. I want to do something." She touched his arm. "Don't you?"

"Yeah, I do." Sam felt a wave of nausea sweep over him. He sat up straight and took a deep breath. He belched and felt better. If she could do something, maybe he could too. He didn't want her to think he was a weak and scared little nobody. He felt challenged. "I'll think about it."

"Good." She smiled at him, and he melted a tiny bit.

Someone called the meeting to order. They turned their attention to the circle of potential speakers.

Chapter 22

When Guy woke up the next morning, he thought maybe it would be possible to keep living. Why had he spent so much of his life scoffing at the value of therapy? To him now, it felt like a lifeline. After he got dressed and had some breakfast, he sat at his kitchen table and considered what to do next. One thing he finally felt courage to do was to go see Jake. He checked the kitchen clock. It was already after 9:00 a.m. Not too early to call. Before he could change his mind, he dialed Jake's number.

He barely recognized the voice that answered as belonging to Jake. His "hello" was barely audible and his voice hoarse. He sounded half-dead. Guy was stunned.

"Jake, it's Guy," he said. Before Jake could answer, he stumbled on. "I want to come see you. Is this a good time?"

"Yeah," said Jake. Then he seemed to wake up. "I heard you were shot. Are you okay?"

"I'll live," said Guy. "I'll tell you all about it in person. See you shortly."

By some miracle, a taxi arrived within five minutes. The ride to Jake's house was also short, and soon Guy was standing in front of a two-story red-brick home with untrimmed bushes in front that spread their arms high and wide. Black shutters lined the windows. The curtains were drawn. Jake led him into the dark living room and snapped on a lamp on the end table. The couch had a flowered pattern and matching chairs in dark blue. Guy sat in one of the chairs, relieved the cushions were firm under him. Jake sank into the end of the couch near him. He could hear Jake's wife and younger child in the kitchen.

Guy really didn't know what to say, but he started with the obvious. "Oh, Jake, I'm so sorry about Gracia." He studied Jake as he watched for his response. Jake hadn't shaved, and he had deep circles under his eyes. He looked somehow thinner. His eyes were dull and barely seemed to take in Guy's presence.

Jake nodded. His eyes focused at last, as if just seeing Guy for the first time. "Thanks." Jake stared off into space a moment. "I think we're still in shock. I barely know what day it is."

"I know how you feel. It's Thursday. I think."

Jake turned back to Guy. "I'm so sorry about your grandson. And that you got shot." He examined Guy's leg. "Are you going to be okay? You look okay."

"Yeah, I was lucky." Guy hesitated, then went on. "Physically I'm going to be fine, but otherwise, I'm a real mess. Losing my grandson has about done me in. You must know. How are you doing? This must be so tough. How's your wife? Your little boy?"

"Jimmy is barely old enough to understand, but he keeps asking where his sister is. My wife is about like I am. We can barely function. Actually, Julie is doing better than I am. She's my rock. And Jimmy gives me a reason to keep going." He gave a big sigh. "I can't even think about returning to work. I can't believe she's gone. They're all gone." A tear rolled down his cheek. "But you were there, right? You volunteer. I thought about calling you earlier but, as I said, I'm barely functioning. Tell me, I want to know everything." He turned to Guy with intensity in his eyes. "You were there with her, for the last moments."

It was Guy's turn to sigh. "Honestly, I don't remember much. I was reading them a story. The intercom came on. We went into the lockdown drill. Before Ms. Warwick could get the door locked, the shooter came in and shot me, and I lost consciousness." He felt tears well up in his own eyes. "I'm sorry. I wish I could tell you more."

"That's okay. It doesn't change anything. She's still dead. I just miss her so much." He began to cry great gasping sobs.

Guy watched, feeling unsure how to respond. He nearly fell to sobbing himself. But he wanted to be there for Jake. Words felt so inadequate. He took a deep breath and reached to touch Jake's knee.

With effort, Jake pulled himself back together. "I'm sorry," he said as he reached for a tissue to blow his nose. "I've been trying to keep it together for Jimmy's sake, but sometimes I just can't."

"I get it," said Guy. "I've been crying a lot myself. My tears seem to be bottomless."

Jake raised his eyes to Guy. "Bottomless, yeah, that about sums it up."

Just then, a small boy appeared from the kitchen and hurtled across the room and into Jake's lap. "Daddy! Daddy! Don't cry." He threw small arms around his father's neck.

Jake wrapped his arms around his son. "It's okay, Jimmy. It's okay to cry. It's good to let the sad out." Jimmy looked at Guy. "Jimmy, this is Mr. Grant, my boss. Say hello."

Jimmy lowered his head. "Hullo," he whispered.

"Hello, Jimmy," said Guy.

Jimmy turned back to look at his father's face, ignoring Guy. "Daddy, I let my sad out too. I miss Gracia. But Mommy says Gracia is in Heaven. Is she, Daddy?"

Jake smiled. "She certainly is, Jimmy. She's our little angel up in Heaven with the other angels."

"What it's like in Heaven, Daddy?" Jimmy tilted his head and waited.

Guy felt himself melt as he watched. He felt pangs of grief for Little Guy, who would never climb in his lap again asking questions that often he didn't know how to answer. At least Jake still had this adorable little boy.

"Well," said Jake.

Guy leaned forward. He had no idea what he would say if he were Jake. He hadn't been religious as an adult. His childhood church days were a dim memory. As he was starting to realize, his religion had been his career, one he wasn't at all sure he believed in anymore. As he watched Jimmy's face with its certainty that his father knew the answer, all the answers, he felt a strange longing rise up inside him for something he could barely name. For something to believe in, for something to have faith in. For something he never knew he needed—and now needed desperately.

Jimmy sat back, his eyes glued to Jake's face, getting ready for his words. He balanced on Jake's knee and fiddled with Jake's hand.

"Well, Jimmy, it's a warm and safe and happy and beautiful place," Jake said. "Some say we come from Heaven, that Heaven is our first home. And that when we die, it's like returning home."

"So Gracia is at home in Heaven now?"

"That's right."

"Can I talk to Gracia in Heaven?" Curiosity filled the little boy's face.

"You can talk to her, of course." Jake paused. Guy hung on his every word. He had no idea what Jake could possibly say.

"Will she talk back to me?" he asked with wide eyes.

"It's a different kind of talking, Jimmy," said Jake. "You will hear her in your heart." He laid his hand over his heart. Jimmy did the same. "It's more in feelings than in words. And we will always feel her in our hearts. Always."

Jimmy nodded as he took it all in. He gently patted his chest over his heart. "I feel her now, Daddy."

"Yes, so do I." Jake smiled and kissed his son on the top of his head.

Jimmy jumped down. "I'm hungry." He turned toward the kitchen. "Mommy, I'm hungry!" Then he was off, his words fading as he ran. "I want a snack."

"What a precious little boy you have, Jake," said Guy. "And you are such a good father."

"Thanks, Boss." Jake said. "He's very special."

"I'm in awe of you. How you handled him just now was amazing."

Jake shook his head. "He's teaching me. My love for him guides me. And, if I didn't have my faith, I don't know how I could get through this. It has surely been shaken, but somehow I've not lost it. Jimmy helps me keep it. I want him not to suffer too much. I want him to feel safe. Like I wanted Gracia to feel safe."

Like I wanted Little Guy to feel safe, thought Guy. He felt a stab of guilt at his failure to keep any of the children safe. "Is there anything I can do for you, Jake? I'm sorry I haven't come by sooner. Or at least called. I feel like a real coward. I didn't know what to say, and I've been such a mess myself."

"That's okay, Boss. I know." He wiped his eyes with a tissue. "But you're here now, and I really appreciate it." He shook his head. "Somehow, you know, this just changes everything. I can't begin to think about returning to work."

Guy sighed. Work was the farthest thing from his mind. "Don't worry about it. I haven't been in myself. Susan and Mike had to come to my house yesterday to get to talk to me. I hadn't even called in. Take as long as you need." He saw Jake's wheels turning in his mind.

"I keep remembering that night I spoke to the school board about arming teachers. Tell me, you were there, when that guy . . . when he . . . at the shooting. What do you think of that idea now?" Jake asked and looked intently at Guy.

Guy felt a bit of relief to turn his attention to problem-solving. "Maybe arming the front office staff would have worked. Maybe they could have gunned down the shooter when he first showed up."

Jake thought a moment. "Wouldn't that have been great? I wish I'd been there behind the counter. I could've had him down in a split second."

Guy pressed his lips together. "You are the fastest sharpshooter I know. God, if only you had been there. The front office might be the best place to have armed staff." He perked up as he considered the question. Then he slumped. "I don't know. It all happened so fast. I was shot before I knew what was happening." Then he shuddered, thinking. "I doubt I could have raised a gun, and if I had had one,

I might have, well, who knows who I would have shot, even as a trained marksman."

"But we've got to do something," Jake said. He leaned against the back of the couch. "I keep playing scenes in my mind of being there myself and taking the guy out. I would have loved that. But I don't know." He stared out the window, then back at Guy expectantly.

Guy wasn't sure how much to share. He had certainly had similar thoughts. He knew there had been no way he could have shot the guy. Knowing the office staff, he knew they'd require a lot of training—a lot. They were such sweet and kind people. He had a hard time imagining them being quick with a gun. To maintain marksman skills, you have to stay in practice. It had been such a surprise. The atmosphere inside a school is not like a war zone, for obvious reasons. A school is for nurturing young minds and keeping them safe.

"Jake, what you say makes a lot of sense. We do need to do something. I just don't know what." Guy paused. He felt the long-held mantle of boss sliding off his shoulders, and with it, any reticence he may have felt for sharing his true feelings with an employee. Jake wasn't just an employee anymore. He was a grieving dad, just as he was a grieving grandfather. Their former roles were dissolved. "To be honest, Jake, I don't know anything anymore. I don't know what could have prevented this horrible tragedy." He rubbed sweaty palms on his pants leg. He choked back a sob. "It led to me losing Little Guy and you losing Gracia." He shook his head. "I just don't know."

Jake raised his eyebrows. "Boss, I don't know either. I just know

I miss my little girl."

Guy felt a surge of kinship rise up inside him; he felt an incredible bond with this grieving man. "Call me Guy, Jake. I don't want to be called boss anymore." Guy extended his hand. Jake grabbed it and squeezed.

"Okay, Guy." Jake smiled weakly. "Nice to meet you, Guy." Gripping Guy's hand even tighter, he asked, "What are we going to do now, Guy?"

"I don't know. But whatever it is, I'd like to do it with you, Jake." Guy reached his other hand to clasp Jake's other hand. They held on to each other, deeply connected. They each shed a few quiet tears.

Chapter 23

Sam knocked on the door of a small red-brick townhouse at the end of a row of townhouses. It was noon on Saturday. He checked the address in his phone to make sure. Yes, this was the right house number. It also had a long ramp from the front door that snaked back and forth in gradual descent to the sidewalk. Yes, this must be it. He knocked again. Then he noticed a doorbell to the right. He pressed it and heard it reverberate inside, then footsteps and the sound of the deadbolt lock turning. The door swung slowly open. Annette brightened when she saw him.

"Sam, come in! I wasn't sure you were coming." She waved him in and locked the door behind him, then led him down a small hall to the living room.

Annette had invited him over to work on speeches for the rally the group was planning. He had said yes, then maybe. Actually, the thought of standing up in front of what he imagined would be a huge crowd terrified him. But his admiration for Annette drew him to her. Both his mother and his therapist had encouraged him to at least go talk with her about it. "You don't have to decide to do it," said Matt, his therapist. "Just go put your toe in the water."

So here he was, sitting on the couch in her living room.

"Elaine is coming," she said. "And Sarah and Derek might stop by."

Sam gripped the notebook he had brought with him, then slowly relaxed his hand and set it on the coffee table. "Cool," he said, thinking he'd much rather be alone with Annette.

A woman in a wheelchair rolled into the room from the kitchen. She and Annette looked a lot alike, only her mother looked old and wan. Her face was deeply lined, and her short hair was streaked with gray. Yet when she greeted them and smiled, her face was transformed. She was still a beautiful woman. Despite what she'd been through, she had a light in her eyes. She rolled close to the couch.

"Hello, you must be Sam. I've heard a lot about you."

Sam blushed with surprise.

"This is my mom," said Annette. "Rachel Green."

"I figured," said Sam. "Nice to meet you."

"Likewise," said the older woman. "I understand you knew my son." A shadow crossed her face.

"Well, yeah, but not well." Sam couldn't imagine what to say.

"Annette told me he tried to recruit you for his murderous rampage." She shook her head sadly.

A spasm of guilt squeezed him and took his breath. His stomach churned. He had to say something. He inhaled deeply. "I had no idea what he was planning. I feel terrible I didn't tell someone, but . . ."

"None of us knew," said Mrs. Green. "I have many regrets, and they go way back. Don't give yourself too hard a time. Rick had been simmering toward a boil for a long time. None of us could have stopped him. Really. If anyone could have, it should have been me. If I had had any idea his intention was mass murder, I would have had him committed." She pressed her lips together and frowned. "But he totally shut me out ever since his father, um, died. Rick was just as stubborn. I couldn't do anything with either one of them."

"Thank you," said Sam with a big sigh. "Thank you for sharing your perspective. It must be so hard for you. I'm so sorry."

"Thank you, Sam. We're all sorry. But I tell you, every day I feel grateful to be alive. We just have to find a way to go on. I certainly never dreamed the man I married would go psychotic and try to kill me." She paused and stared off into space. "And apparently his son has taken after him."

Sam hung on her every word, riveted. He was a bit shocked and immensely impressed at how open she was.

She gathered herself and turned back to them. "But remember, life throws us a number of curve balls. Some we dodge and some we catch, and some hit us. We just have to live the best way we can and try not to get hit by too many. But if we do get hit, we get up, dust ourselves off, and keep going. I'm glad you young people are planning something. I will help you in any way I can."

Sam watched her maneuver her wheelchair in awe. She was certainly a survivor. He now knew where Annette got her strength and determination. Admiration for her flooded him. The mountain of his own problems shrank to a hill. A tall hill, to be sure, but not a mountain.

"Honey, I'm heading to work," she said to Annette. And to both of them, she said, "Have a good and productive planning session." She blew Annette a kiss and rolled toward the front door.

Sam knew the ramp outside was for her. But how did she get to work? Surely, she couldn't drive. Or could she?

Annette spoke as if she had heard his thoughts. "She has a special car she can drive with her hands."

"Wow," he said. "I wondered."

"Yeah, I know, everybody asks that. It even has a lift to help her get inside. I know, it's amazing. But she's been driving for a year now."

"Where does she work?"

"At the 7-Eleven a few miles away. She's the cashier. She loves working there. She's got a great bunch of folks to work with."

Sam frowned as he absorbed her words. A job like that couldn't pay much. He wondered but dared not ask. He waited to see if she could hear these thoughts also.

She laughed. "I know what you're thinking. How do we live on convenience-store pay? Believe it or not, my dad had a big life insurance policy, one that covered everything, even suicide. He might have been crazy, but he did that one thing right. And I think Mom gets some sort of widow's benefit from the government. We do okay."

"Good."

Annette blushed. "I can't believe I'm telling you all this."

"I'm glad you are." Sam's heart began beating faster, and heat rose into his neck and face. He wanted to take her hand, but he wasn't sure.

"I just feel a kinship with you after . . . you know . . . what we both went through."

"Yeah, a weird, horrible thing to have shared, but I feel the same way." Sam held both his own hands to hold back his urge to hold hers. "My family has gone through some stuff also. Last spring my father ran off with his, I don't know, someone from his office. He sort of disappeared."

"That sounds tough," she said.

"Yeah, it has been." He wanted to say more, but he held back. Even this sounded so much less traumatic than having your dad try to kill your mother and then kill himself. And he wasn't quite ready to admit, especially to Annette, that he had nearly killed his dog. He felt too ashamed. "But it's nothing compared to what you've been through."

"It's all relative," she said. "It's certainly something. I'm glad you told me. It makes me feel like you might trust me a little."

"Yeah, I guess I do." Sam felt a warm glow inside. His urge to touch her felt nearly irresistible.

Annette punched him in the arm with her fist. "I don't know what happened to Elaine, but let's get to work."

Sam felt both disappointed and relieved the spell was now broken. He picked up his notebook and pulled a pen from his shirt pocket. "I came prepared to take notes. Where should we start?"

Just then, the doorbell rang. "Maybe it's Elaine," Annette said. "Wait here." She scurried toward the front door.

It was indeed Elaine. And with her was Sam's buddy Mark. Sam was flabbergasted. How did they happen to come together? He soon found out that Elaine and Mark had both been in the debate club. Sam couldn't believe Mark hadn't told him.

"Hey, man," said Mark in response to the surprise on Sam's face. "I joined the debate club maybe a month ago. I thought I told you. Elaine was already there. I only got to two meetings before all this went down. I'm a total novice."

"Annette thought I might be able to coach you all in public speaking," said Elaine as they all gathered in the living room around the coffee table. Elaine and Mark sat in two stuffed chairs that faced the couch. Annette resumed her place on the sofa next to Sam. "I'll share what I know, but I'll warn you, it's not much."

Annette took the lead like a natural. "I was just thinking we should all tell our stories, make it personal. I mean, we could do research and gather statistics and all that, but to me that's boring. Elaine, what do you say?"

Elaine sat up tall. "Yes, statistics can be boring. What I learned was they should be used like seasonings to spice up a story. But personal experience is the real meat."

Sam began to feel hungry. He wished he'd brought some chips or something. Elaine had apparently not only thought about it but had actually packed provisions. She opened her backpack and unloaded a variety of chips and hummus and crackers and cheese and spread it all out on the coffee table.

"Wow, Elaine, thanks," said Annette. "Let me get what I have." She bounced off to the kitchen and returned with a bowl of apples and bananas and a jug of lemonade. "Now we have enough to fuel our brains. Just a minute." She disappeared into the kitchen again and returned with paper plates and cups and napkins. "Dig in, every-one!"

They filled their plates and soon their mouths and stomachs.

"I came with something," said Elaine. She pulled a notebook out of her backpack. "I wrote a rough draft of what I might say."

"That-a-girl," said Annette. "Always prepared, that's my friend. Let's hear what you've got."

Sam sat back in awe. He began to wonder what he could say. His mind was a complete blank. He studied Elaine, eager to listen.

Elaine opened her notebook and stood up. She cast her eyes around the room as if it were filled with a large crowd. "Hello. My name is Elaine, and I grew up in a household without guns. My father always said he'd never have guns in our home because too many toddlers get shot by accident. That naturally seemed to me to be the right way to do things. But then we started having all these mass shootings. I was horrified to hear about them on the news. But all those places were far away." She glanced at Annette. "And then I got to know Annette and learned what had happened in her family. That hit closer to home." She turned back to her notebook. "But still, even though we started having these active-shooter drills, I never thought it would ever happen in *my* school." She paused. "And then it did." She stopped. "What do you think so far?"

"It's great," said Annette. "Keep going."

Sam and Mark nodded, both transfixed.

"That was the most traumatic day of my life. I was sure I was going to die. I feel really lucky I didn't have P.E. first period. I feel really lucky to be alive. When we went on lockdown, of course we didn't know what was going on for a while, but I was terrified. *Terrified.* I felt sweaty and sick to my stomach and like I was going to faint. I wanted to run because I knew I was going to die. I panicked, and then I went kind of numb. It wasn't until I found my mom in the line of cars that came to get us—it wasn't until we hugged that I fell apart. I literally dissolved in tears. I was ready to get home, and when we got there, I went all around the house to lock all the doors and windows. They were already locked, but I had to check. It wasn't until then that I felt safe, that I knew I wasn't going to die." She raised her head to her friends who all nodded to encourage her to continue.

"I was scared, but now I'm angry! I didn't know Rick very well, just saw him a few times when I went over to Annette's house, but I could tell he was a bomb about to go off. He should have gotten some help. He should never have been able to get hold of an assault rifle. All that is just wrong. Wrong." She sat down and raised her eyebrows at her friends.

"Awesome!" said Mark.

"Powerful!" said Annette.

Sam didn't know what to say, so he said, "Ditto!" The idea of giving a speech at their rally terrified him even more. What was he even thinking?

Elaine smiled. "Thanks, guys. Anyone else have a speech yet?" They all shook their heads. "I'd like to propose we all write our speeches and share them next time. What do you say?"

"I'm game," said Mark.

"Me too," said Annette.

Sam said nothing, feeling his stomach churn, feeling speechless.

"How about you, Sam?" asked Annette.

Sam cleared his throat. "I've never done anything like this. I don't know what to say. I could never make a speech as good as yours, Elaine."

"Thank you for the compliment, Sam," said Elaine. "But remember, none of us has ever done anything like this. You just have to tell your story. Say what you said at that first meeting after our vigil."

Sam's breath stopped, then he gasped for air. Fear paralyzed him. Admit in front of the entire world that he could have stopped this shooting and didn't? Impossible.

"Sam," said Annette, squeezing his arm. She spoke as if she again could read his mind. "I feel such deep regret I didn't do something to stop my brother, especially after seeing him that very morning. I know you feel that same way. But I couldn't read his mind. He seemed like he always did, just a bit more angry. I didn't see a gun. Neither of us knew what he was up to. It's not our fault. It's just not. Just tell your experience, pure and simple. That's what I plan to do. You can do it."

Sam melted at her touch and hung on her every word. He hung his head. "Well, maybe."

"No maybe about it," said Mark. "You can do it, and we'll all help you."

"Yes," said Elaine. "Remember, we're all in this together."

Sam felt the butterflies inside him settle a bit. He felt as if his friends had taken him into a warm, sustaining group hug. Maybe he could. Maybe he would. Yes, maybe.

▷ ⊕ ◁

Guy sat at his kitchen table with a sandwich and chips and a can of Coke. It wasn't much of a sandwich, just ham and cheese and mustard on white bread, but he had made it himself. He wore a pale-blue oxford cloth shirt and khaki pants, the only casual clothes he owned. The day before he had been checked by his doctor and given permission to drive. His leg was healing well. His doctor told him he probably didn't need crutches anymore, but he kept them near just in case.

His first trip in his car had been three blocks to the Safeway. Being behind the wheel had felt strange. He drove at a crawl and felt relief when he pulled into the parking lot. Inside the store, he clung to the cart and filled it with items from every aisle. At home, much to his surprise, he had found it easier to carry the grocery bags inside without his crutches. For dinner he had made his signature dish: spaghetti with marinara sauce and a salad. The sauce came from a jar and the salad from a bag of mixed greens, but it was a step up from the frozen pizzas he'd been eating. Being able to make himself dinner and now a sandwich felt like a victory. He felt increasing confidence he could recover and take care of himself. Maybe he could live after all.

His visit with Jake had lifted his spirits as nothing else had, except maybe seeing Dr. Mehlman. He felt a new bond, a grief bond, with his coworker, now friend. Jake seemed as lost as he did. Guy hoped they would stay in touch and maybe together they could help and support each other. Guy's stomach turned every time he thought about returning to work.

As his thoughts fluttered around inside his mind, he stared blankly out the kitchen window. The sun shone on the deck. It was a crisp and cool fall day. He had refilled the bird feeder that stood on a pole on the edge of the deck, the feeder that had been mostly empty for years. But Safeway had had a big bag of bird seed on sale. He had bought it and filled the feeder as soon as he had gotten home. The birds had quickly discovered it. He watched, mesmerized, as the different birds stopped to feast.

He knew so little about birds. There was a red one. Was it a cardinal? Many were dark in color. He had no idea what they were. A wave of sadness rolled over him. The children in Ms. Warwick's class were like birds, chattering and hungry. He thought about her, how skillfully she had been able to gather the children for their lessons.

She had been the mother bird, filling them with knowledge. And now they were gone, mowed down by a crazed gunman. He shook his head. A tear rolled down his cheek.

He wondered how Ms. Warwick was doing. The police officer who had interviewed him had called the day before to say she had survived—or, at least, that she wasn't on the list of those who died. Guy was impressed the officer had remembered to call with all the police force had to deal with right now. Now, as he ate the last of his sandwich, he thought of calling her. He had no idea if this was appropriate. He had no idea what had happened to her that awful day. He had passed out. She could be critically injured and in the hospital. She could be home recovering. They could be wrong, and she could be dead. Her sparkling eyes and bright demeanor flashed across his mind. Had her light been dimmed? Had it been shut off? He ruminated while he drank the last of his Coke. He had been brave enough to go see Jake. Was he brave enough to call her?

Oh, stop it! he thought. *Just do it!*

He scrolled through the contacts on his phone to her number. He paused, his hand trembling. Then he sat up taller in his chair and hit the green phone icon. It rang and rang and rang and rang. When the voice mail came on, he felt both disappointed and relieved. He smiled hearing her familiar voice on the message, saying, "You've reached Kate Warwick. Please leave a message after the beep and I will return your call as soon as possible." *Beep.*

Guy swallowed and cleared his throat. "Hello, Ms. Warwick. This is Guy Grant." He choked on his words, struck by images from that day. He felt suddenly speechless as a dark vortex pulled at him. He threw it off. "I just wanted to know how you are. Please call me back if you can. I am recovering and would love to talk with you." He hung up, surprised by how wrung out he now felt.

Putting his phone in his shirt pocket, he took the newspaper and migrated to the recliner in his living room. Leaning back, he skimmed the paper. He had read just about every article, but maybe he had missed one that said something about Ms. Warwick. He hadn't heard from Laura yet about a service for Little Guy. He felt better, but life still felt pretty empty. He searched the obituaries. It covered several pages, as it had for a week now. The number of confirmed dead rose daily. Maybe he had missed her name. No, it wasn't there. Laying the paper aside, he stared off into space.

His phone began to buzz. Had he really not turned up the volume? He pulled it out of his pocket and answered without checking the caller ID—only to hear a recorded voice telling him they had good news about his college loan. Shaking his head, he hung up and raised the ringer volume. Then the phone rang again. Not to be fooled twice, he looked before he answered. His heartbeat quickened when he saw it was Ms. Warwick. He answered on the second ring.

"Hello, Ms. Warwick, omigod, are you okay?" he stammered.

"Hello, Mr. Grant, yes, I am, or I will be." She coughed. "I am so glad to hear from you. Are you okay?"

He nearly melted hearing her voice. "I'm fine. I did get shot in the leg, but I'm recovering. I can even drive now. Tell me about you."

She sighed. "I got a concussion when I got knocked into the edge of the white board. I've been in the hospital and got home a few days ago." She sighed again. "But I'm still in shock." Her voice choked. "All my children. Gone. I'm still absorbing it all." She paused, sniffling. "And you lost your grandson—that must be awful for you."

"It has been." Guy shook his head, choking back his own tears. "It's unbelievable, hard to take it all in." With effort, he turned his attention to her. "But I am glad you're okay."

"Glad you are too." She fell silent. "I wonder, well, I was getting ready to go to the school, to my classroom. I can hardly bear it, but I need to go. As the investigation is ongoing, a police officer will accompany me. I was able to make special arrangements. Do you want to join me? It's perfectly understandable if you don't want to."

Guy felt horrified at the thought but didn't hesitate. "I'll go with you."

"Oh, thank you. It will be good to have someone with me who was there that day." She sniffled again. "I haven't been there yet. I just couldn't face it." She paused. "I must face it."

Guy could hear Dr. Mehlman inside his mind agreeing with her. They hadn't talked about revisiting the scene of the shooting yet, but Guy already could tell Dr. Mehlman was an advocate of facing your demons. Guy was touched by her invitation.

"I will be honored to accompany you," he said. "Thank you for inviting me." Then, feeling bold, he asked, "Can I pick you up?"

"That's kind of you, but why don't we meet there, say, in twenty minutes?"

"That works for me. See you in twenty."

Guy arrived at the school in fifteen minutes. He pulled up and parked in the circular drive in front of the school. A police car and one other car, which he soon learned belonged to Ms. Warwick, were also there. An officer stood on the curb. Guy recognized him as the young officer who had come to his house. As soon as he got out of his car, Ms. Warwick got out of hers. Officer Parton nodded to them, turned toward the front door, and waited.

Images of the first time he met her rose up and crushed him, along with memories of Little Guy holding her hand and jumping up and down when he recognized his grandfather that first time he had picked up Little Guy after school. He struggled to stay upright as he walked slowly toward Ms. Warwick. He recalled so vividly how radiant she had looked that day. In contrast, today she looked gray and sunken. Her eyes lacked their brightness and instead were full of sorrow. He wanted to hug her but wasn't sure he should. Instead, he squeezed both her arms with his hands.

"Hello, Mr. Grant," she said. "Well, here we are."

He dropped his hands and tried to smile. "Yes, here we are."

"Are you ready to go inside?" She tried to smile in return.

"As ready as I'll ever be." He turned toward the front door. The walkway seemed long, and each step he was about to take felt arduous as scenes from his times here flashed across his mind. He turned to find her standing still, her eyes on the ground. He said, "Would you like me to lead the way?"

She stirred at his words as if awakening from a trance. She raised her eyes to him and then to the front door so far ahead. "No, let me." She shook herself and walked forward. "I'm just flooded with memories."

"I know what you mean," said Guy. He watched her in growing awe as she moved in front of him, following the officer. He had lost his grandson, but she had lost all her children. He found himself unable to move as he absorbed this realization. Also, he felt surprised and a bit ashamed that he noticed the curves of her back and legs. She might be burdened with grief, but she was still an attractive woman.

She paused and turned back. "Are you sure you're up for this?"

"Yes, sorry. I just move slowly these days." He mentally chastised himself and pushed his legs to walk.

The yellow police tape was still in evidence. Officer Parton lifted it and held it for them to duck under. At the front door, he pulled out keys and unlocked it, then stepped aside for them to precede him. He kept a respectful distance. Inside was a strong smell of disinfectant and whatever other cleaning supplies were used. It was an old building, but it was as sparkling clean as they could get it. Ms. Warwick led the way to her classroom. It was open. She stood in the doorway a moment. Guy followed her like a ghost as she walked inside. The officer remained in the doorway. The little tables and chairs were set up as they had been every day. On the white board in front were the same words that had been there that awful day: "Happy Halloween." Guy turned his eyes away to watch her.

Kate Warwick walked slowly around the room in silence. The chair was in the same place where Guy had sat to read the Halloween book to the children. The circle of small chairs was also in the same place. Tears filled his eyes as those memories washed over him. He felt himself crumple inside and forced himself to stay upright. He didn't want to collapse if she could stay standing. This was harder than he had thought it would be. *How much harder it must be for her,* he reminded himself.

She stood by the chair, then sat in it. Relieved, he pulled another chair over and sat next to her. Everything felt in slow motion. He mirrored her movements. She scanned the room. He followed her gaze. On the walls were colorful posters with uplifting messages in simple words for first graders. She had worked hard to make the room a warm and welcoming place for learning. The room looked the same but different. There were bullet holes in the walls and bloodstains on the floor, scars from that horrible day.

He wanted to say something, but what? He waited for her to break the silence. The air felt heavy. He swallowed back the tears that came unbidden. What was it he felt sitting next to her in this deep silence? His mind reached for the word, and then it was there: *reverence*. Grief, yes, but also reverence.

At last, she turned her head to face him. Her eyes were moist as they met his. "Thank you for coming with me," she said. She held herself in a quiet dignity. "When I was in the hospital, I had the most horrible nightmares. I was in a coma, and when I woke from it, I felt so glad to be out of those dreams." She sighed. "But, of course, the nightmares were just beginning. We are still in them. When are we going to wake up?" Now her voice had an edge of anger in it. "When are we going to wake up and stop these nightmares that continue to happen?" She shook her head, her mouth in a grim line.

He couldn't look at her. "I'm sorry," he said. He studied the rug, feeling the weight of his decades-long career with the National Rifle Association. He had participated in this campaign against gun regulations—eagerly participated. Hell, he had been one of the leaders in that fight. From where he sat now, in this empty classroom, he wondered why.

Chapter 24

When Guy got home from visiting the school, he crumpled into his living room recliner. The thought of inviting Ms. Warwick for coffee had flashed momentarily across his mind but then faded. Her last comment and her tone had scared him. She knew what he did for a living, what he had done. Did she hold him responsible for this nightmare? He held her in such high esteem, he didn't think he could bear it if she did. He couldn't even imagine asking her. He sank into the recliner like a limp dishrag. He raised the footrest and leaned back.

Memories of leading his staff in fierce opposition to any gun regulations rose up like monsters to haunt him. All the lobbying, all the carefully crafted talking points, all the Congressional hearings, all the op-ed articles, all the speeches. He had followed all the NRA talking points. He had advocated against background checks, against banning assault rifles, against all the things that might have, could have, would have prevented this horror—the loss of his grandson, the deaths of all these children and their teachers and school staff.

Guy knew little about him, but the kid who did this must have some serious family problems. Clearly, he had needed help. He closed his eyes as the guilt monsters loomed over him and surrounded him, pushing him deeper into a black hole. The black waters rose higher, lapped over his chin, his mouth. He began to feel he was drowning and flailed his arms. "No, no, leave me alone!" He sat up and opened his eyes. *Pop*, the monsters were gone. He scanned the living room. The couch, the coffee table, the magazines scattered in messy piles, all the familiar sights of home. He shook his head. What would Dr. Mehlman say? Had he been hallucinating?

Lowering the footrest, he stood and walked into the kitchen. Outside on the bird feeder sat one tiny brown bird. A brightly colored red bird joined it. They both bent their heads to eat, then flew away together. How Guy longed to fly away with them, into the blue sky, far, far away. How he longed to have someone to fly away with him. He sat at the kitchen table and put his head in his hands. He longed for the comfort of family. But who? Laura was all he had left, and he didn't know if she was even speaking to him. His son lived far away and never communicated, never with him, anyway.

He began to carry on a conversation with his daughter in his mind. *Hello, Laura, I miss you. How are you?* He waited but there was only silence.

He shook his head, and Dr. Mehlman appeared, his gentle voice a comfort. *Why don't you call her, Guy? She might welcome hearing from you. When is the last time you talked to her?*

Guy smiled. *Thanks, Doc. It has been a while. Maybe I will. I'm just afraid of what she'll say.*

Dr. Mehlman replied: *Better find out and deal with it. It may not be as bad as you think.*

He would say that or something like that, Guy knew. He took out his phone and dialed. It rang and rang and went to voice mail. He sighed. Voice mail was his life lately. After the beep, he gathered his courage.

"Hello, Laura, it's Dad. I've been thinking about you." He swallowed and went on. "I've been rethinking my whole life. You may find this hard to believe, but I'm seeing a psychiatrist. He's really helping. Please call me. I want to know how you and Tom are doing and when there might be a service for Little Guy. I miss him so much. I miss you." Guy hung up and watched the bird feeder again. No birds.

The rest of his day passed in a blur. Another ham and cheese on white bread. A long afternoon nap. The phone rang several times. Each time, he jumped and his heart flew into his throat when he answered. One call offered him a cruise down the Danube at a never before so deeply discounted price. Another promised help with his college loan, and yet another a free weekend to see a special deal on a time-share. One caller even sounded to be someone speaking Mandarin. He hung up and vowed not to answer it again. He made another spaghetti dinner, this time with ice cream instead of salad. He watched for birds, but only a few came, and he couldn't name them. Maybe he'd get a bird book. When was he going to see Dr. Mehlman again? It couldn't be too soon. He couldn't wait to say, *See, Doc, I called, I left a message, I got nothing.* Maybe he'd go binge-watch something, something grisly. What was that one he'd heard about? *House of Cards*? Or maybe a comedy would be better. He felt his mood sinking.

He made some popcorn, grabbed a beer, and settled into the recliner downstairs in his den. He pointed the remote at the large screen TV, and then the phone rang. *Ah, jeez, probably another robo call offering to sell me something I don't want.* He felt annoyed and considered letting it go to voice mail. *But maybe.* He picked up the phone. No, it wasn't his cell phone; it was his house phone. No one ever called his house phone. A cordless extension sat on the desk across the room. He got there on the fourth ring.

"Hello?"

"Hi, Dad."

"Laura? Is it really you?" Guy barely made it back to the recliner with the receiver before his legs gave out.

"Yes, it's really me. What's left of me, that is." Her voice sounded thin and hoarse.

"It's so good to hear your voice, Laura. I've missed you. You sound, I don't know . . . how are you?"

"Half alive, if you want to know the truth. I'm not sleeping. I'm barely eating." She sighed.

"Oh, honey, I'm so sorry to hear this." He wanted to reach through the phone and take her in his arms. This urge surprised him. Physical demonstrations of affection had never been part of their relationship. "What can I do for you?"

"Nothing, there's nothing anyone can do if they can't bring Little Guy back."

"I wish I could, Laura. I wish I could." He felt tears well up in his eyes. He wiped them away with his fingers as he scanned the room for a box of tissues. None.

"You can tell me about seeing a psychiatrist. Is this for real? You? NRA guy, seeing a shrink?" Her tone was weary with a hint of mocking in it.

Here we go. He braced himself for whatever he was sure she was about to throw at him. "It's been the best thing I've ever done, Laura. It has been a lifeline."

"Hmpf," she said. "And what did you mean about rethinking

your life?" she said in a softer tone.

How could he even begin to answer something he was just beginning to re-examine? Well, he had said it and now he had to say something. "I just wonder . . . I regret . . ." Despite himself, he broke down in sobs. "I just think maybe I've been wrong, so wrong." He reached in the pocket of his cardigan and found a wadded-up tissue. He wiped his nose.

"Wrong about . . . ?" She sounded curious, her voice a bit more resonant.

"You know, guns." Walking around the room, he opened the desk drawer and found a pack of tissues. Holding the phone in the crook of his neck, he sat down and opened it. He blew his nose, waiting for her to say something. When she didn't, he said, "You know, my life's work. It just looks different now." Silence on the other end continued. "Laura? Are you still there?"

Then he heard her weeping as if from a distance. The weeping came closer, followed by the sound of her blowing her nose. She cleared her throat. "Dad, did I hear you right? I can't recall ever hearing you say you were wrong. About anything."

Guy couldn't read her tone. With difficulty, he pulled himself together. "Laura, I'm so sorry, so very sorry. I was so wrong. I haven't been back to work. I may never go back. Dr. Mehlman is helping me figure it all out."

"Give me his number. I want to thank him." She laughed, and then she wept again. "After Little Guy and all these others have been shot by a lunatic with an assault rifle? And now you say you were wrong about guns? What took you so long?"

Guy didn't know what to say. He really had no idea. It had been an abstraction and now it was a reality. Now he was suffering the consequences of gun violence. That seemed pitiful, inadequate. Laura sounded angry, and he couldn't blame her. He knew she was speaking from her grief and loss. He felt a tad defensive, but more than that, he felt responsible and guilty. And on top of that, he felt his own grief and loss. Or was it the other way around? His grief and loss made him feel responsible and guilty. Tears welled up again, and he struggled to speak. "Oh, Laura, I feel terrible. I feel responsible. I feel guilty. I feel so much regret that I can barely function."

He heard silence on the other end of the line, then soft weeping. Then a voice so quiet he had to strain to hear it. "Dad, I've never heard you speak this much about how you feel. You sound like a different person."

"I'm trying, honey, I'm trying."

"And there are two of us not functioning. Maybe you really should give me Dr. Mehlman's number. Maybe I need someone to talk to."

"Of course, honey, I'll be glad to give you his number."

"I can't even think about a service for Little Guy. Tom wants to do it, and our minister is ready any time." She paused. "I just need to get over feeling I need to put myself in the ground with him." Her voice dissolved into more weeping.

Guy was shocked and alarmed. He held his breath, then gasped for air as his heart began racing. *Laura, no, don't say that!* Those were the first words in his mind, but he held back, remembering how depressed and suicidal he had felt. Expressing his feelings seemed to be working with her. He'd keep it up. He took a slow, deep breath. "I know exactly how you feel, Laura. I've been feeling the same way, that my life is over, that I have nothing to live for anymore. I got referred to Dr. Mehlman when I was in the hospital. Talking to him has really helped. I'll be glad to give you his number. Shall I text it? Call him. Tell him you're my daughter. Maybe that will help you get seen faster."

"Thanks, Dad. I will call him in the morning." She sniffled and blew her nose again. "Funny that you got to a shrink before I did. I didn't think you were the type."

Guy sighed. "I didn't think I was the type either. But I am now."

Chapter 25

"**W**hat if I had told you about Rick, how he was pursuing me?"

Sam sat in Matt Nichol's office on Monday. He'd had a few sleepless nights, his mind churning with these questions. Now he poured them out to his therapist. He leaned forward in his chair, gripping his hands together.

"What if I had read his texts and showed them to you?" Sam said, then stared at Matt.

"Well," began Matt. "We would certainly have discussed Rick and how you felt about him." Matt shifted in his seat. "I take it you're still thinking about what you could have done differently to prevent this shooting."

"Yeah, I am. It's been keeping me up at night. If I'm going to make a speech at our rally . . ." Sam shook his head and examined the rug at his feet. He sighed and looked up. "I thought about telling you, I really did. Damn, I wish I had."

"It's hard to know now if it would have made a difference, but any further ideas about why you didn't tell me?"

Sam grimaced. He decided to open that door a bit more. "I was just so messed up back then. I thought I was crazy, and I was afraid you'd think I was crazy, and I barely knew you and . . . and . . . shit."

"I never thought you were crazy, Sam," said Matt with emphasis.

Sam's face lit up with relief. "You didn't?"

"No, I didn't. I thought you were troubled but with good reason. Your father had left . . ."

"I hurt my dog."

"Yes, all that. It was a lot to deal with. It makes sense Rick was just one more thing to add to how overwhelmed you were already feeling."

"Hmm," said Sam. "Yeah, I guess so." He smiled at Matt for the first time that day. "I'm so glad to hear you didn't think I was crazy. Maybe I'm not crazy after all."

Matt chuckled. "Not a bit crazy."

Sam sat back in his chair and relaxed as he took in Matt's words. "Still, I wish I had told you. I remember sitting here thinking about Rick. He creeped me out big time." He leaned his chin on his fist and thought a moment. "If I could have told you, told you everything, looked at the texts with you, what would you have done?"

Now it was Matt's turn to lean his chin on his fist and think a moment. "You shared a few of them. What do you think we would have seen if we had looked at them together?"

"It would have looked like Rick was crazy, really crazy." Sam narrowed his eyes. "He said something about being famous, about having an arsenal, about taking out more than anyone ever had. Real sicko stuff." As Sam spoke, a wave of guilt hit him. "Oh, God, he should have been committed." He wrinkled his brow and leaned toward Matt. "Could we have had him committed?"

"Maybe," said Matt. "It's hard to say. And remember, hindsight is twenty-twenty. Always. We didn't know what the texts said. We can't change the past. We can only learn from it as we go forward."

"I've sure learned I should have trusted you and told you. I just avoided it. And look what happened."

"Yes, but don't give yourself too hard a time. You did the best you could."

"I want to do better. I hope to God there never is a next time, but next time I will do better." Sam sat a bit taller. "People need to be educated about mental health. About what to do when they suspect someone is about to blow."

"Sounds like a good topic for your speech," said Matt with a smile.

"Maybe," said Sam. "If I give a speech." He wrinkled his brow. "How do you even have someone committed anyway? I have no idea. Can you tell me? Then, if there's a next time, I'll know what to do."

"Sure. If you believe someone is of 'imminent danger to self or others,' call 911. The police will take that person to be evaluated."

"Imminent? What does that mean?"

"That means right away. If you hesitate, they could harm themselves or others."

"It's that simple?" Sam was incredulous. "Doesn't a doctor or therapist have to call?"

"No, anyone can do it. Only a medical professional can do the evaluation, of course, to determine if someone is indeed of imminent danger to self or others and needs to be hospitalized."

"I wish I had known this when Rick stopped by my house before he went to school. I knew he was up to something bad, but I had no idea what to do." Sam tried to imagine picking up the phone as Rick banged on his door. In his mind's eye, he saw his hand trembling as he dialed. "Wow. That would be hard to do."

"Yes, I know," said Matt. "It's never easy. But sometimes it's the best option."

Sam looked at Matt. "Have you had to do it?"

Matt nodded. "Not too many times, fortunately, but yes."

"People need to know this." Sam's eyes glazed over as he considered this, then they brightened and he sat up tall. "I could share this in my speech." He slumped and leaned back in his chair. "That is, if I give a speech."

"You certainly could." Matt smiled. "It would be a public service, Sam."

"Hmm." Sam turned inward a moment. "A public service. I could do a public service."

"You certainly could," said Matt, smiling. "That is, *if* you give a speech."

Sam closed his eyes as his mental wheels started moving inside. They were stiff and needed oil and creaked as the long unused pistons began their up and down motion. But slowly, the wheels started, and in a slow crescendo they accelerated. He opened his eyes. "People need to know this. What to do. I didn't know. But now I do. I could tell them."

"You could do a good job, Sam," said Matt. "And I'll help you."

"You would?" asked Sam, his eyes big.

"Of course. That's what I'm here for."

Chapter 26

"I'm going with you," said Annette. She and her mother, Rachel Green, sat at the breakfast table on Monday morning, empty plates in front of them and the lingering smell of eggs and toast and bacon in the air.

"You are welcome to come with me," said Rachel. "I just want you to know you don't have to. Rick is likely to be in a bad mental state. It may be a difficult visit." She gave a big sigh and put her head in her hands. "I still can't believe we're doing this, visiting Rick in jail. My son, the mass murderer." A single tear ran down her cheek. She wiped it away, then pulled herself up tall. "But I still love him, and I really want to see him."

"I know," said Annette, patting her mother's arm. "I really want to talk to him, to find out what in the world he was thinking."

"I'll be surprised if he will say much about that, but you can try."

"Any idea why he finally gave permission for family to visit? I mean, didn't he refuse until now?" Annette leaned her head on one hand, her eyes intent as she listened. She downed her last sip of coffee.

"I'm sure he wants something, but I have no idea what. We're not allowed to bring anything in. Matter of fact, there is even a long list of acceptable clothing. I'm planning to wear what I have on." She waved her hand over her brown corduroy pants and red cable-knit sweater. "I'm also going to leave everything in the car except my driver's license and keys. I recommend you do the same. They require a picture ID but nothing else."

Annette smiled. "Yeah, I read the list on the jail website. They want us to dress like proper Victorian ladies." Annette wore black leggings with a fuzzy white-and-blue eyelash sweater. "Will this do?"

"The sweater is good, but didn't you see they specifically said 'no leggings'?" She shook her head. "Very strict."

"Too form-fitting? Leggings?" Annette raised her eyebrows. "He's my brother, for God's sake. He has never even looked at my legs as far as I can tell."

"I wouldn't be sure about that, but anyway, that's the rule." Rachel smiled.

Annette's eyebrows remained high, her eyes wide. She opened her mouth to speak but then closed it. "Never mind, I don't even want to go there." She looked at the clock on the wall. "What time is our appointment?"

"Ten o'clock. But we have to be searched and go through the magnetometer, so I want to get there at least ten minutes early. We need to leave very soon."

Annette pressed her lips together. "Magnetometer? A metal detector just like at the airport, eh? Let me go find my baggiest and least 'form-fitting' pants. Do you want me to do the dishes first?"

"No, I'll just put them all in the dishwasher. Better go get ready."

When they got to the adult detention center, a barrel-chested white male officer with deep wrinkles and gray hair checked them in. He stood behind a counter, a serious expression on his face. His name badge said "Officer Todd Dean." Annette felt butterflies begin to riot inside her. She'd never seen the inside of a jail except on TV. The reality was starkly intimidating.

The navy-blue corduroy pants she wore with her eyelash sweater must have been acceptably baggy because Officer Dean didn't seem to pay a bit of attention to their respective attire, except to give a slight nod. The place seemed clean but smelled of sweat with a hint of disinfectant. The room was dim, despite the fluorescent tube lights on the ceiling. The plastic coverings were a dingy gray. The carcasses of bugs that had found their way to the light littered the plastic, adding to the dull atmosphere.

When they showed their identification and announced they were there to visit Rick Green, Officer Dean paused and stepped out from behind the counter. He said nothing but stared hard at them and cast his eyes from their picture IDs to their faces and back several times. Annette's hands grew moist. She could only imagine his thoughts. *You're that monster's family? What kind of monsters are you?* Surely they bore some measure of responsibility also. She wished the floor would open up and swallow her. Why did she want to come here? He had them sign in the visitors' book and pushed a button on the intercom. Soon, a short, squat female officer with brown skin showed up. Her badge read "Officer Mildred Johnson."

"They're here to see Green," he advised her. She frowned at them and shook her head.

"Come with me," she said. She led Annette and Rachel through a door into a room that did indeed bear a resemblance to airport security. "Step right here one at a time," she said, indicating a circle on the floor. "Well, I mean roll right here," she said to Rachel. "Can you stand up?"

"Is that necessary?" Annette was quick to ask.

"It's okay, Annette," said Rachel.

The woman shrugged. "I guess not. Stay seated, raise your arms." Rachel did and the woman proceeded to pat her down. Then she looked at the magnetometer and shook her head. "Wait over there." She pointed to a spot to the side of the entrance to the machine. Rachel rolled as requested. "You next," she said to Annette.

Annette stepped onto the circle and got her own pat-down, then walked through the metal arch. She was relieved not to hear any beeping. Her heart was beating so loudly she wondered if it was audible. There were several chairs before another door. Annette sat down and watched her mother, gripping her hands tightly in her lap.

Officer Johnson consulted Officer Dean, who pulled a long, wide wand out of a drawer. The woman ran it over Rachel, trying in vain to avoid scanning any metal on her wheelchair. She frowned and groaned and ran the scanner several times until she was able to satisfy the device. She opened a gate beside the magnetometer for Rachel to roll through.

She led them down a hall and through another locked door into a small room divided by a long table with chairs on either side and a plexiglass wall extending down the middle. It reminded Annette of a ticket counter at the train station. There was a small gray circle in the middle of the plexiglass at mouth level. It had an even smaller opening, where presumably your voice could carry through to the other side. Between each of the four visiting areas, a partition extended high enough on each side to give some sense of privacy. This place smelled heavily of disinfectant. The uncovered fluorescent lights overhead were blinding. Rachel and Annette squinted as they exchanged glances.

The officer pointed them to the first section. She pulled the chair out to allow Rachel to roll her wheelchair in and put the chair behind and to the side. Annette sat in the chair. There was barely room for her next to her mother's wheelchair.

"Maybe I'll just stand," she said.

"Suit yourself," said the officer. "Your family member will be brought out shortly. I'll be here by the door until your time is up." She took her place in front of the door through which they had just come, applying to her face a look of detached boredom.

"So much for private conversation," Annette whispered to her mother.

Rachel nodded and turned her eyes to the only door on the other side of the room, where they presumed Rick would soon appear.

A large circular clock on the wall had a ticking second hand. The time read exactly ten o'clock. They heard a loud click as the door opened. Rick shuffled out with two officers in blue uniforms holding either arm. He wore an orange jumpsuit. His hands were cuffed in front of him. His feet were in shackles as well. The officers escorted him to the chair and pushed him into his seat. They said nothing as they retreated to their places in front of the door, barely six feet away.

Annette felt stunned as she examined her brother. Her body stiffened, and her throat closed up. Her hands went reflexively to hold her mother's shoulders. She couldn't believe how bad he looked. His body odor preceded him. His eyes were dull, and his hair stood up in spikes all over his head as if it hadn't seen a comb since he'd arrived. He kept his handcuffed arms in his lap as he gradually focused on them.

"Hello, Son," said Rachel.

"Hello," echoed Annette, moisture rising under her arms.

Rick narrowed his eyes and passed his gaze over them for a moment. Then he spoke in such a soft voice they had to lean forward to hear him. "I don't belong in here," he said. "You've got to get me out of here!" His voice rose in a slow crescendo. "They treat me like some sort of criminal! This was not how it was supposed to be." He hung his head.

Annette felt strangely sorry for him. *What could he be thinking? He committed murder—why does he think he wouldn't be treated like a criminal? Especially in jail? Who does he think he is? Has he lost touch with reality? How did he think it was supposed to be? Does he realize he will be facing the death penalty? Or life in prison?* These and many more questions swirled inside her mind. Yet she hesitated to ask them. She waited for her mother to speak first.

Rachel's eyes filled with tears as she watched Rick. Shaking her head slowly, she choked them back with effort. "How did you think it was going to be, Rick?" Her voice was soft and tender.

"Not like this," he said. "Not stuck in here, handcuffed and shackled." He frowned and gritted his teeth. "Not after the way I was treated. It's not fair!" he shouted.

"What do you mean?" asked Rachel.

"Hmmpf. You wouldn't understand," he said and closed his eyes.

"I would." Annette took her opening. "If you meant at school, I saw what happened. How your friends turned on you, teased you, taunted you. I understand. I was there."

Rick opened his eyes and kept them on his sister. "You weren't there." He spit out his words.

"Yeah, I know I was a year ahead, and we didn't have classes together." She stood tall. "But I saw you in the cafeteria eating alone." She addressed her mother. "You were in the hospital for such a long time, Mother. Things got really bad for Rick at school."

Rachel listened in disbelief. "Why didn't you tell me, Annette?" Rick said nothing and glared at them both.

"I didn't want to bother you. You had your hands full trying to get well. And then you had to sell our big house, and we had to move to our townhouse." She paused and took a deep breath. "Knowing how things are now, I wish I had." Her voice trembled. "I was afraid I'd lose you, too, Mother. I didn't think, well, I thought I could help him myself."

Annette clasped her hands together tightly and spoke to Rick. "I reached out to you, Rick, don't you remember? I wanted to help. I tried to get you to talk to the school counselor, but you refused. You blew up at me. Then you wouldn't talk to me, like I was your enemy or something. You got so angry at me every time I tried to talk to you, I finally gave up. You just withdrew more and more."

Rick sneered. "You thought I was crazy, Annette. Why would I talk to you? You're crazy if you think that."

"I didn't think you were crazy, Rick, I thought you were suffering!" Annette sat down, put her head in her hands, and wept.

Throughout this exchange, Rachel's head swiveled between her son and daughter. When they stopped, she sat in a heavy silence, taking deep breaths and squeezing her fingers with her hands and making fists and squeezing them again. After some time, she laid her hands open on her thighs and cleared her throat. "I knew you were suffering, too, Rick. I was not out of it that much."

Rick sat quietly and listened, his face tight and guarded, his eyelids at half-mast.

"I knew you needed help, Rick." Her voice was tender and firm. "I even consulted the school counselor, don't you remember? I believe she called you into her office once, but she told me you wouldn't say a word."

Rick made fists and laid them on the counter in front of him. The handcuffs clinked. "That lady was a wimp. She was all touchy-feely with '*Tell me your feelings*' and '*Let me help you*' garbage. She was weak. I would never talk to some idiot like her. She would never stop those big kids from torturing me. Every day they laid in wait for me. I knew one day they were gonna kill me. No one would stop them. I had to do it." He sighed. "I thought I had someone to help me, but he refused. He was also a wimp." His eyes glazed over, and he looked off into space. "I knew I was destined for better things; I knew I was going to be famous. I saw what those other guys did at those other schools. Ha, I would outdo them all! Dad did one thing right. He taught me to shoot." He began to grin widely and chuckle to himself.

Annette thought back to all the guns her father had kept. One room in the basement of their old house was like a gun cabinet, with guns mounted on all the walls. He was not only a collector but also a sharpshooter. He had taken Rick every Saturday to the firing range once he got old enough. He had never taken her. To him, guns were for men. She had never wanted to go, but a part of her had felt jealous of the attention their father had lavished on her brother.

"Where did you get the gun you used, Rick?" asked his mother. "I thought I had gotten rid of all the guns your father had when we moved."

Rick laughed. "You thought you had, huh? You were wrong. Besides, even if you had, it's really easy to get more."

"Where did you keep them?" asked Rachel.

"I had my secret place to stash them." He grinned. "Where you would never find them."

"Oh, Rick," said Rachel. "How I failed you. How badly I failed you." She sighed and closed her eyes.

Annette reached for her mother's hand. "We both failed him, Mother."

Rachel turned to Annette. "It wasn't your responsibility, Annette. It was mine. You're not the parent, I am." Rachel squeezed her daughter's hand and released it. She took a deep breath and looked at Rick. "You asked us to come today, Rick. What can I do for you?"

Rick's eyes widened. "What do you think? I want you to get me out of here!"

Rachel sighed. "The judge denied bail. I can't get you out." She leaned back in her wheelchair and patted Annette's hand that lay on her shoulder. Annette squeezed her mother's shoulder. "And honestly, Rick, I love you, but . . ." She paused and took a deep breath.

Rick glared at her. "What?"

"Rick, do you realize why you're in jail? Do you understand what you have done?" Rachel bit her lower lip with her top teeth. "I'm not sure I feel safe having you at home after what you did. I hate to say it and I still love you, but it's the truth." She sat back in her wheelchair.

Annette gathered her courage and leaned forward. "Why did you do it, Rick? Why did you kill all those people, those children and teachers? What were you thinking?"

Rick's mouth hung open as he continued to glare at them. "What do you mean? You said you knew how they treated me. They deserved it! No one's gonna mess with me again. I showed them—I showed everyone. I may be a fuck-up, but I can shoot." He shook his head and closed his eyes. Half to himself, he muttered, "You just don't get it. Even my family turns against me . . ." He opened his eyes and pierced them with his gaze. "You don't know what it's like in here. It's worse than it was at school. They got even bigger bullies, they got rapists in here. If I stay in here one more day, it will drive me crazy!" He slumped back in his seat. "Maybe I should have done what dad did. Maybe I should do that now. That way I would get out of here."

"No, Rick, no!" cried Rachel. "You need help. Please. I want to get you some help if you're thinking like that."

Annette sighed deeply. She laid her hand across her mother's shoulder, felt her shake with sobs. She found herself going numb. In a way, she was glad Rick had been willing to talk. It was talk that should have happened a long time ago, but at least he was no longer acting like a stone wall to his family. Yet she was deeply troubled that he showed no remorse, that he seemed to feel justified. It boggled her mind. Part of her also felt relieved he was locked up, but she heard his desperation and wondered if jail was safe for him. Had he been raped? Was he really suicidal? She didn't know who he was anymore. She didn't know why it had taken her so long to realize that her brother had become a truly dangerous person.

Annette pulled on her mother's arm and nodded toward the door. "Maybe we should just go," she whispered in her mother's ear. Rachel nodded.

Rick opened his eyes and glared at them. "Yeah, go, leave me here. Don't be surprised if the next time you see me, I'm dead." His expression turned inward.

"Rick, please don't say that!" cried Rachel.

"Mom, let's go," said Annette.

Rachel turned to Officer Johnson, who in turn waved at the two guards. In a flash, they were on either side of Rick. They lifted him up and moved him toward the door. Rick shook them off, but they grabbed him again harder. "Time to go, buddy," said one of them. They were built like football players and had no trouble picking Rick up and carrying him out of the room. In no time, the door closed behind them and clicked to lock.

Only then did Annette realize she had been holding her breath. She exhaled, took a deep breath, and stood. She stepped aside to allow her mother to roll her wheelchair back and turn toward the exit. As the officer led them back the way they had come, Rachel began to speak. "My son is suicidal," she began. "He needs to be on suicide watch. Who do I need to tell?"

"Hmmpf," the officer said. "Good luck with that."

"But who do I need to talk to?"

"Oh, that'd be up to someone way above my pay grade. Ask Officer Dean." She pressed her lips together. "I do feel sorry for y'all, but, if you were to ask me, that boy don't deserve to live."

"Excuse me?" asked Annette.

Officer Johnson whirled around, her hands on her hips. "I lost my niece and nephew because of what your son did. I know I'm not being professional admitting this to you, but it's the truth."

"Oh, I'm so sorry," said Rachel with a gasp.

"You didn't do it, ma'am, but it got done. I shouldn't have said anything." She wiped her eyes and led them out.

When they got back where they had started, Rachel, her voice now thin and faint, spoke to Officer Dean behind the counter with the same question. She peered up from her wheelchair, her head barely above the top of the counter.

He sighed and shook his head slowly. "Ma'am, I can tell you're a good mother, and I do recall the hard time your family has already been through. I see what that boy's father did to you, putting you in that wheelchair. And now this." He raised his shoulders and let them fall. "I wouldn't blame you if you didn't want to see your son ever again. I admire you for coming."

Annette's eyes widened. *He knew about their father, about their family tragedy?* She stood up next to her mother, standing as tall as she could. "Did you hear what she said? He's suicidal." She placed her hands atop the counter.

The officer looked at her kindly. "You the big sister?"

Annette nodded.

"Well, honey, I feel sorry for you. I been here over thirty years now. I've seen a lot and I know a lot from what I've seen, and I've never seen anyone like your brother. I'm not a bit surprised if he sounds suicidal. Most of those school shooters shoot themselves before they can be arrested. We will watch him and do our best to keep him safe, that's our job." He gave them a sad smile. "I wish you weren't having to go through this. I wish none of us had to go through what that boy did. Have as good a day as you can now." He turned back to his desk, dismissing them.

They drove home in a heavy silence. When they got there, Rachel gathered whatever papers she had with any information she'd been given after Rick was taken into custody, sat at the kitchen table, and started making phone calls. Annette brewed a fresh pot of coffee for them both. Setting two steaming cups on the table, she sat beside her mother and began peering over her shoulder to see what was there.

Rachel had the phone glued to her ear. "No answer. The voice mail is full," she said as she hung up.

"Who did you call?" asked Annette.

"The public defender office." She flipped through the papers in front of her.

"Has he been assigned a lawyer yet?"

"They were supposed to," said her mother. "I don't know who to call, but I figure I'd start there. I just need to do something, anything."

Annette stared at the paper in front of her without seeing it. "I guess everywhere we go, we could run into someone like that officer. Still, she shouldn't have said anything."

Rachel sighed and wiped away a tear. "She shouldn't have, but I don't blame her." She sighed again. "Now I worry about his safety in there even more."

"But I agree I don't want him home," Annette quickly added.

Rachel nodded. "I'm going to call Dr. Webb."

This time, Rachel got the receptionist and left a message for their family doctor. He had known their family for over twenty years, had delivered both Annette and Rick. He had been there with them through many hard times. He would certainly understand and try to help. She set down the phone and took a sip of coffee. "Thanks for this, honey. I needed it."

"So did I." The warm coffee slid down her throat and warmed her inside. Her numbness melted a bit. "Mom, I can't believe how Rick talked." She gripped her mug in both hands. "It's like he feels no remorse."

Rachel shook her head. "I know. It's disturbing." She fell silent. She lowered her eyes to the beige woven mat in front of her and fiddled with the flowered cloth napkin. The corners of her mouth turned down as her eyes glazed over. She looked sapped.

Annette saw the change in her mother's demeanor and considered her next question carefully. She reached for her mother's hand. "Mom, we haven't talked about this in a long time, and I don't know if it's okay to bring it up." She paused.

Rachel turned her eyes to her daughter. "Honey, ask me whatever you want. It's okay."

Annette took a deep breath. "How did Dad talk to you before . . . you know?" She felt as if she had dropped a huge boulder into the space between them. Her stomach knotted as she waited for her mother's reply.

Rachel sighed. "Before he shot me? For a long time, he didn't talk at all. I knew he was having some kind of trouble at work. He radiated anger at me whenever we were alone, but he wouldn't tell me what was making him so angry." She closed her eyes briefly. "It felt really scary. I suggested we see a counselor, but that just seemed to make him more angry." She looked at Annette. "He accused me of thinking he was crazy. Sound familiar?" Annette nodded. "I had about decided to go see a counselor alone. Then one day, he just snapped." She sighed again.

"Oh, Mom." Annette took her mother's hand in both of hers. "Oh, Mom." Her heart sank as painful memories flooded her. She hadn't been home when it had all happened. She'd been at a movie with friends, using the driver's license she had just gotten. She couldn't remember where Rick had been. Probably out somewhere with his friends. But she remembered clearly being unable to pull into the driveway at home because an ambulance and two police cars were there. And how everything had seemed to go into slow motion as she parked next to the curb and watched two stretchers being brought out of their house and taken away, all the time going through a list in her mind of what could have happened. She had sat in the car, frozen. It wasn't until later that she learned her father was dead and he had shot her mother before killing himself. It was even later that she learned her mother would survive. She did remember sitting long hours in the hospital waiting room feeling numb. Rick had finally appeared to sit with her.

It took her some effort to shake those images from her mind and return her attention to her mother. She gazed at her mother and felt a wave of love and gratitude for this woman who had nearly been killed but had come back strong and determined and was sitting here with her. Annette felt her mother's strength flow into her. "I'm with you, Mom. We will get through this together. Somehow."

Rachel smiled through moist eyes. "Thanks, Annette. I hate what you've had to go through, but I am grateful to have you here, and I'm very proud of the woman you have become."

Annette felt tears in her own eyes. "Thanks, Mom. You're the one who went through the worst. I'm so grateful you survived. I admire you so much." She threw her arms around her mother for a long hug. They held each other a moment and cried together.

"We'll just have to make sure he gets on suicide watch. As soon as possible." Rachel smiled through her tears. "And talk to his lawyer."

Just then the phone rang. Rachel had it to her ear in half a second. "Oh, Dr. Webb, thanks so much for calling back . . . Yes, yes . . . suicidal, yes. . . . Psychiatric consult? You'll try to arrange it? . . . Thank you." She hung up and smiled at her daughter. "Dr. Webb is a saint. He can make it happen. Rick is finally going to get some help!"

Annette's numbness returned. She couldn't help but think her mother was wasting her energy. Even if Rick got help, it was way too late.

Chapter 27

Guy sat in the large fifth-floor conference room of the National Rifle Association and groaned inwardly as NRA President Pierre LeChien stepped up to the podium. It was Tuesday morning, and the room was filled with over one hundred staff and members. As head of the NRA-ILA, Guy had a prime place at the head table, along with the division heads of firearms training, safety and education, media and publications, volunteering, and women's interests. The dark-paneled windowless room was lined with the American flag and flags from all fifty states. Portraits of the NRA founders, past presidents, and the current president hung on the walls.

Guy didn't want to be there. He would rather be anywhere else, mainly at home in bed with his head under the covers. He felt weary, so weary. Weary of this job, weary of his life. He had tried to get out of coming, feigned illness, claimed he had conflicting doctors' appointments—anything he could think of. All lies, but he tried. When, in probably their sixth conversation, President LeChien threatened to send his car and driver to pick him up and bring him to the meeting, he gave in and agreed to come. It was a call for all hands on deck; it was an emergency, a crisis. Gun rights were in peril. Everyone must be there. Guy sighed as he watched LeChien riffle though his papers. He should just resign and wasn't sure why he hadn't. He just didn't have the energy.

"Welcome all," LeChien began. He stood tall in his crisp dark-blue suit and red, white, and blue tie, his gelled gray hair combed back from his face. "Welcome, patriots—American patriots willing to do the hard work to defend freedom. I congratulate you. The NRA today is five million strong; we have done more to advance freedom than any organization in modern history. Thanks to the hard work of all of us, now over forty states have passed laws guaranteeing the rights of individuals to carry firearms. Decades ago, the federal and state governments had the power to go into people's homes and confiscate their guns. You may remember how that was done after Hurricane Katrina. We worked hard and changed those laws. Thanks to the US Supreme Court decisions of DC v. Heller in 2008 and McDonald v. City of Chicago in 2010, the Second Amendment right for individuals to own firearms to protect their home and families cannot be denied. And this is all thanks to the hard work, sacrifice, and leadership of American patriots such as you."

Guy quit listening. He'd heard it all before many times. Hell, he'd said it all before himself. He knew what was coming next: *Now the NRA faces a threat greater than any against the freedoms we hold dear blah blah blah.* Out of curiosity, he tuned back in to see if he was correct.

LeChien paused to take a sip of water. "Now our opponents are committed to doing everything possible to tear down your freedoms, your liberty, values, heritage, your way of life, to dictate every aspect of your life. They aren't interested in debating the issues, of winning hearts and minds to their point of view. No, they want to get free-dom-loving Americans like us out of their way. They want to impose their values and their will on you and your family forever."

LeChien paused again as the crowd roared. Guy listened. Yes, he had roared like this himself in the past. Now, he felt a new detachment. A part of his mind he was newly acquainted with stretched and began to sit up and take notice and wonder. Who exactly were these opponents? He recognized this strategy: be general not specific, incite fear and outrage. He tuned in further.

"Our opponents are determined to use a scorched-earth policy to destroy the NRA. They want to brand us as a terrorist organization." LeChien stopped and cast his eyes around the room. "A terrorist organization. What do you say to that? Are we a terrorist organization?"

"No!!!" roared the audience.

LeChien grinned. "That's right! We are an organization of freedom-loving American patriots!"

Guy smiled. He had never thought about these arguments in quite this way before. He must have swallowed them whole without thinking. Little Guy's adorable face came into his mind. His daughter Laura and Ms. Warwick appeared next. Would LeChien consider them opponents? The families of all the students and teachers who were killed. Were they the enemy? And what about the shooter? He began to wonder if LeChien was going to stay anything about this tragedy that had prompted him to call this meeting.

"Now, I must say something about the recent and tragic school shooting." LeChien gave the crowd a moment to settle and refocus before he went on. "Our thoughts and prayers go out to the families who lost loved ones in this horrible event."

Guy felt a sudden stab of anxiety. Would he be called out as one of those family members? Would LeChien make reference to him and the loss of his grandson? Thanks to that nosy young reporter, LeChien must know about it. He hadn't told him. He hadn't even talked to him except that moment today briefly when he had tried in vain to stay home. That LeChien hadn't offered one word of condolence to him when they'd talked, that he'd only pressured him to be here today, made Guy suspect he had blinders on. All he could see was the NRA mission. *The way I used to be.* He flushed in shame.

He lowered his gaze and sank deeper in his chair, hoping to avoid being identified. LeChien turned in Guy's direction and cleared his throat, preparing to speak. Guy closed his eyes, shook his head, and sank lower. LeChien turned back to his podium. Guy breathed a sigh of relief but kept his head down.

LeChien frowned as he began to speak. "Gun control has become a big topic in the aftermath of this sad event. It even turned the tide of the recent election against us. But let's remember, guns don't kill people, people kill people." He glanced at Guy. Guy saw this through narrowed lids and quickly closed his eyes tight. LeChien returned his face to the audience. "And, in this case, it was a disturbed student, probably mentally ill but certainly embittered, who committed this heinous act. We don't need more gun control. We need more mental health treatment." He raised his head to the audience for emphasis. "Our opponents want nothing better than to turn the narrative to the need for stricter gun laws. It's more treatment for these disturbed and unstable young people that is most needed. Better parenting. Training for teachers to identify the warning signs earlier. Guns are not the problem."

Guy nodded. He certainly agreed with the need for more treatment. This tragedy had completely changed his mind about therapy. Dr. Mehlman had become his lifeline, his guru. From what he'd learned from news coverage of the shooter, if he had been in treatment, this whole story could have turned out differently. Now his daughter was seeing one of Dr. Mehlman's associates. She had even called to thank him for helping her get this help. He strongly supported having mental health treatment widely available and affordable.

But to his mind now, guns were also part of the problem. How that disturbed young man was able to get the firearm he used was a travesty. That should never be allowed to happen ever again. If gun regulations needed to be strengthened to keep that from happening again, he was for it. The image of Little Guy rose up in his mind, and with it, tears that continued to seem ever present. He felt his grandson's small body in his lap, leaning against his chest. Then, just as suddenly, he felt its absence, a hole in his heart that would never be filled.

A question from the audience pierced his reverie. He choked back his tears and refocused on Pierre LeChien as he repeated the question. "Have I heard about the rally planned for December 1? I certainly have. It's just a bunch of high school kids and may not turn out to be much, but I think we need to prepare and have a presence there that day." He paused to recognize someone on the front row.

A tall white man with a buzz cut spoke. "I'm Bob Nolan, a member of the Virginia Civilian Defense Coalition. We are organizing our group for a counter-demonstration. Don't underestimate what these kids are doing. It's likely to draw a huge crowd, possibly from the entire country."

Guy's ears perked up. The man speaking looked vaguely familiar, but he couldn't place him. He hadn't heard about this rally. And he'd never heard about the Virginia Civilian Defense Coalition. He listened closely.

"Tell us more about your organization?" asked LeChien.

"We're newly formed, or, I should say, newly refocused," said the man. "Our mission is to protect the citizens of Virginia from those forces you spoke about so eloquently. Those who want to endanger us by removing the means to protect our home and families. We began as a shooting club a few years ago, you know, sort of like how the NRA started." He frowned and sounded somber. "But when we heard about this rally the kids are organizing, we decided it was time to act."

LeChien nodded his approval. "How can we help?"

"We have big ideas for our counter-demonstration, but we know you guys are way ahead of us in knowing how to do something like this. We'd like to join forces, get someone from the NRA to advise us," said Nolan.

"That sounds great," said LeChien. "We can certainly consult." He waved at those at the head table. "Hang around after our meeting today and we'll huddle. Maybe we can help with some funding."

"That would be super," said Nolan. "Thank you." He sat down, grinning broadly.

Guy's spirits sank. He did not want to hang around and huddle with this guy from the Virginia Civilian Defense Coalition. *Who is he?* Bob Nolan's name was familiar. Where had he seen him before?

"Other questions?" asked LeChien. "Anyone else want to join a counter-demonstration?"

Dozens of hands shot up, along with murmurs of "I do!" and "We will!"

"Great!" said LeChien. He looked around for his assistant. "Can we get a clipboard with a signup sheet circulating now?"

A young man in a shirt and tie scurried forward. "Yes, sir! Here it is!" He waved a clipboard at his boss and handed it to the first person on the front row.

"Good job, Jim." And to the audience: "I have the best intern this year. Jim West, take a bow."

The young man showed his teeth in a huge smile, draped his arm across his waist, and lowered his head almost to his knees. The audience applauded.

LeChien ran his gaze over the audience. "Yes, you in the back. What's your question?" He leaned forward with his hand cupped around an ear. The question was inaudible to most, so he repeated it. "What lobbying efforts do we have planned? Good question. Let me ask our esteemed head of the ILA, Guy Grant." LeChien turned to Guy. "What can you tell us, Guy?"

Guy was startled. What could he say? Guy felt his entire body turn to ice. He shivered as he stared at LeChien, who stared back waiting for his response. What did he used to say? Something vague probably. *We have several bold new initiatives that are under consideration that will be game changers.* Could he say that now? It would be a lie, of course, but it wouldn't be the first time.

Someone beside him pushed the microphone stand on the table in front of him closer to his mouth. His heartbeat accelerated. His face felt flushed. The words he wanted to say filled his mind. *My grandson was killed!* He looked over the audience. The familiar faces began to blur. Bright pricks of light blinded him. He heard someone cry out, "He's not well!" Suddenly, that someone was behind him catching him as he fell back and then pulling Guy's arm across his shoulder and leading him off stage. Waves of murmuring filled the room like a flock of birds crying out as they took flight. The next Guy knew, he was lowered gently into a chair and offered a bottle of water.

"Drink this," said a familiar voice. Guy's eyes opened and focused to find Jake leaning over him.

"Jake, what happened?"

"You fainted," said Jake. "I saw it coming. Lucky I got there before you hit the floor."

"Jake," said Guy gratefully. "Get me out of here. I didn't even want to come."

"There's nothing I'd like to do better," said Jake. "I didn't want to come either."

Jim West appeared at Guy's side. "Are you okay, Mr. Grant? Can I help you?" he asked.

"I just need to get him home," said Jake.

Guy nodded and weakly said, "Yes, I just need to go home and rest. Thank you anyway."

Jim returned to the stage, where LeChien was trying to call the meeting back to order. LeChien paused a moment while Jim whispered in his ear, then returned to the crowd.

"Guy Grant will be fine," he reported. "Now where were we?"

▷ ⊕ ◁

Jake glanced at Guy next to him in his car's passenger seat. "How're you feeling now? Your color looks a little better. You were white as a sheet when you fell."

250

"I still feel a bit woozy, but this water helps." Guy took a sip. "God, I'm so glad you were there. Thanks for rescuing me."

"My pleasure. I wanted an excuse to leave anyway." He shook his head. "I can't stomach that place anymore."

"Apparently neither can I."

Jake pulled into Guy's driveway. When he stopped the car, he scooted around to Guy's side and gave him a hand up. Guy smiled as he slowly unfolded his frame to stand up. "I got it now, Jake. Thanks. Come in a minute?"

"Sure. I need to debrief that experience with you."

In short order, they were sitting around the kitchen table with glasses of ice-cold Coca Cola and a plate of Oreos.

Jake took a long swallow and chuckled. "Ah, I haven't had a soda in years. My wife forbids it. Nothing but vitamin water at our house." He smiled at Guy. "I see you are into health food."

Guy laughed. "Yeah, right." He took his own long swallow. "I can offer you a baloney sandwich on white bread also."

"No, thanks." Jake shook his head. "I'm with my wife on that one. We eat sliced turkey on whole wheat at our house."

"How did LeChien get you to come today? He threatened to shanghai me to get me there." Guy leaned back in his chair waiting to hear Jake's story. He picked up an Oreo and popped it into his mouth.

"Sort of the same way, only he hit me in my pocketbook. Threatened to put a hold on my next paycheck. Man, I want to resign, but I've got a mortgage and a family." He gave a big sigh. "I need to revise my résumé and start looking, but I just haven't had the energy."

"I know just how you feel. I don't know what to do with myself. I feel weary, so weary." Guy patted Jake on the arm. "Here, have a cookie. It will boost your blood sugar."

Jake examined the plate of cookies. "I haven't had one of these in years either. They used to be my favorite." He picked one up and pulled the two chocolate discs apart. "I would eat the filling first." He demonstrated his technique. Soon he had the cookie demolished. "Man, that's good."

"Yeah, I love them, probably too much." Guy patted the belly that protruded over his belt. He downed another one. "Mmm . . . yum." Then he crinkled up his brow. "Say, who is Bob Nolan? That name is so familiar."

Jake drew his lips into a firm line. "Don't you remember? He's the Alexandria School Board member—and NRA member—who recruited me to speak to the school board about arming teachers."

Guy's jaw dropped. "Oh, yes, that guy." He raised his eyebrows. "And have you ever heard of his organization? What is it, the Virginia Civilian Defense . . . something."

"Yes, the Virginia Civilian Defense Coalition. They are starting to make some noise. I've read some articles about them. They're a perfect match for the NRA."

"Articles? Where? I read the *Post* cover to cover every day."

"I think I saw them in the *Alexandria Gazette*. There's some reporter following the story about the shooting and everything related."

"Hmpf, I bet it's that same guy who put me on the front page. Who wheedled his way in here to get an interview." Guy saw he still had the reporter's card tucked in between the sugar bowl and the salt shaker. He plucked it out and showed it to Jake. "Here it is. Neil Simpson. What a royal pain in the ass."

"Could be. You sure you're not a fan? Keeping his card?"

"I keep everything, didn't you know?" Guy shrugged. "You never know when something you've kept might come in handy."

"You're not married to Ms. Neat and Tidy." Jake smiled. "I love her, but she sure does like to throw things out."

"Hey, what do you think about this rally the kids are organizing?" Guy watched Jake closely. Guy himself had never been to a protest rally in his life. He had no idea if they did any good. To him, they'd mostly been an annoyance. He had thought about them as full of hippies and anarchists and communists. People he didn't want anything to do with.

Jake sat silent a good while before he answered. The atmosphere between them felt suddenly heavy. "I've never wanted to go to any of those protest rallies. I thought they were stupid. They just didn't appeal to me." His eyes filled with tears. He looked down at his hand as it encircled his glass of Coke. A few tears fell before he could speak. He let them fall. "But maybe, just maybe . . ." He raised his eyes to Guy. "Maybe it could be a way to honor Gracia."

Guy watched Jake in stunned amazement.

Jake went on. "I don't know. I didn't go to the candlelight vigil they had at the high school. I thought about going, but I felt too raw."

Vigil? They had a vigil? A candlelight vigil? thought Guy. He had no idea. He felt something break loose inside him. Little Guy's image rose up inside him, and with it, his own tears. He hung on Jake's every word.

"But now, now I just have this urge to make a big sign with a huge photo of my little girl. And show the world . . . ," he choked out. "Show the world the beautiful child I lost." A tinge of anger entered his voice. "And do my part to make sure this never happens again. There are things more important than being able to have a gun collection." He made a fist and brought it down on the table with a thud.

Guy felt the foundation he had built his life upon crack. He froze as a wide fissure opened up beneath him, and he fell through.

Chapter 28

Guy pulled into the driveway of Laura and Tom's house and walked slowly up to the door, his head hung low. Today, Saturday, was Little Guy's funeral, and he dreaded it. Laura had asked him to come early and ride with them to the church, for which he was grateful. But to him it felt like a final goodbye to this beloved grandson he had barely gotten to know before the boy was snatched from his arms, his heart. He berated himself. Why had he spent his life chasing some ill-conceived ambitions when he could have been spending time with Laura and Tom and Little Guy? Sure, he had achieved fortune and fame, but what good was it without people to love, to share it with, to nurture and support?

Before he rang the doorbell, he shook off these dark thoughts and forced himself to stand up straight. Today he wanted to be a pillar of strength for his daughter and son-in-law. Today was not about himself, it was about taking care of them. He pressed the doorbell and heard the sound reverberate through the house.

The door creaked open. Tom stood there in his crisp navy suit. "Hi, Guy, glad you're here." Tom's face was lined, and there were dark bags under his eyes. He gave Guy a wan smile as he ushered him inside. "Everyone is in the kitchen. Go on back."

Everyone? Guy had no idea what everyone he would find, but he passed through the living room and into the kitchen. He tugged on the labels of his own crisp navy suit and straightened his dark blue tie. The kitchen was big with a large island by the stove, a refrigerator on the right, and a large round table on the left. Around the table were Laura, his ex-wife, Maureen, and her husband.

Laura got up and greeted him with a big hug. She was dressed in funeral attire in a long, slim, black-velvet dress. Around her neck hung a gold chain with a locket. She whispered in his ear as she embraced him, "Sorry, Dad, I guess I forgot to mention that Mom and Ralph were coming."

"That's fine," he whispered back as he hung onto her an extra moment while he absorbed this news. He hadn't seen Maureen in years. After they had divorced and the kids were launched, she had remarried and moved with her new husband to Boston. This had to be a dozen years ago. Guy thought he remembered Ralph was a surgeon at Mass General or something. He didn't believe he had ever even met the man. Of course Maureen would be here. Little Guy was her grandson as well. He started to imagine all the holidays they had probably spent together in Boston. Ralph had maybe even taken them on fabulous European vacations. He felt pangs of jealousy and felt equally silly for feeling them because he had no idea what had gone on. He himself hadn't been around to find out.

Laura made introductions. "Dad, you know Mom, and this is Ralph Richardson, my stepfather."

Guy smiled and extended his hand. "Nice to meet you, Dr. Richardson." Inside, he observed him critically. The man certainly had an imposing presence as he stood and gripped Guy's hand. He was tall, silver-haired, and handsome. He exuded confidence and self-assurance. He wore a dark suit that Guy recognized from a designer collection. He had acquired a couple, though not many, for himself over the years. He was still amazed at how much you could spend for such a suit.

"Nice to meet you too, Guy, please call me Ralph." He smiled as he retook his seat.

"Dad, please have a seat," said Laura as she sat back down. She poured him a glass of water from the pitcher in the middle of the table, matching the water glasses of everyone else. Tom slipped in quietly next to her.

Guy eased himself into the chair she had indicated and turned his eyes to Maureen. She had the same blond curls as Laura with only a hint of gray. Her face was lined with age, but her makeup was impeccable. She wore a sleek black dress with long sleeves. Around her neck was a black-and-gold scarf held in place on one shoulder by a gold heart-shaped pin studded with diamonds. He felt incredibly awkward. Maureen radiated health and contentment underneath the undeniable layer of grief. Ralph must be good to her. Certainly better than he ever was. He was at once aware of his flabby belly that he had barely been able to fit inside his pants. Ralph undoubtedly had six-pack abs under his suit. *They probably go to the gym together every morning before work*, thought Guy, torturing himself.

She smiled at him. "Hello, Guy."

He pulled himself together. "Hello, Maureen. You're looking well."

"Thank you, Guy, that's kind of you to say." She glanced at her husband.

Ralph nodded at her and addressed Guy. "What she's going to say next is that I make her go to the gym with me every morning, but that's not exactly correct. She comes of her own free will." He draped his arm around the back of her chair and squeezed her shoulder.

Maureen raised her eyebrows at him. "You can certainly read my mind, honey. But honestly, I know I wouldn't go if you weren't going."

I knew it, thought Guy. *Maybe I need to start going to the gym. I hear there's one near my house, and you can hire a trainer.* Then he mentally scoffed at himself. *That will be the day.*

"It's good you could come for Little Guy's funeral," said Guy. "He was such a special little fellow."

The atmosphere in the kitchen darkened as if a cloud had rolled in.

"He certainly was," said Maureen. Her eyes became moist.

The five of them cast their eyes down and sat a moment in silence. Then there was a *ping*. Laura picked up her phone from the table and tapped the screen.

Her face lit up. "It's Sean! He's almost here!" she said. "He expects to arrive soon, very soon. Just in time."

Guy sat stunned. Sean, his son, was also coming. He hadn't seen or heard from him in more years than he could remember. "Where's he coming from?"

"Boston," said Laura. "You know Sean. He's cycling."

Cycling? Boston? thought Guy. He was sad to realize he really didn't know Sean. He had no idea he was in Boston. The last he knew of Sean he was backpacking through Europe. Guy realized that must have been at least a decade ago. Or more. Didn't he do that right after college? And cycling? Sean rides a bicycle long distance? He had no idea.

The confusion must have shown on his face. Before he could ask, Maureen volunteered. "He came to Boston some years ago. He's in a PhD program at Boston University studying glaciers."

Guy's jaw dropped. "Glaciers? You can get a PhD in glaciers?"

Laura rescued him. "I think it's a specialty within environmental science, Dad. Sean joined a research team and spent several years in Antarctica. That got him interested in going back to school."

"He took up cycling once he came to Boston," said Maureen. She glanced again at her husband. "Ralph often cycles to work and got Sean into it, I think."

"I may have showed the way, but that young man outpaced me pretty quickly," added Ralph. "He's quite the adventurer and a natural athlete."

Guy's head was spinning. He took a sip of water as he tried to collect himself. Images of Sean as a little boy swirled inside his mind. He felt embarrassed at how few he could call up. Sean must have been ten when he and Maureen separated. He reached into his memory bank for when he had last seen his son. He did attend his college graduation, didn't he? He honestly couldn't remember.

He took another sip and set his glass down. "Well, this is turning into quite the family reunion."

He felt like the outsider to this family, but he had to admit that was his own doing.

Tom spoke for the first time. "Yeah, weddings and funerals, that's when families come together."

Ah, Guy did remember Laura and Tom's wedding. He had been there, he felt sure. How long ago was it? He did some mental arithmetic. It had to be seven or eight years ago because Little Guy was six—had been six. Anyway, it had been in the same church where Little Guy's funeral was to be held. He must have seen Maureen and Ralph then. Why did he have no memory of them?

Then it hit him; he had left before the reception to fly off on some NRA mission. He had been there long enough to walk Laura down the aisle but not long enough to socialize. What a fool he had been. Mentally he smacked himself upside the head. He had missed so much. He was an idiot.

But did Sean come? His memory was fuzzy. "How about at your wedding to Tom, Laura, I can't remember, was Sean there?"

"No, he was in still in Antarctica then," said Laura. "I don't think we saw him until some Christmas after he'd gotten to Boston." She paused to ponder. "Little Guy was a baby." She smiled, remembering. "Sean loved being an uncle. That holiday we were all in Boston, and Sean carried Little Guy around so much I had to pull him away to nurse him." Tears filled her eyes. "I'm so glad he's going to be here. He told me he wouldn't miss it for the world. I tried to get him to fly down, but that's Sean."

Guy emptied his water glass and wondered if they were going to have anything stronger to drink. A wave of grief and loss rolled over him. Before he broke down, he excused himself to go to the bathroom. There he saw himself in the mirror and was shocked to see an old man staring back at him. How old was Sean now? He had to be in his mid-thirties. When he exited the bathroom, he heard the doorbell and a clatter of chairs as everyone rushed toward the front door. He came into the living room just in time to see Tom open the door and a tall, slim, fit man roll his bicycle into the house. It had two panniers fastened over the back wheel stuffed full. He was dressed neck to ankles in cycling attire and a heavy parka. His blond curls were tangled from the helmet, but Guy recognized some of his own facial features mirrored back at him.

"Hey, guys!" he called out. "Where can I put this?"

Tom gave him a quick hug. "Welcome, Sean." He took the bike from him and rolled it into the dining room. "We'll leave it in here for now."

"Thanks, Tom," said Sean. He had barely released the bike and helmet to Tom and unzipped his parka when Laura was on him with her arms around his tall frame, weeping. "Ah, sis," he hummed softly as he dropped his parka on the floor and took her in his arms. "I'm so glad to be here." He patted her back and rubbed it softly. "There there. It's okay, Laura. We're all here."

She took his face in her hands and planted a big kiss on his lips. "I'm so relieved you made it, Sean. It means the world to have Uncle Sean here."

"Of course I'm here. Where else would I be?" He raised his head to the gathered assembly. With his arm draped over Laura's shoulder, he leaned in to kiss his mother. "Hi, Mom." He released Laura, checking to make sure Tom was there to receive her. He was and put his arm around her waist. She leaned into her husband in a way she had probably been doing a lot more often lately. Sean turned to Ralph, extended his hand to shake, and gave him a half hug with the other arm.

Guy hung back, watching this family ritual of greeting, not really sure what to do. Not really sure he belonged. Other than the familiar facial features, he barely recognized this tall, handsome lad—this man. He flushed with embarrassment to realize his son felt like a stranger. He was a stranger. In this context, his life felt empty, lonely. He watched in awe, waiting and hoping for his turn to be recognized. Sean caught his eye. He stepped forward. Maureen and Ralph moved aside to let him through.

Sean smiled widely at him. "And who do we have here?" he asked.

Guy smiled back. "Yes, it's me, your old dad."

"Dad, it's been a while."

They stood in front of each other for an awkward moment. Sean examined his father. Guy felt incredibly uncomfortable under his son's scrutiny. He braced for accusations, blame, for questions of why he'd been missing in action with his own family for so many years. If not now, that reckoning was sure to come sometime. Not knowing what else to do, he extended his hand. Sean ignored it and pulled him into an embrace, towering over him. Guy felt horrified to feel tears well up. But then he gave into them and began to weep. "Oh, son, it's so good to see you again."

"Yeah, Dad," said Sean, his own voice quivering with emotion. "It's been too damn long. Welcome back."

▷ ⊕ ◁

Within a half hour, Sean had showered and changed, and they all piled into Maureen and Ralph's van for the short trip to the church. It was a large red-brick building with a tall spire reaching to the heavens. On top was a small cross. In front was a large sign: Westwood Presbyterian Church.

They parked and were soon escorted by the senior pastor, Dr.

Alan Clifford, into the lounge, where they would wait until time for the service to start. There were two couches, a love seat, and a few stuffed chairs arrayed in a circle around a large coffee table. On a table in the corner was a pitcher of water and small glasses. Guy watched as people took their places, taking an empty wing chair for himself.

Laura and Tom had met with their pastor several times, first for his comfort in their shock and grief and finally to discuss the service. Dr. Clifford was introduced to those whose acquaintance he hadn't yet made. He gave them all a warm welcome. He was short in stature, with wavy dark-brown hair parted in the middle of his square clean-shaven face. He wore a long black robe with a red cassock around his neck, its two ends in front. He exuded calm, caring, and comfort. Guy felt immediately drawn to him. As Dr. Clifford described the order of service, he relaxed. Sean was going to speak as well as Little Guy's teacher. An electric current ran through Guy when he realized that meant Ms. Warwick. He hadn't seen her since their visit to the classroom, but she had haunted his thoughts and his dreams.

When the minister led them in prayer, Guy bowed his head and prayed fervently that he could have a chance to talk with her further, that she and his family would forgive him. He prayed for guidance to repair the damage he had done, through his absence, through his work with the NRA. He surprised himself, not sure he had ever prayed before, not sure a prayer of his would even be heard, much less answered. But he prayed with all his heart. His longing to do something, he wasn't sure what, rose up like a force within him. "Amen." He joined in the ripple of voices as the prayer ended. He felt soft and tender in a way he couldn't remember ever feeling before.

Dr. Clifford stepped out briefly and returned with Kate Warwick. There were handshakes, hugs, and tears as she met and greeted her student's family. When she got to Guy, she extended her hands to his. He covered her hands with his own.

"Hello, Guy," she said, a sad smile on her face. "Nice to see you again."

"Thank you so much for being here, Ms. Warwick," he said, his eyes moist.

"It's Kate, please."

"Kate, thank you." Guy drank in her eyes, her nose, her mouth. He held on to her hands.

She turned to the rest of the family. "Did you all know this man was my classroom volunteer?"

Maureen, Ralph, and Sean all looked from her to Guy. Laura and Tom nodded knowingly.

"Dad," said Sean. "You took time from work to volunteer in Little Guy's classroom?" He sounded incredulous.

"He certainly did," said Kate. "He was a big help. The children loved having him there, especially his grandson, as you might imagine."

"Wow, Dad. Good for you," said Sean, his eyes wide. He took a step closer to his dad.

Kate went on. "Then you probably don't know he was there that terrible day." She closed her eyes and shook her head. "That horrible, horrible, tragic day." She opened her eyes. "The shooter hit him too." She turned to Guy and squeezed his hands. "I'm glad you're here today, that you survived." She smiled.

Guy felt weak in the knees. Tears threatened to overflow his eyes, but he held them back. "And I'm glad you survived also, Kate." That she would say something positive about him to his family was beyond his wildest dreams. He wanted to kiss her. Instead, he escorted her to the wing chair next to his.

The group settled and retook their seats. Sean pulled a folded paper from his pocket and studied it. Maureen and Ralph talked quietly together on the love seat. Laura paced the room with Tom at her side. Guy had a moment with Kate, although by the time he calmed himself enough to speak, Dr. Clifford reappeared to lead them into the sanctuary, where the front row had been reserved for them.

The large room was lined with stained-glass windows depicting scenes from scripture. The mid-day sun shined through them in shades of red and blue, yellow and green. The stage in front held a pulpit in the center and three maroon chairs behind. A low mahogany wall stood between the chairs and the choir loft with its pipe organ. On the back wall of the choir loft, the array of pipes from the organ stood waiting. In the center back wall was another stained-glass window showing Jesus flanked by three angels. It was a beautiful and serene place.

The sanctuary was full. Guy hadn't known what to expect, but the presence of so many people, most of them strangers to him, felt comforting. He cast his eyes around the room before he sat to face the front. From halfway back, Jake waved at him. Guy waved back and put his hand to his heart. When he took his seat and faced the front, his eyes were drawn to the stained-glass window and rested there. He imagined Little Guy in the arms of Jesus and the angels, as loved and cared for as he had been on earth.

He held onto that image like a lifeline as the service began. There were the usual scripture readings and hymns and words of reassurance from Dr. Clifford about our heavenly home. But the main focus was on celebrating Little Guy's brief life. Guy soaked in the many anecdotes and stories told by Uncle Sean and teacher Kate, most of them new to him. There was Little Guy as an infant, refusing to go to sleep when the family was together for Christmas, only doing so when Uncle Sean held him and walked him around the rooms of the house over and over. And only going deeply to sleep when Sean lay down with him and went to sleep himself. There was Little Guy as a toddler on his first trip to the beach, seeing the biggest sandbox he'd ever seen and falling face down in it in delight, moving his arms and legs until he was coated head to toe in sand. There was him as a student, learning to read before anyone else in the classroom and falling in love with reading. There was him in bouncing ecstasy when his grandfather came to volunteer.

Kate smiled at him from the pulpit as she finished her remarks with this story. Guy felt his heart would melt. These stories, no matter how cute and lovely, felt to Guy like a kind of torture, like fingernails on the blackboard reminding him of all he had missed of his grandson's life and all he would never have again. Then he completely lost it and broke down in sobs. He wailed. The loss of Little Guy was just the tip of the iceberg. There was his marriage and years with Sean and Laura and Tom and Little Guy. And now embarrassing himself by making a scene at his grandson's funeral. He hung his head in shame, certain he was a complete and total idiot.

Hurrying down from the pulpit, Kate sat beside him with her arm around him. Laura began to cry. Tom put his arm around her and passed the box of tissues she had brought for herself. Guy plucked a few gratefully and let her keep the box. He knew she needed it more than he did.

When the service concluded, Dr. Clifford invited them all to attend the reception downstairs in the fellowship hall. As the crowd milled around, Guy got a cup of punch and a few cookies and found a chair against the wall. He barely knew any of these people and felt totally drained. He watched Laura and Tom surrounded by people who obviously knew and loved them. He saw Sean introduced and greeted, clearly a man who knew no strangers. Maureen and Ralph seemed to be in the midst of the action as well. He wondered if he should make more of an effort to socialize. Should he get up and refill his cup? Where was Kate Warwick? He scanned the crowd but didn't see her. He hoped she hadn't left. Then he saw her deep in conversation with Sean. Then he saw Sean catch his eye and head his way.

"Dad," said Sean as he sat down next to Guy. "Are you better?"

Guy nodded, flushing.

"Wasn't that a lovely service?"

"Yes, it was," said Guy, turning to face his son. "And you did a beautiful job speaking."

"Thanks. It's easy to talk about that kid. We had a special bond." Sean tilted his head and gave a sad smile. "I don't know how Laura and Tom are going to get through this. It's rough." He shook his head. "But Dad, you volunteered in the classroom? I never knew you to take off work for anything. But then it's been, what, ten years? A long time. Tell me about you." He gave his dad his full attention.

Guy felt suddenly shy. He didn't know how to begin or what to say. Or if this was the time or place to say what he really wanted to say. How his whole life felt like a mistake. How paralyzed by regret he felt. *And blah blah blah.*

"I'm sorry, Sean, I'm really, really sorry."

Chapter 29

It was the last Saturday in November, a week before the rally. Sarah and Derek, the rally leaders, had called the organizing group together for last-minute planning. Sam, Annette, Elaine, and Mark gathered in the downstairs rec room in Sarah's house. It was a large room with a pool table pushed into the corner and an array of couches and soft stuffed chairs around a large, square coffee table. The dark-paneled walls were decorated with colorful tapestries. Sarah and Derek had ordered several large pizzas and offered soft drinks. A few others trickled in with more pizza, drinks, chips, and bags of chocolate-chip cookies. Soon the room was filled with young people on all the couches and the available rug space. The air was buzzing with excited chatter.

Sam and Annette sat together on one of the couches. He had offered her a ride and was happy she had accepted. Sam clutched a folder with a copy of his speech inside. With Matt's help, he had worked hard on it. He and Annette had practiced their speeches in front of each other, and he was pleased he had been able to use this excuse for some one-on-one time with her. He was even more pleased that she had given his speech high approval. They had also practiced with Mark and Elaine and listened to their speeches. All this practice had built his confidence. He was nervous about delivering it at the rally but felt ready.

Sarah stood up and started the meeting. She wore jeans and a bright yellow T-shirt bearing a black circle with a red slash across it over a drawing of an assault rifle. "Thanks for coming everyone. I hope you all had a good Thanksgiving. My mother wanted me to offer turkey sandwiches, but honestly, I don't think I can eat another bite of turkey. So I got pizza. I hope that's okay."

There was a chorus of laughs. Derek laughed the loudest, his brown skin shining in the light from the window. "I'm with you, Sarah," he said. "We went to my grandma's house and came out more stuffed than the turkey. I'm ready for pizza!" To show he meant what he said, he picked up a big piece of meat lovers and took a big bite. "Dig in, y'all!"

The rest of them took their own slices on their paper plates and poured big cups from the choices of Coca Cola, Sprite, and Mountain Dew. They milled about filling plates and cups, crowding around the coffee table like a flock of birds chittering and pushing each other to reach the feast. Sam watched Annette choose a slice from the vegetarian pizza, but he joined Derek with the meat lovers. It took a while to get everyone settled again. The pizza boxes sat empty, as if vultures had descended and flown off with every bit.

Sarah wiped her mouth with a paper napkin and stood up again before she spoke. "Let's hear reports." She consulted a list in her hand. "I double-checked that the permits are in order. We got a lot of donations, an unbelievable amount, so there was plenty of money to get a stage set up with a sound system and porta-potties and all that on the National Mall." She nodded to someone on the edge of the crowd. "Hey, Ted, you did a great job setting up the website and GoFundMe page for us."

A tall, skinny boy with a long black ponytail nodded and hung his head as if trying to make himself invisible.

"I think we're pretty much ready as far as those details." She pointed at her shirt. "Ted did a great job designing these shirts, don't you think, guys?"

Everyone nodded. "He sure did," said someone next to Ted who patted him on the back. Ted shrunk more if that was even possible. "We have lots of shirts for everyone to wear at the rally. And even some to sell. Don't leave here without one. We have all sizes."

A few started to get up, but she shook her head. "Let's do that after our meeting, please. We have a lot to cover today." She pointed at Derek, seated next to her. "Give us your report, please."

Derek grinned and kept his seat. "I got a flood of local bands wanting to play. We only took high school bands, but we still had more than we could use. I got a folk group, a rock group, a hip-hop group, a rap group. I decided one of each would be best."

"Great, Derek. Fabulous job!" Sarah waved toward the speech-writing group. "I have a big surprise, but first let's hear from you guys."

Elaine, chair of the speech-writing committee, began. "We have all written speeches, just our own stories, mainly, with some very useful information tucked in." She smiled at her friends. "These guys should be on the debate team. They will knock you over. Dynamite speakers! We have practiced a bunch too, so I think we're all ready, right, guys?"

"Yes, you bet," said Sam.

"Practicing really helped calm my nerves," said Annette. "I'm hoping we can do it here today also."

"Ditto," said Mark.

"Yes, indeed," said Sarah. "We'll do that later." She turned back to Derek. "Any idea which band should open? I'm thinking we'll have music, maybe a couple bands, then speeches, then more music, then the last speeches. Oh, and we want to end with some sort of call for action. We'll have to figure out who would do that and how to phrase it and all that. What do you think?"

Derek consulted his list. "I propose we open with something loud, maybe the Braddock Bandits. They call themselves a rock band, but they do a little bit of everything: soul, hip-hop, grunge, heavy metal." He studied his list and chewed his lip. "Then maybe something quieter, like Night Sounds, sort of a folk and pop band with some blues thrown in." He raised his eyebrows and waited.

"Sounds good to me," said Sarah. "What do you rest of you think?"

An affirmative buzzing of *yes, hell yes*, and cheers rose up from the group.

She smiled. "Okay, thanks." She nodded toward the speech writers. "Now, who wants to give the first speech?" She caught herself. "I don't mean now; we'll do that later. I mean at the rally."

Elaine and Mark and Sam and Annette all looked at each other. Mark shrugged. Elaine spoke. "I think either you, Sam, or you, Annette, should go first. What do you think? I mean, Annette, you have the most powerful story to tell, talking about your brother. Yes, you, and then Sam, you're talking about mental health and how to get help for someone. What do you say?"

Sam felt his palms grow clammy and his stomach knot. Here it comes. They were really going to do this. He looked at Annette who had her head down, her long hair shading her face. He couldn't read her.

When she raised her head to speak, tears were in her eyes. "I'll go first. Right now, it's hard to imagine I can get through my speech without choking up. But I'll do it." She pressed her lips together. Determination radiated from her.

Elaine put her arm around Annette's shoulders. "You have written such a powerful speech, Annette." She addressed the room. "I nearly cried listening to it. It shows how tragic it is that guns are so easy to get, especially for someone as troubled as your brother, Rick. And how easy to hide. And how easy to use. Her speech is perfect to be the first one." She turned back to her friend. "We can practice it over and over until you can say it in your sleep, and it won't be so emotionally charged."

Sam patted her knee. "I'll help you practice every day if you want."

Annette smiled at him through her tears. "Thanks, Sam."

"Will you go second, Sam?" asked Elaine. "You have a story to tell about your relationship with Rick, and then you have such useful information." She again addressed the room. "I had no idea what the procedure was to get someone help who you thought was going to do something really dangerous and bad. What was that phrase you told me?"

"*Of imminent danger to self or others,*" said Sam. He could say that phrase in his sleep, he had said it so many times.

Sarah's face softened. "Sam, I'll be forever grateful if you do go next. People need to know this." She faced the entire group. "You can just call 911. Who knew?"

Faces with open mouths and surprised expressions popped up like little birds in a nest eager to be fed.

Sam gave a nervous smile. "I will. I'll keep practicing and practicing." He nodded to Annette. "Why don't we help each other?"

"Of course," said Annette, returning a somewhat less nervous smile.

"Great!" said Sarah. "I think we're in good shape. Thanks to everyone for all your hard work." She took a deep breath. "Now, I have a big surprise." She paused as they leaned forward to hear. "I know we decided we would only have student speakers. But someone has volunteered I think we might make an exception for."

Derek frowned. "Sarah, this is our rally. You know we turned down congresspeople and senators and school board members and teachers. I thought we agreed we wouldn't have any adults speaking. I mean, the adults have had decades to do something about gun violence and have done nothing. In a few years, we'll be the ones running things. It's time to show we can."

"I know, I know," she said. "Hear me out."

"This better be good," he said, tucking his arms across his chest.

Sarah smiled. "I'm not sure how this man found me." She paused. "Maybe it was through that reporter, Neil something."

"Neil Simpson," said Derek.

"Yes, thanks, Neil Simpson. He's been a big help, helping us publicize our rally. He wrote that big article in the *Alexandria Gazette* that got reprinted in the *Washington Post*. Anyway, our web address was in the paper, and I got an email that I missed for a couple days . . ."

"Hey, just tell us, Sarah," said Derek impatiently.

She took a deep breath. "Okay, well, this man with the NRA wants to speak at the rally."

"What do you mean?" said Derek. "The NRA?" He raised his voice and stood up. "They're part of the problem. They *are* the problem. What are you thinking?"

"I should have said he *used to* be with the NRA." She held up her hands. "Don't judge until you hear the whole story. I admit I was skeptical myself. I didn't answer his email at first. I didn't call him like he asked. I felt the same way you do. The NRA is not on our side."

Grumbling rumbled through the group. "That's for sure," said a voice in the back.

"Go on," said Derek as he sat back down.

"But then somehow, he got my phone number and left me this sad voice mail. I think he was even crying." She shook her head and raised her eyebrows. "It was so weird." She took another deep breath. "He said he lost his grandson in the shooting, and he had quit the NRA and wanted to help us."

"What?" asked Derek. "Did you even talk to him?"

"Yes, I called him." She paused. "It was so weird. Stranger than fiction."

"Go on, go on, tell us!" said Derek.

"Yeah, yeah, tell us," murmured the group.

"Okay, well, he poured out this heart-wrenching story about volunteering in his grandson's first-grade classroom, and, get this, he was there the day of the shooting when his grandson and all the other kids got killed. He got shot." She stopped a moment and cast her eyes over the group. "This man sounded so anguished. He said when his grandson was killed, he began to realize his whole life had been a mistake, and he wants to do something to make up for it."

A murmur of "Wows" rippled through the group.

"He read about what we're doing, and he thinks it's great. He practically begged me to let him help us. I think we should let him speak."

"Wow," said Derek. "This could be big. Former NRA guy renounces them and joins us. Imagine the headline."

She took another deep breath. "I even invited him here to talk with us." She glanced at a text on her phone. "My mom just sent me a text. He's upstairs right now with her in the kitchen." She looked around the room. Everyone sat in a stunned silence. "Can I bring him down?"

The stunned silence erupted in replies of "Yes, bring him down," and "Okay, sure, let's hear him!"

"I thought that's what you'd say," said Sarah. "I'll be right back."

▷ ⊕ ◁

Guy's right leg jiggled as he sat at the kitchen table with the nice dark-haired lady who had answered the door when he knocked. Ms. Hunter, he thought she had said her name was. He hadn't slept well in days and couldn't trust his memory. He clutched the mug of coffee she had offered him. He didn't think he'd ever been so nervous. His mind was buzzing. She had explained that the young people were meeting downstairs. Her daughter would come get him if the group agreed to have him join them.

She chattered on to him in a friendly manner. This calmed his nerves but only a tiny bit. She explained she was a social worker and had helped them at their initial meeting but had then stepped back. They didn't need help from adults. She was in awe of them and thought providing money for pizza would be her contribution. But her daughter, Sarah, had rejected her help. They had raised so much money, they could buy their own pizza.

Guy listened with a plastic smile on his face. He zoned out, her voice becoming a hum in the background of his thoughts, grateful she wasn't asking him any personal questions. He figured Sarah had told her everything. He couldn't believe he was actually sitting here, hopefully soon to be talking to these young people. It had not been easy to find them and get in touch. After the long newspaper article about their upcoming rally, written by that annoying and persistent young reporter, Guy had gone to the website mentioned in the article. He had left email after email. As much as it galled him to do this, he had finally called that reporter, Neil Simpson, and begged him for a phone number. That was like battering down a castle wall. Protect your sources, sure, he understood.

Guy finally poured it out—that he had quit the NRA and wanted to help them in their efforts. They made a deal. The phone number in exchange for an interview after the rally. With a big sigh, Guy had agreed. Then came the repeated calls and leaving voice mails until he broke down and poured it all out in a voice mail. Then, only then, had this girl, Sarah, called him back. And she was so nice and so smart and so determined. He couldn't help but imagine Little Guy would have been like her if he had gotten a chance to grow up. She had listened and asked questions and clucked in sympathy and finally invited him to come here today. That had been only yesterday, but it felt like years ago.

He took a sip of his coffee. It was only slightly warm now, but he didn't care. Ms. Hunter had been quick to refill his mug whenever he set it down. He thought this was his second cup, but he couldn't be sure. And he didn't need any more caffeine. He was jazzed up enough as it was.

He woke from his reverie when Ms. Hunter glanced at her phone and spoke. "Sarah is on her way to get you, Mr. Grant. Shouldn't be long now. She just texted me."

"Oh, good, thank you," said Guy with a sigh.

A door off the kitchen opened, and a tall, slim girl with long black hair tied back in a ponytail appeared. She smiled as she spoke. "You must be Mr. Grant."

He nodded. "I am indeed." He noticed her attire. "I like your shirt. Where did you get it?"

"Thanks, I like them too. We had them made for the rally. We have this fantastically talented but very shy guy who designed them." She laughed. "I like to praise him because he deserves it, but it just embarrasses him." She extended her hand to Guy. "Welcome. I'm excited you're here."

Guy shook her hand. It was strong and sure. "Thank you for letting me come. I so admire what you young people are doing and I'm eager to find out how I can help."

"Well, follow me and we'll join the group downstairs." She frowned. "We had pizza, but I'm afraid I can't offer you any. It's all gone."

"I would be happy to make you a turkey sandwich," said her mother. "We have lots of turkey."

"That's quite all right," said Guy. "I've already eaten." That was a lie—he had barely been able to eat a piece of toast with his coffee. He had grabbed his last banana on his way out. He was too anxious to even feel hunger.

Sarah led him down the stairs, where Guy saw a crowd of maybe thirty kids waiting. One quickly moved to offer him a seat, but Guy shook his head with a smile. He preferred to stand.

"Hey, guys, this is Mr. Guy Grant, lately of the NRA." Sarah smiled and nodded at Guy. "He wants to help us. Let's hear what he has to say." She sat down and waited.

Guy felt horrified to feel tears rise up in his eyes. He took a deep breath and stuffed them back. "I, um . . . I, um," he stuttered. There was not a sound, not a wiggle, as the young people waited to hear him speak. He studied their faces. Young, some beautiful or handsome, some with pimply faces, some with long hair or short, some White, some Black, some Asian. They appeared earnest and sweet to him. One in back kept his head down. *Must be the shirt designer,* thought Guy. He took a deep breath and began.

"I was at Parkwood Elementary School volunteering in my grandson's—" he choked and paused, gathered himself, and continued. "I was in the classroom when the shooting happened. My grandson was killed along with every one of his classmates. I was also shot, but as you can see, I recovered." He trembled and felt suddenly faint. He moved his arm beside him as he wobbled. A young man quickly squeezed closer to the girl next to him and patted the space he had vacated. Guy sat down on the couch and wiped his face with his hands. He closed his eyes briefly and took a deep breath. He sat up tall and cast his eyes over the room.

"I can't help but feel this shooting was my fault. And the fault of my former organization." There was a ripple in the group in response. "You see, I spent my entire life working for the NRA, protecting the Second Amendment and all that. I even thought it would be a good idea for teachers to be trained and have guns in school." He shook his head. "I was ambitious, I worked hard, I became the top lobbyist. Whenever I called anyone in the halls of power—the White House, the Congress—I got a call back." He swallowed. Someone handed him a cup of Coke. He smiled his thanks, took a long drink, and continued. "Now I realize all I had done was drink the Kool-Aid." He paused and looked at them. "Are you even old enough to know what that means?"

"Yes," said Sam from his place between Guy and Annette. "We studied it in history. This crazy religious fanatic, Jim Jones, killed himself and all his followers down in South America in 1978. With poisoned Kool-Aid. They all died."

"Yes," said Guy. "That's it. I drank the Kool-Aid. My mind was poisoned. And, as a result, I lost my grandson, and so many others were murdered." A lone tear rolled down his cheek. He let it. "Now I can't tell you what I was thinking. I was wrong. My whole life has been wrong. It was all a mistake. I feel so guilty. I have to do something to atone—I have to before I die. I want to help you. Please, let me help you." He sank into the back of the couch, his energy spent. But he kept his eyes on them, intent, imploring. "I've got to do something."

A deep stillness filled the room as they returned his gaze. For several moments, no one moved or spoke. Sitting close up next to Guy, Sam broke the ice. "Want to give a speech?" He nodded to

Annette, Mark, and Elaine. "We're the speech-writing committee." He turned to Guy and smiled. "We're just telling our personal stories mostly. Your story might just trump any of ours." Not waiting for Guy to answer, he addressed Sarah. "Why don't we have him speak last? What a surprise that would be. What do you think?"

"That would really be something," said Sarah. "We could keep it a secret. Make sure when Neil Simpson writes any more articles, he doesn't spill the beans."

"I've talked to him a bunch," said Derek. "I think he will work with us on that. He seems like a good guy."

Guy sat stunned. *Neil Simpson. Is he everywhere?* he wondered.

Sarah spoke to Guy. "Would you be willing? I mean, we have told everyone we only want young people to speak, but I think we want to make an exception for you."

Guy had to clear his throat before he could speak. He took another sip of his Coke. He pictured himself on the stage by the podium leaning into the microphone. He had given lots and lots of speeches over the years, but never one like this. His stomach knotted in anxiety just thinking about it. Could he? Only yesterday, after he had told Sarah he would come today, had he submitted his formal resignation letter to Pierre LeChien. He did it by email. He had also sent a paper copy via registered mail that hadn't had time to arrive. But the response to his email was instant and overwhelming. His phone had started ringing constantly. He had refused to answer any calls from the NRA. He would have to face them sometime. Maybe he would face them from onstage at the young people's rally. He smiled. The idea appealed to him. That would show them.

Sam patted his knee. "We get together to practice. None of us are used to giving speeches, certainly nothing like this. You could join us and practice with us. Practice really has helped me feel more comfortable."

Sarah spoke to the group. "What do you guys say, want Mr. Grant to speak?"

"Yes," said Annette.

"Yes," said Elaine.

"Yes," said Mark.

"How about a show of hands?" asked Sarah. "All in favor, raise your hand." All the hands shot high.

Guy felt awe and admiration rise up inside him for these young people. His stomach relaxed. Ms. Hunter was right; they didn't need adult help. But here they were, helping him, giving him the chance he needed to speak his newly found truth to the world. At their rally. To be the only adult speaking. To do something to repair the damage of his lifetime.

"I would be honored to speak at your rally," said Guy. Sam handed him a napkin. Only then did Guy realize he was crying.

Chapter 30

The day of the rally came bearing blue skies and crisp, cool air. The bright sun promised above-average temperatures for early December. Sam, Annette, and the rest of the organizing group came early to make sure everything was in order. They vibrated with anxious energy. The stage was set up with the Washington Monument behind it and facing the US Capitol at the far end of the grassy expanse.

Sam climbed onto the stage to get the feel of where he would stand to give his speech. Annette came with him. Derek was busy helping the Braddock Bandits set up their equipment and test the sound. Sarah walked slowly around on the stage with clipboard in hand, checking off items in turn. With a sudden shout, she headed down and ran out of sight. Sam stepped behind the podium.

Annette smiled at Sam. "How does it feel?"

He took a deep breath and scanned where the audience would be. "Awesome," he said. "Terrifying." He stepped back from the podium. "Here, take a turn, see what it feels like to you."

She grasped the sides of the podium with both hands and gazed over the mall. "Awesome is right. So is terrifying." She drew herself up tall and raised her eyes to the Capitol building at the far end. "But important." She nodded at Sam. "Let's not forget that what we're doing matters. That helps calm my fears." She stepped back.

"Yes, and we certainly practiced our speeches enough." He

smiled. "I think I could recite mine in my sleep." He patted his jacket, where his speech waited. "My cards are here in the inside pocket. I intend to pull them out in case I get such stage fright that I need to read my speech. How about you?"

She opened her jacket to reveal her belt bag. "My cards are right here. Are you going to keep your jacket on when you speak? It hides our T-shirts. I brought a heavy sweater to put on under my shirt, but it looks like it'll be a warm day." She shrugged her jacket off to show off her bright yellow shirt with their logo: a black assault rifle with a black line encircling it and a diagonal red line striking through it. She put her jacket back on. "But maybe not that warm."

"I had the same idea," said Sam. He removed his jacket to show his heavy black sweatshirt under his yellow t-shirt. He kept his coat off, plucking his speech cards out and lifting his shirt to place them in the front pouch of his sweatshirt.

Sarah marched over carrying a large cardboard box, a satisfied smile on her face. Sam moved quickly to help her set it down, only to find it was not at all heavy. "At the last minute, I ordered some sweat-shirts with our logo. They arrived last night. They are just for those of us onstage, but I think there are enough. Find your size."

Sam dug through the box and handed Annette a medium-sized sweatshirt. "I usually wear large. Ah, yes!" He pulled his out.

Sarah sighed and shook her head. "Look down there," she pointed. "That's what made me run off. Can you believe they put the porta-potties in the wrong place? Halfway down the mall in a horizontal row facing the stage, as if we weren't going to have many people. I barely kept my temper when I saw them." She smiled. "I made them move them to the side." She raised her hand to her forehead to shade her eyes. "Yep, they are just getting the last one in place." She pointed. "Right in front of the National History Museum. See?"

"Good job, Sarah!" said Annette as she pulled her sweatshirt over her head.

Elaine and Mark rummaged through the box for their sweatshirts. Elaine waved. "Sarah, you are awesome to order sweatshirts."

Sarah grinned. "We aim to please." She wandered off, her phone to her ear.

"And we are mighty pleased," said Mark. "This is much better. You guys ready?"

"As ready as we'll ever be," said Annette. She cast her eyes around. "Have you seen Mr. Grant yet? I thought he'd be here by now."

Sarah strode up looking exasperated. "I left him several messages. I just now heard from him. He said traffic is horrible. He's trying to find a parking place now."

"Maybe that's a sign we'll have a big crowd," said Sam.

Sarah smiled. "Thanks, I hadn't thought of it that way." She frowned. "But he should have left earlier."

"He'll get here. Relax," said Derek. "But we've got bigger problems. One of the guitarists with our first band just broke a string and doesn't have a spare."

"Oh, jeez," said Sarah. "I always carry a spare, don't you? What's wrong with them?"

They looked over at the Braddock Bandits and sighed. The second band, Night Sounds, had arrived and was conferring with them. They all held their breaths. Then the guitarist gave a thumbs up, grinning from ear to ear.

They gave a long, collective exhale, then a collective cheer as they saw Mr. Grant, wearing a dark blue suit, mounting the steps onto the stage.

"Sorry I'm late," he panted. He paused to catch his breath. "You won't believe the traffic. Get ready for a huge crowd." He surveyed the stage and the view. "You all have done a great job. The setup is fabulous. I love that we're looking out from the Washington Monument to the US Capitol, kind of from the past to the present. It's perfect."

"Sarah did it," said Sam. "We just showed up with our speeches." He examined Guy closely. "How are you? You look a little ragged."

"I'm okay. I think," said Guy. "I admit I didn't sleep well last night." He shook his head, his lips pressed together. "I'm getting some harassment from the NRA. But really, I should have expected it. I just didn't think the boss would come to my house."

"Wow," said Sam. "You mean Pierre LeChien himself? What did you do?"

They gathered around Guy in a circle, leaning close to hear every word.

"I ignored him, didn't want to be bothered with him. He finally went away but left me a lovely threatening note." He smiled. "So much fun."

"What did he threaten?" asked Annette, her brow furrowed in concern. "Did he threaten to shoot you?"

Guy shook his head. "No, he wasn't that specific, called me a lot of angry names." Guy thought a minute. "I kind of like it." His face lit up. "I love it."

They gave a collective sigh and relaxed.

"You do look happy," said Sarah. "We're so glad you are here."

"What can I do to help?" asked Guy.

"Just sit in one of the chairs behind the podium and relax," said Sarah. "Have a sweatshirt if you like." She handed one to him.

Guy looked at it. "Maybe under my suit jacket?"

Sarah frowned. "On second thought, the suit look is better, more professional. But keep it if you want."

"I will. Thanks," said Guy. He tucked it under his arm.

Sarah looked down the mall. People were starting to arrive. "Hey, look at that." She checked the watch on her Fitbit. "And we've got nearly fifteen minutes until the rally starts. Wow. This is exciting."

Guy scanned the crowd. Sam kept a protective eye on him. Guy heard his name and saw Jake trying to get his attention from in front of the stage. Jake held a huge poster with Gracia's photo on it and big letters that read: GRACIA MAY CUMMINGS, SIX YEARS OLD, VICTIM OF GUN VIOLENCE, OCTOBER 31, 2018. Guy went to the edge of the stage, then sat and draped his legs off the edge. "Jake, glad you're here."

"I submitted my resignation also." He grinned from ear to ear. "Best thing I've ever done."

"I know how you feel. And I love your poster. I wish I had made one for Little Guy." He felt himself tear up as he stared at Gracia's adorable face.

Jake laughed. "How's this?" He turned his poster around to reveal a large photo of Little Guy with similar words: GUY GRANT IVEY, SIX YEARS OLD, VICTIM OF GUN VIOLENCE, OCTO-BER 31, 2018.

Guy took a deep breath and put his hand to his heart. "Thank you."

"It's the least I could do," said Jake. "What are you doing on the stage?"

Guy longed to tell him he was speaking, but sworn to secrecy, he resisted. "Oh, just helping them some, but they don't really need my help."

Jake nodded. "Yeah, young people can be amazing. But good for you."

"Where did you get that photo? It's wonderful."

"From me," said Laura, appearing behind Jake with her husband.

"Laura, Tom," said Guy. "I didn't know you guys were coming."

Laura smiled. "We wouldn't miss it for the world, would we, Tom?"

"Of course we had to come," said Tom. "This is a big event."

Guy frowned. "I didn't know you had even met."

"We met at the funeral, Dad," said Laura.

Guy slapped his head. "Of course."

"Didn't we meet at some school meeting as well?" asked Jake.

"Maybe so. But at the reception after the funeral, to find out we had both lost children in that horrible shooting," said Laura, "that was something." She touched Jake's arm. "I remember Gracia from school. She was such a lovely girl."

"And likewise, I remember Little Guy," said Jake. He pulled his handkerchief from his pocket and dabbed his eyes. With a big sigh, he gathered himself back together. By this time, Tom was on his other side, draping his arm across Jake's shoulder.

Tom waved to the kids. "I'm so glad you guys have put this together."

Sam stepped closer to get introduced. "Nice to meet you. We had to do something. We lost a lot of our friends. But it's not like losing your child. I'm so sorry."

"Maybe you heard. I quit the NRA also." Jake nodded toward Guy. "He was my boss. Now he's my role model. I'm so glad to be out of that job."

"Good for you," said Sam.

Annette, Elaine, and Mark soon joined Sam at the edge of the stage.

"Elaine is head of the speech-writing committee," said Sam. "We're the first speakers."

"Annette, do you want to share, um, you know?" asked Elaine.

"I might as well. I'm soon going to be telling a huge crowd." Her voice trembled slightly. "My brother was the shooter."

"Your brother?" said Laura. "Rick Green is your brother?"

Annette nodded.

"Oh, you poor dear," said Laura. "Did you have any idea?" She paused. "Never mind, no need to go into it now."

"You'll hear it all in the speech," said Elaine.

▷ ⊕ ◁

The Braddock Bandits' rousing rock performance had the crowd dancing and singing along for the rally's opening act. They closed to a roar of applause from a crowd extending nearly to the foot of the Capitol. Derek helped them quietly exit stage left while the Night Sounds gathered their instruments and waited for their turn to perform. Sarah stepped up to the podium to open the rally while Sam, Annette, Elaine, Mark, and Guy sat in the line of chairs a few feet in back. Sam held Annette's hand, as much to calm his nerves as to calm hers. Elaine sat still as a statue. Guy's leg jiggled as he waited his turn.

Sarah cleared her throat, leaned into the microphone, and began in the loudest voice she could muster, "Welcome everyone!" The crowd cheered. "I'm Sarah Hunter. Thank you for coming." She nodded toward the band. "And thanks to the Braddock Bandits for getting us warmed up." The crowd cheered louder. She paused a moment with her hand over her heart as she surveyed the audience. "That so many of you came out today is beyond our wildest dreams. After the tragic events of October 31, we, the students of Parkwood High School, wanted to do something to say, 'ENOUGH IS ENOUGH!'" Another roar and a few echoes of her words came from the crowd. "We want this tragedy to be the last school shooting EVER!" She held up her hands to quiet the roar. "We have a few brave students willing to tell their stories. Our first speaker is Annette Green." Sarah smiled at Annette as they changed places.

Sam gave Annette a big smile and blew a surreptitious kiss as she walked to the podium. He felt vicarious butterflies in his stomach knowing he'd be next. He sat up a bit straighter and kept his eyes glued to her.

"Hello, everyone, and thank you for coming," she began. She gripped her speech cards and inhaled slowly before she spoke. "Rick Green has been indicted as the alleged shooter, and I'm sad to say, he is also my brother." There was an audible murmur from the audience. "I knew he was troubled, but I promise you, I had no idea what he was planning. If I had, I would have moved heaven and earth to stop him, believe me." She paused to let her words sink in as they had rehearsed. She glanced at the crowd but felt her nervousness threaten to overwhelm her, so she fastened her eyes on the Capitol dome in the distance.

"Some of you may know what happened to my family a few years ago when my father shot my mother and killed himself," she went on. "After that horrible time, after we had buried our father and knew our mother would survive, Rick just seemed to withdraw and become more and more angry. Both Mother and I urged him to get treatment. We even dragged him to family therapy. I loved having a place to pour it all out myself, but Rick refused to talk and withdrew even more. Mother got rid of all our father's guns—we thought. But guns are all too easy to get in our society." She paused and regarded the audience. They remained stone silent, as if hanging on her every word. She took a deep breath and continued. "We didn't know what to do to help Rick. He kept getting into fights at school and spent a lot of time in detention as a result. It was hard enough for Mother and me to find some sense of normalcy. But I assure you, we had no idea, no idea at all, what he was planning."

As she spoke, Sam ran his gaze over the crowd. He felt a weird sense of danger, sort of a "spider sense." He felt his entire body tense up and a feeling of doom fill him. *He's locked up, you fool, he can't be here. And you are NOT Spider-Man.* He saw the counter-demonstrators at a distance on the right by the Smithsonian Castle. Maybe that was the source of his "spider sense." They were a small group, he guessed maybe no more than fifty. Not much danger there. They had a giant sign he really wanted to read. *Stop it. Danger is all in your mind.* Realizing his speech would be soon, he turned his attention back to Annette.

"After the candlelight vigil, I went to the organizing meeting in real fear that I'd be blamed for not stopping my brother. The guilt that consumed me almost stopped me from going." She cleared her throat and reached for her water bottle from a small shelf underneath the podium. After taking a sip, she continued. "But I'm so glad I did, and I'm so glad I told my story, and I'm so glad to be here to tell it to all of you. My brother should never have had access to guns, any gun. We need to make gun access more difficult. Please join us in raising your voices. Contact your representatives and senators to demand stricter gun regulations. Without a gun, Rick might have gotten in fights, but he wouldn't have been able to do what he did. Enough is enough! Thank you."

She stepped back. Applause rang out loud and long. She gave a slight bow and returned to her seat. Sam grabbed his speech cards, stood, and waited while Elaine gave him a brief introduction. "Our next speaker is Sam Schuyler. Please give him a warm welcome."

The audience clapped loudly as Sam took his place at the podium. "Hello, everyone, and thank you for coming." He raised his hand, and the crowd quieted. "As Elaine said, I'm Sam Schuyler. I went to school with Rick. I even got into a fight with him once at school when he said nasty things about a girl I liked. A girl he shot in his rampage. A girl who died like so many others that horrible day." He sighed. "Because of that fight, I shared some detention time with him as well. But we were not friends."

He paused and sighed. "I got a bad feeling about him and stayed away from him. I'd already gotten in trouble once because of him. I didn't want any more trouble. And he was trouble." Sam looked out over the crowd. "He was also troubled, very troubled. For some strange reason, he pursued me, like he wanted me to be his friend. I have to say he stalked me, came to my house uninvited one Saturday afternoon. My mom also saw he was troubled."

He stopped and shook his head. "He also came by my house the morning of the shooting, acting like we were friends, wanting me to come with him. To do what I had no idea. I slammed the door in his face and escaped through the back door into my car. He chased me, and I eventually lost him."

Sam cast his eyes over the crowd. He saw several friends; he saw his mother. He even saw Matt, his therapist. There was not a sound as the audience listened. "I guess I should count myself lucky because I got violently ill in first period that day. Must have been that real bad intestinal virus that was going around then. Remember that?" A few near the stage hollered *yes!* and *sure do!* "The nurse got my mother to come get me. I was home hugging the toilet when the massacre happened. I was lucky."

He took a deep breath. "But few were lucky that day. When I found out what Rick had done, I felt horrible that I hadn't done something. I felt guilty; I felt helpless. But I had no idea what to do. Thanks to my therapist,"—he waved and Matt waved back—"I know now. And I want all of you to know. If you think someone you know is about to do something to harm themselves or others, you can call 911. The police will take that person to the hospital for a psychiatric evaluation. If the psychiatrist agrees they are dangerous, they will be involuntarily committed to the hospital psychiatric unit. That person will get help, and the community will be protected. Anyone can do this." He stared out at the crowd. "Anyone. Any citizen. This is not just something doctors can do." He took a drink from his water bottle. "There's a law that states that for anyone you suspect to be *of imminent harm to self or others,*' you can call 911. It's that simple."

There was an audible reaction from the crowd. A stirring, people speaking to those next to them. Sam went on, "If I had known then what I just told you, if I had called 911 when Rick came by my house, that day could have turned out very differently. I hope there won't be a next time, but if there is, I know what to do. And now so do you. Remember this: just call 911. Thank you."

Sam stepped back. The audience erupted in applause. He bowed and returned to his seat next to Annette.

"Good job, Sam" she whispered. Elaine, Mark, and Guy echoed her words.

Sarah leaned into the microphone. "We will now have a brief musical interlude before more speeches, including a special guest speaker. Stay tuned and enjoy listening to Night Sounds." As they began to play their soothing folk and blues tunes, Sarah conferred with her friends. "Wow, guys, good job. Annette, you were amazing. Sam, you knocked it out of the park."

"Thanks," said Sam. "I'm glad my part is over. But I want to go spy on the counter-demonstrators and sort of see who is here. Anyone want to come?"

"I'll come," said Annette.

"I'd come too," said Mark, "but my speech is coming up next."

"Mine too," said Elaine. She squinted down the mall. "But don't be gone too long, okay?"

"We promise," said Annette.

Sam took Annette's hand and they headed out. They paused briefly to receive congratulations from a few of their family and friends but kept going. Winding their way through the throng, Sam pushed Rick out of his mind. They passed an array of homemade signs. GUNS DON'T BELONG IN SCHOOLS! ARMS ARE FOR HUGGING! SAFE SCHOOLS FOR ALL KIDS! WE DON'T PUT KIDS IN WAR ZONES SO GET WAR GUNS OUT OF SCHOOLS! WE NEED SENSIBLE GUN LAWS NOW! A few people recognized their shirts and thanked them. They kept going.

"See, there are the counter-demonstrators," said Sam when they got in sight of the Castle but were still hidden within the crowd. White men dressed all in black milled around inside the area designated by yellow tape. Two of the black-clad men held a giant sign that read, WE SUPPORT THE RIGHT TO BEAR ARMS. VIRGINIA CIVILIAN DEFENSE COALITION. Two park police officers stood at attention at either end of the tape.

Annette stopped. "I'm getting scared. These shirts make us a target."

"Let's go," said Sam, placing his arm around her back and turning them both around.

"We need to support our friends as they speak. And especially Mr. Grant."

Annette murmured agreement. "Mr. Grant's speech is sure to create a stir. We can't miss it."

When they got back, they made themselves busy handing out the 5x7 cards that Mark described in his speech. This was their call to action with websites and phone numbers and suggested scripts for speaking with Congress. There were also lists of organizations working on the issue of gun control for further involvement. They had worked hard on compiling this information. They didn't want anyone to be uninformed about possible actions to take.

Elaine's speech was a reading of the list of those who died in the shooting. She spoke slowly and articulated each name carefully. Her voice choked as she read the names of some of her closest friends. The crowd responded with a reverent silence, broken only by a few audible sniffs and sobs as individuals heard the names of their loved ones.

Sam listened as he handed stacks of cards to people to take and pass on. Like seeds being scattered on fertile ground, the cards spread through the huge crowd. Hearing the names of his own friends, a wave of sadness rose up inside him. He tried to shake it off. Handing out cards gave him a welcome distraction. But it didn't completely work. His "spider sense" persisted. He knew it was nuts, but there it was. Elaine's recitation faded into a background hum as Sam ruminated. He fell down the rabbit hole into a dark place. His old familiar demons began to taunt him. He shook his head and thought of what Matt would say. *Find something positive to focus on. Focus on the present moment. Know you will know the right thing to do when you have to cross that bridge.* With gratitude for Matt's wise teachings, Sam raised his gaze to the sky, the clear blue sky, to his friends on stage. He climbed out of the hole and saw the beauty around him. He saw Sarah at the podium and Mr. Grant standing behind her.

"And now it's time for our special guest, Mr. Guy Grant," said Sarah. "Mr. Grant, until very recently, was the head of the lobbying arm of the National Rifle Association, the NRA, the Institute for Legislative Action, or ILA. He has since resigned that position. He has a story to tell about why. Please give him a warm welcome."

A feeling of shock vibrated through the crowd. Their applause was tepid, but many heads tilted forward to listen.

Guy took the podium and cast his eyes over the vast crowd. He cleared his throat and began to speak.

Chapter 31

Kate pushed her way through the crowd to get closer to the stage. Hearing the names of all her students read aloud had almost done her in. She clutched her handkerchief, now sodden with her tears. She was as shocked as anyone to hear Guy's name announced and see him step up to the podium. She stretched her memory in a vain attempt to recall the last time they had talked. Had it been at his grandson's funeral? Maybe. No, he had certainly said nothing then about speaking at the rally.

She heard a soft voice behind her. "Mom, wait up." It was Emma, who had insisted on accompanying her today. Emma had forbidden Kate from riding the metro and had insisted on driving; Kate thought that was an overreaction. That Emma thought she must protect her mother made her feel a bit like a child being required to hold her mother's hand. However, Emma worked downtown and knew a few secret parking places. They had had to walk ten blocks but had gotten here in plenty of time. The size of the crowd made Kate glad to have a companion. She turned to find her daughter parting the sheaves of people to get to her.

When Emma reached Kate's side, Kate shushed her and pointed at the stage. They stilled themselves to listen, behind only a few people who were kind enough to leave a space. They had an excellent view of the stage.

⊕

Sam slipped away when Guy began speaking. Mark saw Sam's departure out of the corner of his eye and joined him.

When they got off stage, Mark grabbed Sam's arm. "Hey, what's up?" he whispered.

"I just have this bad feeling something is going to happen. I know it sounds crazy." Sam turned a quizzical face to his friend.

"Okay, buddy, I'll be crazy with you."

While Guy spoke, they wandered around not too far from the stage, surveying the crowd and studying facial expressions.

⊕

"I'm here today, not as chief lobbyist of the NRA, but as a grieving grandfather who lost his only grandchild in this horrible shooting." Guy kept his focus over the heads of his audience. He was on the edge of a waterfall of tears and didn't want to be swept away.

A ripple of surprise and sympathy murmured through the crowd, followed by a sudden hush.

"Also, I am here as a survivor of this horrible shooting. You see, I volunteered in my grandson's classroom. I was there the day of the shooting, and I was shot." He took a deep breath and cast his eyes over them. He'd been hoping to catch sight of Kate. Of course, he had no idea if she was planning to attend this rally. He didn't think she was the rally-going type. But then, neither had he been before October 31. She had been in his mind all day, all week. He had thought about calling her to talk to her about what he was doing. But Sarah and the others had made him promise not to tell anyone. Not anyone. He thought about calling her just to invite her for dinner or coffee, but he didn't trust himself to keep the secret if he saw her. If he saw her now, it might just nudge him over that waterfall. Raising his eyes to the blue sky and the few wispy clouds, he inhaled the beautiful day.

A stunned silence came from the crowd, waiting.

Guy went on. "Fortunately, as you can see, I recovered. I loved volunteering in the classroom of the amazing Ms. Warwick. Our schools are full of these talented educators." He smiled as he remembered. "And I volunteered to make up for lost time. Up until this fall, I had not been a very good grandfather. I hadn't been a good father either. The only thing I was good at was pursuing my ambitions. It was like I had blinders on. I believed fervently in the message of the NRA, in unlimited freedom to bear arms and all that garbage." He paused and closed his eyes a moment. He opened them and punched his next words. "Because it is garbage. I'm ashamed that it took losing my beloved grandson, Little Guy, to wake me up to the reality that guns are dangerous and need to be regulated."

Guy looked around the crowd to verify they were all with him. He had given lots of speeches in his long career and had learned how to read an audience. He heard some "boos" and caught sight of the counter-demonstrators. He couldn't read their sign, but it triggered a memory. *Ah, yes, the group that came to the recent NRA meeting. Not too many of them.* He ignored them.

"The NRA, my former employer, has been a big force in this country in opposing sensible gun regulations, opposing background checks, opposing the ban on assault weapons. Their cries of freedom have meant freedom to be shot by some deranged person in a movie theater, in a school, in a shopping mall. They've equated guns with patriotism. It's nonsense. It's dangerous. I'm deeply ashamed I ever promoted this world view."

He shook his head. "I'm not talking about guns for sport, for hunting, or even target practice. That's fine. I'm talking about guns for killing people, guns meant for the battlefield being brought into our schools. They say guns are for protection while ignoring the issue of how to protect people from gun violence. In this school shooting, the final count shows that over ninety children and adults lost their lives." He took a breath and closed his eyes. Little Guy's image shone on the screen of his mind and in his heart. He felt the tug of that waterfall pull him toward the edge. Then he opened his eyes and caught sight of a familiar face, her radiant eyes beaming up at him, locked onto his face. Kate Warwick. The waterfall took him.

He stood there with tears streaming down his face. Then he felt a hand on his back and an open water bottle placed in his hand. It was Annette, who quickly sat back down. Guy took a long drink and turned to his audience. In all his years of giving speeches, this had never happened to him. He sighed as he cried, took another sip, and then, through bleary tear-filled eyes, saw the crowd waiting and Ms. Warwick's face crumpling with his.

"I'm sorry," he said. "I was hoping this wouldn't happen." He glanced at his speech and decided to take a detour. He inhaled deeply. "I was going to give you a bunch of statistics and data, which probably would have bored you. Instead, I'm going to tell you my truth, my bitter truth."

He pulled his shoulders back and stood tall, as if about to dive off the high dive. "Losing my grandson, my namesake, almost did me in.

I felt responsible. I felt guilty. I felt my entire life had been a mistake. I wondered if life was worth living." He blinked back his tears. "Yes, I became seriously depressed. My physical wounds healed, but not my emotional and spiritual wounds. If it hadn't been for my psychiatrist, I might not be standing here today. But he helped me re-examine my life and begin to find a way to create a new life."

He pressed his lips together. "People don't often talk about mental health problems. I used to think anyone who went to therapy must be crazy. But not anymore. It doesn't mean you're crazy. If something happens in your life and, as a result, you're depressed and anxious and suffering or even suicidal and you won't go for help, now that's crazy."

He turned back to his prepared remarks. "I am here for atonement, to atone for my mistakes, for my misguided beliefs and actions, for my years of lobbying for the NRA. I am proud to say I no longer work for the NRA. Enough is enough! I don't know how many years I have left in my life, but I fully intend to spend them working for gun safety, for reasonable gun regulations, to prevent any more tragedies like this school shooting that robbed me of my beloved grandson and cost the lives of so many others—children and educators." He waved one of their information cards in the air. Sam and Mark held up stacks of them from a small table in front of the stage. "Be sure to pick up one of these cards before you leave. It will tell you how to get further involved as I intend to do. I invite you to join me. Enough is enough!"

Guy stepped back from the podium to wild applause. He gave a slight bow. Then there was the sound of a gunshot.

Chapter 32

"**E**nough is enough!" Guy concluded. Mark and Sam saw someone crouching on the steps to the stage. Someone Sam recognized, creeping up step by step, pointing a gun. Any sound he made was drowned by the applause as Guy stepped away from the podium.

Sam roared and sprang. Rick heard him and paused. Sam the tiger knocked Rick on his back. A shot flew heavenward. The gun flew with it. The tiger grabbed his throat. Chaos erupted everywhere. People ran and fell and screamed and pushed. The Park Police ran forward in hot pursuit.

And it took a while, after the tiger was pulled off and its prey was handcuffed and taken away and the gun retrieved and the crowd had dispersed, for Sam to return to his human form.

▷ ⊕ ◁

Sam, dazed and disoriented, found himself sitting in a chair on the stage. Annette sat beside him holding his hand. Guy sat on the other side with his arm around the back of the chair. His friends sat in a hastily formed circle of chairs around him. Ms. Warwick and her daughter were there, as well as Jake, Laura, and Tom. He shook his head free of cobwebs and began to focus on each face in turn.

Guy spoke first. "I think you may have saved my life, son," he said. "Thank you."

"He may have saved Annette's life," said Mark. "I saw what he saw. Rick was aiming at his sister."

"At me?" said Annette, startled.

"Yeah," said Mark. "At you."

Annette turned a whiter shade of pale. She squeezed Sam's hand. "I can't believe it. My own brother."

Sam's eyes found Annette's, and he found his voice. "I wouldn't let anything happen to you, Annette."

She smiled, and her eyes, her entire face, smiled at him. "You saved my life."

For a moment, they were in their own private world.

Guy glanced around the circle. "How the hell did he get here? I thought he was in jail. And where the hell did he get a gun?" He raised his eyebrows. "Only Park Police are allowed to have guns on the National Mall."

"Those are the first questions in our investigation," said an older Park Police officer as he approached the circle. "I'm Officer Rivers." He pressed his lips together in a grim line. "You are correct, Mr. Grant. The suspect was in custody, and only Park Police carry guns on the National Mall."

Mark stood to offer him his chair, but the officer waved him off.

"I have a few questions for this young man," he said, nodding at Sam, "Is this a good time? We can do it here unless you'd rather come to the station."

Sam sat up in his chair. "Of course. No, here and now is fine. I'm sure others will have things to add."

This time, the officer accepted the chair next to Sam that Guy vacated. Guy went to stand behind the chair Ms. Warwick sat in and placed his hands on her shoulders. She patted his hands. Emma saw them and smiled.

"This is just a preliminary inquiry. Tomorrow I want you to come to the station for a more in-depth interview and to sign a written statement." He waved his head toward the others. "And the rest of you tomorrow as well." He pulled a notebook and pen out of his pocket. "Just tell me what you saw. Just the facts, please, if you can."

Sam began to tell the story. He didn't disclose his "spider sense." He didn't describe the volcano that had erupted inside him and the tiger that had been unleashed. He would have to discuss all that with Matt in his next session. To the officer, he spoke simply: he had seen Rick, jumped on him, the gun had gone off skyward, and no one was hurt. Those were the facts.

Annette saw her mother in her wheelchair as close to the stage as she could get, craning her neck to listen. "Can someone help my mother get up here?"

Derek quickly jumped off stage and rolled her up the ramp. When he got her settled next to her daughter, Annette turned back to the officer. "Officer Rivers, what will happen to my brother?" she asked.

"Yes, please, tell us. I saw what happened," said Mrs. Green.

"He's on his way to the DC jail now, under a tight guard. Further charges will most likely be filed. Probably starting with attempted murder and on from there."

"Any idea how he got here?" asked Sam.

"That will certainly be part of our investigation," said Officer Rivers.

"How could he escape custody?" said Mark. He shook his head.

Officer Rivers nodded as he wrote. "We will certainly inquire about that. It's highly unusual." He cast his eyes on the others. "Anyone else have something to say that can't wait for tomorrow?"

Sarah spoke. "I do. I hate to think what would have happened if Sam hadn't been on the ball. Who knows how many shots Rick would have gotten off, how many more people could have been hurt or killed? Sam Schuyler is the hero of this story. Please put that in your report, Officer. That's Schuyler, S-C-H-U-Y-L-E-R."

Officer Rivers smiled for the first time as the rest of them added their agreement. "I certainly will."

Sam blushed and hung his head. He didn't know what to say.

Mark did. "Hey, guys, isn't that a taco truck over there? Anyone hungry?"

Sam knew what to say to this. "I'm starving. Let's go."

After providing Officer Rivers with their names and contact information and promising to arrive at the station no later than 9:00 a.m. the next day, they hiked through the now-empty National Mall, buzzing with shock and relief, growing hungrier as they went.

They didn't notice the occupants of a parked car watching them.

Chapter 33

Rick sat on a top bunk at the DC jail, his legs dangling over, staring at the three other guys who shared this tiny space. The one in the bed below him lay on his back talking to the bed springs. Tall and skinny with deep circles under his eyes, he had warned Rick when he had first been shoved inside this hellhole that there were implants inside the springs that could hear his thoughts. "Be careful what you think," he had warned. He was currently talking animatedly to these springs.

Another man lay curled in the fetal position on the other top bunk, moaning and groaning. He was obese and shook the bed as he rocked back and forth. Rick wondered if he was ill and if the bed would collapse on the man in the bed below. These bunk beds were far from sturdy as it was. The man on the lower bunk had his head buried in a book. He at least seemed like he might be sane. Then he had a coughing fit that had him curl up and spew whatever he was coughing up in all directions. He laid the book face down on his lap. Rick could see it was the Holy Bible and sighed. Maybe he wasn't sane after all.

Rick lay back on the thin mattress and bunched the tiny pillow into a ball under his head. He gazed at the ceiling with lines and cracks in the concrete and wished he could make himself the size of an ant and crawl through. But he doubted even an ant could get out of here. He'd been here only a few hours, but it already felt like an eternity. It was moldy and dank-smelling and didn't even have a window. The toilet in the corner was crusted with black as if it hadn't been cleaned in years. Roaches crawled everywhere. Compared to this shithole, the Alexandria jail was a palace. Judging from the snarky attitude of the guards that locked him in this cell, he doubted he would ever get out. If he had that gun again, he might turn it on himself.

He thought he'd been so clever. They were going to put him in the loony bin. They'd given him just enough warning for him to calm his panic and come up with a plan. He'd decided to act *happy* about going to St. Elizabeth's, to kick up the drama and put on a show. To convince them he'd been longing to get help, to talk them out of keeping the shackles and handcuffs on him or, even worse, a strait-jacket. The orderlies from the hospital were easy, and the best part was that they were young. Handcuffs and shackles stayed with the jail. When the guards turned him over to the young orderlies, after the paperwork got signed, he was put into the back of the hospital car. It didn't take him long to figure out that the back doors were locked on the inside. A heavy plexiglass partition separated the back seat from the front. He couldn't get out unless he could persuade them to let him out.

The trip to St. Elizabeth's would take a while, so he began telling his sob story. He wasn't the shooter—it was a case of mistaken iden-tity. He bore a slight resemblance to the shooter, sure, but it wasn't him. He said this so many times, they began to believe him. Hell, he began to believe it. His story included abuse of all kinds, from his uncle, his father, from the other inmates, even from the guards. He made them believe he was depressed and upset and hopeless. When they drove by a wooded area, he even convinced them he was about to puke. They stopped on the side of the road, those fools, let him out, and he was gone.

It didn't take him long to shake them. He climbed a tall white pine tree with low-lying branches until he was up high and invisible within the green canopy. He watched them run around squealing like a bunch of pigs. He knew reinforcements would arrive soon. When they returned to the car, they were sure to call for help. He climbed down and crawled through the thick undergrowth, feeling a bit like Brer Rabbit in the briar patch, and headed for the nearest bright lights. He found posters everywhere about the rally organized by the Parkwood High School kids happening later that morning. When he read his sister's name on the list of organizers, he knew what he was going to do.

When he got there, he was stunned by the size of the crowd. He'd never seen so many people in one place. It must be thousands or even millions. He hid in the middle of this so-called counter-demonstration group to make himself as invisible as possible.

Then he had heard some biker-looking guy bragging that he had snuck in a gun. He'd stuck it in his backpack on the ground, leaving the zipped compartment half open. How dumb. This guy should be locked in the psych ward, not him. One problem solved.

It had been ridiculously easy to slip the gun out of the backpack and into his waistband underneath his jacket. He even saw Sam and Annette winding through the crowd, asking to be shot. A bolt of fury had hit him. He had blinked, and they had gone.

On the stage, Annette had been an easy target. Rage had burned inside him as he remembered their visit to him in jail. Mother had refused to get him out, but in the past, he had always been able to get her to do what he wanted. Annette dragged her away before he could do that. He would never forgive either of them. They both deserved to die.

And, thanks to that asshole Sam, here he was in this dungeon. He closed his eyes. *I give up. I quit,* he thought. *If this is my life, I don't want it.*

▷ ⊕ ◁

After the group got their tacos, Guy invited them back to his house. All shaken by how the rally had ended, they trailed after him in their cars across the 14th Street Bridge and over the Potomac River into Alexandria. Kate and Emma joined them as well as Laura, Tom, and Jake. The group somehow fit into Guy's living room. Guy indicated where the bathrooms were. Annette and Elaine offered to make a quick trip to the nearby Safeway for ice cream and cookies. Sam and Mark and Derek insisted they also get chips and salsa. And hot dogs. And soda.

"You guys are bottomless pits," observed Elaine. She held out her hand for more cash. Guy put several twenties in her hand before anyone could stop him.

"This is my treat," he said to the girls as they left. "I'm afraid, for beverages, about all I can offer until they come back is water. Anyone thirsty?"

"I'll get it, Dad," said Laura, scurrying into the kitchen. Then they heard her cry out in dismay. "Dad, do you ever wash your dishes?"

Guy started to get up.

"No, you sit down, Mr. Grant. I'll help," said Sarah as she hurried to join her.

"Thanks, Sarah," said Guy. The clatter of dish washing was music to his ears.

"Mr. Grant," said Mark, "what's your Wi-Fi password? We want to play Minecraft."

Guy squinted and shook his head. "On your phones?"

"No, on the Switch," said Sam, rooting around in his backpack.

Guy gave them his password and started to ask what a Switch was but shrugged his shoulders.

Jake took a seat next to him. "It's a Nintendo game device."

"Oh," said Guy, looking mystified.

"You don't need to know." Jake patted Guy's arm. "Are you okay? You had a close call there at the end."

Guy considered the question. "I'm not sure I know yet." He took a deep breath. "I'm glad it's over and that kid didn't shoot anyone else."

"That's a blessing. In my opinion, the rally was a big success. Any idea what you're going to do next?" asked Jake.

"Something the opposite of what we did at the NRA. Maybe check out one of these gun control organizations." He pulled one of their cards out of his pocket and held it up. "How about you?"

"I'd love to do that if I could get paid. I do have a family to support."

"Hmm," said Guy. "Maybe we could make that happen. Let's do some research."

"Yes, between the two of us, we know everyone in Washington. I like that idea. A lot," said Jake with a smile.

Laura and Sarah appeared with a tray of glasses and a water pitcher. They set them on the coffee table. Before they could begin to distribute glasses of water, the front doorbell rang, followed by a banging on the door.

"That must be the girls," said Tom. "I'll get it. I guess the door is locked."

He opened the door only to step back as Pierre LeChien barged through. Trailing behind him, both looking sheepish, were Mike and Susan from Guy's office. LeChien paused to locate Guy and stomped over to him. Seeing Jake, he spoke in a booming voice. "Ah, I might have known I'd find you two together. Neither of you have answered any emails or phone calls or responded to any attempt to communicate. What the hell is going on?"

Guy stood up. He was at least two inches taller than LeChien. "I thought my email was clear. I have resigned my position with the NRA." He regarded with some amusement this man huffing and blowing in front of him, a big bad wolf trying to blow his house down. "I didn't expect you to like it. And, I might add, I did not invite you here today." He narrowed his eyes. "I respectfully ask you to leave."

Jake stood up next to him. Sam and Mark and Derek joined them.

"Do you need us to escort you to the door?" asked Sam.

"Yes," added the others. "We'd be happy to do that."

"We'll do it," said Susan and Mike in concert.

LeChien paused and examined the room. "Hmmpf," he said as he turned to leave. "Expect to hear from our attorneys," he said as he went out the door under Susan and Mike's escort. "Remember, we have a contract."

Susan and Mike returned wearing big grins. "Hey, Boss," she said. "We got him in his Mercedes and watched him drive off. We drove separately. We didn't want to be with him. He coerced us. We're really on your side." She paused and looked at Jake. "I remember Gracia so well from our office picnics. I just can't stand it that she's gone."

Jake gave a sad smile. "Thanks, Susan."

"Neither can I," said Mike. "She was a real sweet little girl." He shook his head. "I can't get her and those kids out of my head. I'm out. I'm not staying on the NRA payroll. It's been a hard month."

"I'm out too," said Susan. "Enough is enough. My resignation letter is waiting to be sent."

"We were there today," said Mike. "Unfortunately, we were with LeChien. He thought we were joining him in surveillance of you, but really, we were watching him, hoping to keep a lid on him. We kept a low profile, watched from his fancy car, but we heard your every word. Inspiring, Boss!"

Guy felt his heart swell. "Stay and let's talk. We have ice cream and cookies coming."

Susan turned to Mike. "Let's do it."

"Sorry about LeChien's tirade," said Mike. "We all know he's full of hot air. Man, he sure gave us an earful."

Guy frowned. "About me?"

Susan nodded. "About a lot of things. You, the resignations that have begun. Through the grapevine, I have heard of quite a few."

Jake chuckled. "Hard to tell who the really crazy ones are here."

He sat back down. "And last I heard, it's not illegal to resign a job. What a joke."

"Right," said Guy, smiling as he sat.

Annette and Elaine came in, their arms full of grocery bags.

"Who was that?" asked Elaine. "He looked familiar."

"Nobody important," said Guy. "Certainly not as important as cookies and ice cream."

Susan and Mike chuckled. Mike grinned at the young people. "We're the latest defectors from the NRA, Mike Gunn and Susan Britt. Mr. Grant is our boss, well, was our boss. I'm in awe of what you guys pulled off today. You're amazing."

"You certainly are," added Susan.

The young people grinned.

Somehow everyone found seats. The young people sat on the rug.

"Thanks," said Annette. "Welcome. We've got ice cream and cookies and chips and salsa. And ginger ale and coke."

"Did you forget the hot dogs?" asked Mark, his brow wrinkled in concern.

Elaine rolled her eyes. "Relax, we got them."

Laura fetched clean bowls and a big scoop. "Who wants Rocky Road? Who wants Mint Chocolate Chip?"

"I want a scoop of each," said Sam, leaning over the coffee table.

"So do I," said Derek and Mark in unison.

"Hey, you guys," said Sarah. "Let's serve Mr. Grant and our guests first. Remember your manners."

Once they were all served, Guy called them to attention. "We had a great day today, thanks to you. But this is only the beginning. I wonder if you have thought about what's next?" He ran his eyes around the room and paused a moment.

"I have," said Sam. "I don't know how, really, but I want to fight for safe gun regulations."

"So do I," said Derek. His words echoed as everyone else spoke up in agreement.

"Let's plan a time to meet soon and toss ideas around," said Sarah. "We can meet at my house, I bet. How about tomorrow afternoon? Maybe 3:00 p.m.?"

Her suggestion was followed by choruses of "yes" and "I'll be there" and "that works for me."

"Okay, 3:00 p.m. tomorrow," said Sarah. "Don't be late. We have work to do."

Guy sat back in his chair. He looked around the group now assembled in his living room. His former coworkers, these amazing young people, his daughter and son-in-law, and Kate Warwick. These were his people now, and they would be his companions in this new life.

As Dr. Mehlman had taught him, he knew he had a long road ahead of him to recover from his grief and the trauma of being shot. Each of them would have similar journeys. When he thought of his grandson and all those beautiful children who'd been needlessly slaughtered, he felt a catch in his heart. His nights were dark. He knew the only way to pull himself out of the pit of despair would be to do something. Together they would take action, as long as it took, no matter what setbacks and obstacles they encountered. As this determination filled him, a wide grin filled his face, and a warmth of satisfaction flowed through his entire body as he absorbed the reality of his new life purpose.

Chapter 34

A year later, on a Saturday morning, Guy sat around a large conference table with the same group that had met that Sunday afternoon the day after the rally. His former coworkers, the rally organizers, his family, and Kate. He called to order the first annual meeting of the American Gun Safety Association, or AGSA.

It had been a productive year. They'd found several rich donors and foundations, enough to rent office space and provide salaries for everyone who wanted one. With the Capitol Hill connections of those who used to work for the NRA, they already had a bipartisan bill for extensive gun regulations, including a gun license provision similar to a driver's license. It now was waiting for a vote in both the US House and the Senate. Over ninety representatives had signed on to co-sponsor the bill in the House and over sixty in the Senate. They had high hopes for its passage. But even if it didn't pass this time, they were ready to press ahead with other legislation.

Kate sat next to Guy, a shiny diamond ring on her left hand, as radiant as she had been the first day he had met her. After the rally, they had started spending more and more time together. She had taken a break from teaching to help AGSA get started. Guy, determined to do better this time, had made her the center of his life.

As the anniversary of the school shooting approached, he had taken her out to a fancy restaurant. It was a sad day for them both, but he hoped to give it a happier association. After they had finished the main course and were waiting for dessert, he had gotten on one knee and proposed. Surprised and delighted, she had accepted immediately. The waiter, who had been primed, had arrived with a bottle of champagne, two flutes, and a small crystal bowl containing a sparkling diamond ring.

Sam sat across the table from Guy next to Annette. They, too, had become an item. After high school graduation, he had started classes at George Mason University, mainly to be near her but also to work part-time with AGSA. She was in her second year at Northern Virginia Community College and also worked part-time with AGSA. Wherever they went the following year, they would go together.

Guy smiled at the assembled group. "Let's take a moment to appreciate how far we have come in a year. Together, in a short time, we have built a powerful organization. I am very proud of all of us."

Jake spoke up. "The NRA seems to be going up in smoke. Illegal financial activities have been uncovered that threaten their nonprofit status. None of us ever heard from LeChien after we resigned. I guess he has bigger fish to fry now."

With smiles all around, they paused for a moment of silence. Guy reflected on the changes of this year. They had formed a strong bond, and with it, the ability to lift each other up when the mountain seemed too high and the well of grief too deep. They fell down at times but picked themselves up with each other's help and took another step forward. The silence was deep and long, providing sustenance to them all.

It was only broken when Tom said he had an announcement to make. Laura sat beside him, glowing. Tom cleared his throat. "I'm happy to say that Laura and I are expecting. Our baby is due in April, maybe just in time for your wedding, Guy and Kate."

As words of congratulations erupted around the table, Guy's face broke into a huge grin without noticing the tears welling up. A new job and new purpose. And now a new grandchild.

Acknowledgments

Giving birth to a novel involves more than simply the author. I'm grateful to my writing group, Novel Gazers, for walking through the manuscript with me chapter by chapter and giving valuable feedback. They include Doug Brower, Terry Kitson, and Sam Leaman. I could not have done it without their wise counsel. Thanks also to first readers Mary Jo Klingel and Lori Hoyt who cheered me on and gave valuable suggestions on how to make it better. Great appreciation to my developmental editor, Eve Porinchak of darlingaxe.com, for her expertise. Also I thank Diana Wade, designer, and Kathy Brown, proofreader, for their help to make this book not only compelling to look at but accurate. Bob Kern of TIPS Publishing Services gave invaluable help with the technical aspects of self-publishing for paperback and ebook. Also appreciation for the North Carolina Writers' Network for their conferences and workshops that taught me much and provided me a community of writers. Finally, I thank my husband, Dave Curtin, for his faithful love and support in whatever I do.

About the Author

During her forty years as a clinical social worker, Alice Carlton worked with many individuals and couples in distress and gained much insight into human nature and relationship difficulties. Retirement offered her an opportunity to devote herself to creative writing. She is a member of the NC Writers' Network. She has published a novel, *The Poetry Cure*; a story in *Motherscope Magazine*; and poetry in *Friends Journal* and in *Iris*, the UNC Journal of Medicine, Literature and Visual Art. She lives in Chapel Hill, North Carolina, with her husband, one dog and two cats.